PRACTICE
TO
DECEIVE

By David Housewright

Penance
Practice to Deceive

David Housewright

PRACTICE TO DECEIVE

A Foul Play Press Book

W. W. Norton & Company

New York   London

For information about permission to reproduce selections from this book, write
to Permissions, W. W. Norton & Company, Inc., 500 Fifth Avenue,
New York, NY 10110.

The text of this book is composed in Century Schoolbook
with the display set in Goudy Old Style
Composition by Gina Webster
Manufacturing by Courier Companies, Inc.

Library of Congress Cataloging-in-Publication Data

Housewright, David, 1955–
Practice to deceive / David Housewright.
p.   cm.
ISBN 0-88150-404-1
I. Title.
PS3558.08668P7   1997
813′.54—dc21   97–12864
CIP

Published by Foul Play Press, a division of W. W. Norton & Company, New York

W. W. Norton & Company, Inc., 500 Fifth Avenue, New York, N.Y. 10110
http://www.wwnorton.com

W. W. Norton & Company Ltd., 10 Coptic Street, London WC1A 1PU

1 2 3 4 5 6 7 8 9 0

For Eugene and Patricia Housewright

For Renée

ACKNOWLEDGMENTS

Special thanks
to Chris Engler, Dr. John Fromstead, Dale Gelfand,
Gus Grell, Phyllis Jeagar, Lou Kannenstine,
Alison Picard, Mike Sandman, John Seidel,
Mike Sullivan, and Renée Valois.

ONE

She had lived long past the time when her death would have been tragic. The things she valued most—family, friends, health, even her money—were lost to her now. She had outlived them all. What remained was a small house filled with mementos collected over eight and a half decades, memories that grew increasingly dim with each passing day, and an unquenchable thirst for revenge.

That's where I came in.

I met her on the redwood deck my father had built on the back of his house in Fort Myers, Florida. She was sitting in a wicker chair, silent and still, shaded by the huge umbrella my father had arranged for her comfort. Her hands were folded in her lap. When my mother introduced us, I cautiously took one hand in mine, careful not to shake or squeeze it for fear her fingers would crumble like dry leaves.

"Mrs. Gustafson, this is my son Holland," my mother said. "He's here to help you."

Mrs. Gustafson nodded slightly, and I gently replaced her hand atop the other. My father pulled his chair next to mine; the legs scraping against the wood floor. Mrs. Gustafson flinched at the sound.

"It's only Jim," my father said. Then he leaned toward me and whispered, "She's partially blind."

"What can I do for you, Mrs. Gustafson?" I asked.

"She wants you to get her money back," my mother answered for her.

"What money?"

"The money that rat stole from her," Mom said, spitting out the word "rat." You can't get much lower than that with my mom.

"Can you tell me about it, Mrs. Gustafson?"

"This guy, calls himself an investment counselor, he was supposed to manage her money for her—only instead he stole it," my mother said.

"Mom . . ."

"Two hundred and eighty-seven thousand dollars."

"Mom, I'm speaking with Mrs. Gustafson."

"Just trying to help," she told me and retreated to the other side of the deck, rolling her eyes in exasperation. I expected her to slide into the "I'm-just-a-rug-for-my-children-to-wipe-their-feet-on" speech with which I was so familiar, but she restrained herself. In deference to her guest, no doubt.

I knelt in front of the ancient woman and patted her hands, surprised that they stayed intact. "What happened, Mrs. Gustafson?" I asked.

"My money . . ." she whispered.

"Yes?"

"My money is gone."

"Someone took your money?"

"All my money."

Dad set his hand on the woman's shoulder. "Do you want me to tell the story?" he asked. Mrs. Gustafson nodded.

"This guy, calls himself an investment counselor," my mother called from the other side of the deck, "ran away with her retirement fund, two hundred and eighty-seven thousand dollars. . . ."

"Honey . . ."

"She said we could tell it."

"She said *I* could tell it," my father reminded her.

"What's the difference?"

Between my mother and father—mostly my mother—I learned that Mrs. Irene Gustafson was a transplanted Minnesotan like my parents; she had lived, in fact, just off Rice Street in St. Paul, where my father and his friends had wreaked havoc during their misspent youth. "So that was you," she had said to him when they became acquainted a few years back.

Mrs. Gustafson had moved to Fort Myers after her husband died, doing so on the advice of her son. "Why spend another winter in Minnesota when you can bask in the Florida sunshine?" he'd asked. Why, indeed? Mrs. Gustafson took her savings, her husband's insurance, and the money she earned selling her home, and gave it to her son. He used part of it to buy a small, two-bedroom house in Fort Myers and invested the rest. Every couple of months he, his wife, and his two sons would come down to visit. Sometimes they flew, sometimes they drove. And each time he would set her down and go over her assets, making sure she understood her financial situation.

Then they stopped coming. A drunk driver killed the entire family when he ran a stop light just outside Jackson, Tennessee. I winced at the telling. That's how my wife and daughter had been killed—by a drunk driver who mistook red for green.

That was ten years ago. Mrs. Gustafson was her son's sole survivor, so all his assets had gone to her. It had amounted to about as much as you'd expect a young family to accumulate: life insurance and little more. Yet added to what she already had, Mrs. Gustafson was now quite well off, especially when compared to most of her retired friends who lived month to month on Social Security. She insisted she would have traded every penny for just one more day with her family, but people always say that when they profit from the misfortune of others.

Mrs. Gustafson hadn't known what to do with her money—she never did pay much attention to her son's bimonthly financial seminars—so she put it all into a passbook savings account. That's what you do with money, isn't it? You put it in the bank? Fortunately, a column by Ann Landers showed Mrs. Gustafson the error of her ways. She contacted an investment firm, and they put her into income-producing investments, giving her a comfortable lifestyle for nearly a decade. Now, Mrs. Gustafson was eighty-five years old, and the money was gone.

"What happened?" I asked.

"This guy, calls himself an investment counselor, stole her money, two hundred and eighty-seven thousand dollars," my mother said.

"You keep saying that."

"Well . . ."

"Are you sure he stole it?"

"It's gone, isn't it?"

"That doesn't mean he stole it; the stock market is a volatile concern."

"'Volatile concern,'" my mother mimicked me—like I used to mimic her when ordered to clean up my bedroom.

"Who is 'this guy,' anyway?"

"Levering Field," Mrs. Gustafson mumbled.

"Excuse me?" I said and leaned toward her.

"Levering . . . Field" she repeated slowly; her voice was barely audible, and I wasn't sure I'd heard it right.

"Levering Field," my father confirmed.

"What kind of name is that?" I wondered. No one on the deck could remember hearing it before.

"He works out of Minneapolis," my father told me. "I gathered all the monthly statements he sent to Mrs. Gustafson's during the past seven years. I have them for you."

"Is there anything irregular about them?" If anyone would know, my father would. He gave me one of his trademark it-depends-on-your-interpretation shrugs; it was the same shrug he gave when I asked his opinion about quitting college to become a cop.

"How did you meet this man?" I asked Mrs. Gustafson.

"She didn't," my father told me. "At least not face-to-face. She picked him out of a telephone directory."

Mrs. Gustafson shook her head sadly.

"Why Minneapolis? Why not Fort Myers?"

"Home," she mumbled. "It was closer to home."

"I understand," I said. But what I did not understand is what they all expected me to do about it. Investments go sour all the time.

"You're a private eye aren't you? Get the money back," Mom told me.

"Mom, it doesn't work that way."

"What way *does* it work?"

"First of all, we don't know the circumstances. I'll try to find out for you," I told Mrs. Gustafson. "If we can prove wrongdoing on Mr. Field's part, we can take our information to the SEC or attorney general, depending on who has jurisdiction. The prosecutor will decide if there are grounds for indictment or further investigation. Let's assume there are. Let's assume Mr. Field is arrested, tried, convicted. Let's even assume that the court orders him to pay restitution. None of that means Mrs. Gustafson is going to get her money back."

"Then what good are you?" my mom wanted to know.

"Ma, beyond what I just told you, there's not a helluva lot I can do."

"What's the use of being a private eye if you can't help people?"

"Arguing will not help Mrs. Gustafson," my father reminded us.

I turned back to her. She had not moved, but bright tears clung to the wrinkles of her face.

"I'm sorry, ma'am," I told her. "I'm just not sure I can help you."

"Help me. . . ."

"Ma'am . . ."

"It's all gone. Everything . . . My husband's money, my son's . . . All gone . . ."

"I know."

"Can't let him do that, get away with that. Can't let him . . ."

I took Mrs. Gustafson's hands in mine. The tears continued to fall freely. A drop splattered on the back of my wrist.

"Won't you get my money back?"

"I don't think so, ma'am. I'm sorry."

"Well, why not?" Mom wanted to know.

"You won't help me?" asked Mrs. Gustafson.

"Can you tell me why not?" Mom continued.

"I don't know how," I admitted.

Mrs. Gustafson sobbed. "He robbed me! Can't we rob him back?"

"THIS IS INSANE," I announced to the ceiling. Dad was taking Mrs. Gustafson home. Mom was frying chicken. "I can't believe I promised that poor old woman I would help her. How can I help her? I can't help her."

"You said you would."

"You made me say that."

"Holland, you know I have never once made you do anything you didn't want to do."

That stopped me. "Mom, just off the top of my head, I can think of at least twenty things I've done because you made me, including taking home economics in high school."

"A man should know how to take care of himself."

"Do you know how embarrassing that was—how much abuse I took from my friends because of that?"

She smiled the same smile she always used when she was about to inform me that mothers always know best.

"None of your friends can cook," she informed me. "None of your friends can do laundry."

"I don't think they're losing sleep over it."

"That's because they have wives to look after them. If they didn't, they'd all starve. But not you. After Laura died, you were able to take care of yourself, you were able to feed yourself. You think your father could take care of himself if I was gone? He'd be dead in six months. They'd find his body laying on the kitchen floor, a can opener in one hand and empty cupboards everywhere."

"I doubt it."

"The man can run corporations, but he can't scramble eggs; he'd burn down the house if he tried. But you can scramble eggs. Why?"

"Because I took home economics in high school?" I volunteered.

"You're lucky to have me for a mother."

I paced some more, wondering what to do about Mrs. Gustafson while my mother fried her chicken. "It's your favorite," she told me. I tried to explain that it wasn't my favorite, but she insisted. After a few moments of silence, she informed me that she recently had a long talk with Lee.

"Who's Lee?"

13

"Lee? Letitia Taylor? Your sister-in-law?"

"Oh, yeah, Lee. What'd Lee have to say?"

"Lee says you're dating a lawyer named Cindy."

All my defense mechanisms locked into place. I pivoted toward my mother, instinctively moving into a karate stance, knees bent, weight evenly distributed. "Her name is Cynthia," I corrected her.

"What's wrong with 'Cindy'? She can't be called Cindy like regular girls?"

"Cynthia is not like regular girls."

"I'll say." Mom wiped her hands on a towel and moved to a kitchen drawer. In the drawer was a magazine devoted to the Twin Cities. On the cover of the magazine was a photograph of Cynthia standing outside the Federal Court Building in downtown Minneapolis. The headline read THE BLACK AND WHITE WORLD OF CYNTHIA GREY.

The article centered around a lawsuit Cynthia was waging against a woman's clothing manufacturer on behalf of a dozen former female employees who claimed they'd been sexually harassed—actually assaulted in several cases—by male co-workers. The suit contended that management had not only ignored the women's complaints, but that the company's oversexed, underdressed, women-as-boy-toys advertising "contributed to an atmosphere that condoned, if not promoted, sexual harassment" in the company's Twin Cities plant.

The writer, a man, was careful to note that there was merit in the lawsuit, that it might even rewrite sexual harassment law. However, his portrayal of Cynthia was somewhat less than flattering. He accused her of grandstanding, of using the case solely to promote herself in the media without regard to her clients. In his words, Cynthia was obsessive, humorless, frustrated, and self-righteous. And the photographs accompanying the article—Cynthia scowling behind her desk, Cynthia scowling in front of the federal court house—reinforced his claims.

Cynthia was delighted.

The writer was lazy. He had interviewed maybe a dozen people for the article, fellow lawyers mostly, a few clients, and the defendant she was in the process of pounding into submission—no one who had known Cynthia longer than two years; no one who could tell him about the unflattering life she lived before she became obsessive, humorless, frustrated and self-righteous.

"She has some mouth on her, this girl," Mom claimed, paging through the article. "Claimed she didn't want to be *merely* a housewife. What's wrong with being a housewife? I'm a housewife and you kids are lucky I am. The world is falling apart because women aren't housewives anymore, because they aren't staying home."

Mom tossed the magazine on the kitchen table and folded her arms. "Something else Lee told me; I wanted to ask you if it was true or not."

"What?"

"Is this Cynthia the same lawyer who defended the drunk driver who killed Laura and Jenny?"

"Yes."

"How could you?" She was angry now.

"What?"

"How can you spend time with someone like that?"

"Someone like what? Ma, she's not the person described in the magazine article. She's very caring, she's very sincere—"

"I don't care."

"She carries iodine in her purse in case someone has an accident."

"I don't care! She tried to save the man who killed my granddaughter."

I took a deep breath. Nothing I could say would make

much difference, but I thought I'd give it a try and then let it go.

"I started seeing her a few months ago while I was working a case. My first reaction was the same as yours. I wanted to punch her out. But after speaking with her for a while I realized I wasn't angry anymore, not at her or the rest of the world. Besides, Mom, she's a lawyer. It's her job to defend people who aren't very nice. Sometimes I work for the same people."

"It's wrong," Mom told me.

"It isn't wrong."

"I don't care what you say."

"Wait until you meet her—"

"Meet her! I have no intention of meeting her."

"Ma . . ."

She turned her back on me, returning to her chicken. But I knew she wasn't finished. I waited. Finally she looked back, grease dripping from the wing she held with metal tongs.

"Lie down with dogs and you'll wake up with fleas," she told me.

MY FATHER HAD arranged all of Mrs. Gustafson's monthly financial statements in chronological order. I started with April, seven years ago. Mrs. Gustafson had opened a discretionary account with Levering Field, giving him full authority to make investments on her behalf. He seemed to have done well for her: long-time dividend payers, short-term bonds, mortgage-related securities, moderate-risk mutual funds—including one in which I had invested. She was averaging about nine percent annual return with negligible risk. That's a lot of money for a little old lady living alone in Central Florida; her biggest bills were property taxes and a Medicare supplemental insurance payment, about thirty-five hundred a year.

"What am I looking for?"

My father was lying on his sofa, reading *The Wall Street Journal.* He turned a page and said, "Seek and ye shall find" without looking up.

"Hey, this isn't my algebra homework. You can help me without worrying that I won't learn how to do it myself."

Dad smiled. "The last six months."

The last six months were telling. In month one, Field began liquidating Mrs. Gustafson's positions in all her investments, storing the cash in a money market savings account. By month two, the process was complete. In month three, Field bought twenty-five units of Willow Tree, LP at ten thousand dollars each.

"What in hell is he doing?" I wondered aloud.

"Keep reading," my father said.

There was no return on the investment in months four or five. In month six, Field reported a net loss of the entire investment and notified Mrs. Gustafson that he was closing her account.

"What happened?"

"The statement is not very informative, is it?" my father volunteered from the sofa.

"Best guess."

Dad neatly folded his paper and slid into a sitting position. "I never guess. It's a sign of weakness."

I didn't reply.

"Apparently, Field put all of Mrs. Gustafson's money into Willow Tree through a private placement," my father said.

"Private placement?"

"An investment scheme that's not registered with the SEC."

"How does that work?"

"Willow Tree was a limited partnership. Limited partnerships are usually used for real estate development.

17

Developers need financing to buy the land, so they offer a number of limited partnerships, as many as thirty-five. Basically, you give them your money, they run the company, and pay you back out of the profits."

Based on the tone of his voice, I suggested, "You don't approve."

"Know what they say about that kind of investment?" he asked rhetorically. "At first the general partners have the knowledge, and the limited partners have all the money. When it's over, the limited partners have the knowledge, and the general partners have all the money."

Dad leaned forward and smiled. I smiled back. My father is probably the single smartest man I know, but he generally conceals his intelligence beneath a decidedly blue-collar facade, declaring with pride his Rice Street roots, admitting freely that he'd been a rowdy gang kid going nowhere fast until he was saved by a squeaky-clean Catholic girl from the right side of the tracks. Actually that's Mom's version of the story. Anyway, what he does not admit is that in the subsequent years, he earned a drawerful of degrees and certificates from the Universities of Minnesota and St. Thomas. As a result, business competitors tend to underestimate him. So do the unions with which he negotiates as a freelance consultant working on behalf of management—they think they're dealing with one of their own until it's too late.

I hadn't even learned about my father's educational background until I was a sophomore at St. Thomas and met one of his former professors. "Jim Taylor? Best student I ever had," the professor had told me. When I mentioned the incident to Dad, he just shrugged the way he does and said, "It's nothing to get excited about." That's when Mom, who had been sworn to secrecy, took me to their bedroom and showed me Dad's trophies, plaques, and paper.

"Why didn't you tell me about all this?" I asked him.

"I didn't do it to impress you," he'd said.

We never discussed the matter again.

"You researched all this, didn't you?" I said now. My father did not say if he had or hadn't. Instead he told me, "Willow Tree was created to build low-income housing in and around the Twin Cities. It was grievously underfinanced and incompetently managed. It was unable to convince a single city or county board to rezone property for their use; it couldn't get proper building permits, construction costs skyrocketed—they went out of business without putting up so much as an outhouse.

"That's point one," Dad continued. "Point two . . ." He closed his eyes and recited from memory, "'In recommending to a customer the purchase, sale, or exchange of any security, a member shall have reasonable grounds for believing that the recommendation is suitable for such customer . . .' NASD Rules of Fair Practice, twenty-one fifty-two, section two." He opened his eyes again. "Field put everything Mrs. Gustafson had into Willow Tree."

"He should have known better," I volunteered.

"It's a violation of fiduciary responsibility!" my father exclaimed vehemently. The last time I'd seen him so angry, I was sixteen years old and trying to explain to him and the Fort Snelling State Park rangers exactly what I was doing in the park at one A.M. with a young lady in the back seat of my mom's car.

"Investment counselors work under a concept called 'the shingle theory,'" Dad added more calmly. "The theory is that when someone hangs out a sign saying he is an investment counselor, he is promising that he will look after the interests of the client and follow high professional standards. Obviously, Levering Field did not do that in Mrs. Gustafson's case—you don't put elderly people living on the relatively fixed income of a retirement plan into risky ventures. That makes Field guilty of misrepresentation at best and fraud at worst."

"I know the rules apply to stockbrokers," I said. "But if Field is just a personal investment counselor—"

"I don't give a shit if he's a goddamn janitor!" my father exploded. "If he's investing other people's money, he has a responsibility to do the right thing!" Dad stood up, punched the air a few times, circled the sofa twice, reclaimed his seat, and said, "So, there."

"Maybe he didn't realize Willow Tree was risky," I suggested.

Dad shook his head. "Due diligence," he said calmly. "Field was obligated to research the product he was investing in, and he didn't. If he had, he would have known better. Christ, if I can figure it out . . ."

"I wonder why he did it."

"What do you think? He did it for the money. He earns five percent commission off any trade he makes. Hell, he could have charged more; we don't know."

"No, I mean why did he do it to Mrs. Gustafson? And why now?" I leaned back in the chair and regarded the hundreds of books carefully arranged on shelves along the wall.The books belonged to my mother. My father never reads them, only *The Wall Street Journal* and *National Geographic*.

"What happened six months ago?" I wondered aloud.

"Mrs. Gustafson had a stroke," my father answered as if he expected the question. "At her age, the doctors thought she wasn't going to make it. But she's a tough old bird. They were amazed at how quickly and completely she recovered. She lost some vision, some mobility, but mostly she's all right."

"Does she have any family?"

"No one."

"No nephews, no nieces?"

"No one."

"Does she have a will?"

Dad shook his head.

"Think Field knew that?"

"Part of his job is to know the customer."

"That sonuvabitch," I said under my breath.

"You understand now, don't you?"

"That sonuvabitch," I repeated. "Field thought she was going to die and leave all that money to the State of Florida. So he cashed her in, trying to make as much off of her as possible while she was still breathing. But she survived, and now she's screwed."

"That's what I think, too."

I studied my father's face for a moment. He did not look away.

"What am I doing here?" I asked. "You already have it figured out. Call a lawyer. Call the attorney general; see if a crime's been committed."

Dad shrugged. "I thought you might want to run over to Hammond Stadium with me, catch the Minnesota Twins in a couple of Grapefruit League games."

"Spring training? Who are you kidding? You don't even like baseball. The only reason you took my brother and me to games when we were kids was because you thought it was your parental duty."

"That's true."

"So?"

"So?"

"So, why am I here?"

"Can't you guess?"

"No."

"Try."

"No, you tell me."

"All right," he said. Dad left the sofa and moved to the desk. He stood in front of it. It made me uncomfortable looking up at my father, so I stood, too.

"I would never ask anyone to do anything I was not willing to do myself if I had the skills."

"OK."

"From what I know of you, you're very good at what you do. Tough, resourceful, persistent, sometimes ruthless."

"OK."

"If you weren't my son, you'd still be just the kind of man I would hire for this job."

"What job?"

"I want you to get Mrs. Gustafson's money back."

"How?"

"By hook or by crook."

"By crook?"

"By whatever it takes."

I sat down.

"Hi," I said.

"Hi, yourself."

I was always pleased to hear Cynthia Grey's voice. It was very soothing, almost like a melody played on a musical instrument, a clarinet, Artie Shaw doing "Summertime." You listen to the voice, not the words.

"I didn't wake you, did I?" It was eleven-fifteen P.M. in the Twin Cities.

"No, I was watching Leno. How are you?"

"Fine. Listen, I'm coming home tomorrow."

"I thought you were staying with your parents the entire week."

"Something came up that I have to deal with. Can I see you?"

"You had better," she told me.

"No, I mean professionally."

She hesitated. "Sure. What's up?"

"It's one of those things you have to explain in person."

"You're not in trouble again, are you?"

"Not yet."

"Uh-huh."

I changed the subject. "How have you been?"

She hesitated again. "OK."

"OK?"

"Yes," she said, but the word was weak and followed by an audible gasp.

"Cynthia?"

"It's nothing," she said. Her weeping was now unmistakable.

"Cynthia? Cynthia, are you all right?" I was alarmed. Cynthia Grey never cried. Never. Not even when someone had shot at her.

"Yes, it's just . . . I can't . . . I've been crying since noon and I can't stop."

"What's wrong? Tell me what happened."

"Nothing's wrong . . . It's just . . . It's just—"

"What? What happened?"

"They offered a settlement," she informed me between sobs.

"The clothing people?"

"I took it to my . . . clients. Told them they could do better . . . in court . . . but they voted unanimously to accept it."

"How much?"

"Sealed," she said. She was weeping freely now. "Sealed. No admission . . . of wrongdoing. No statements . . . to the media."

"Cynthia," I said softly, wishing I was there, wanting to wrap my arms around her, wanting to comfort her.

"I don't believe it. After everything that's happened . . . to me, after . . . everything that I've been through . . . it comes to this. I just don't . . . believe it."

"Most out-of-court settlements are sealed, aren't they?"

I asked, trying to be understanding from fourteen hundred miles away. "No admission of guilt? Isn't that why companies settle out of court, so they don't have to admit their guilt?"

"Oh, hell, Taylor. I don't care . . . about that."

"Are you upset that your clients caved?"

"No . . . They were anxious to get on . . . with their lives . . . I don't blame . . . them."

"What's wrong, then?"

"*Nothing's* . . . wrong."

"Then why are you crying?"

"I'm rich," she said. "I'm filthy . . . stinking . . . rich."

TWO

I'VE NEVER HAD much luck with Cynthia Grey's office manager. Her sensitivity is well organized and alert to offense, and she always finds something in my speech or actions to protest, no matter how carefully I monitor myself. Not to mention she holds me personally responsible for the killing of one of Cynthia's clients. I had nothing to do with his death, but he was involved in a case I was working on, so she blames me just the same. It's not that she cared for the guy. I doubt she ever spoke to him beyond, "Ms. Grey will be with you in a moment if you care to take a seat." But clients getting killed is bad for business, especially if they haven't settled their accounts first, and she is opposed to anything even remotely bad for business. Besides, she is the keeper of Cynthia's schedule. Part of her job is making sure every court appearance, every deposition, every meeting, happens when it's supposed to happen, and whenever I come around, usually unannounced, well, there goes the schedule.

Yet despite her animosity toward me, she seemed genuinely thrilled when I walked into the office suite, like I was a high school pal she hadn't seen since the last reunion.

"Taylor!" she cried, coming to the door, wrapping her arms around me, hugging me to the very marrow of my soul. "It's good to see you," she announced. Her eyes were moist and blazing with light, her smile was bright enough to read by. Scared the hell out of me.

"What's going on?" I asked, my hand moving instinctively to my right hip where my gun would have been if I had been carrying it.

"Same old same old," she sang back. "How are you?"

I set my suitcase on the floor; I had come straight from the airport by cab. "Same old same old," I said.

"How was Florida? Sunny?" The woman was practically giddy.

"That's why they call it the Sunshine State," I replied.

"I bet you're here to see the lovely Miss Cynthia. I'll buzz her," she said and fairly skipped to her desk. She picked up the telephone receiver, punched two numbers, waited, and said, "Hey, Cynthia, guess what. Taylor is here. . . . I sure will." She replaced the receiver. "Go right in," she said, waving toward the door. I walked slowly to the door, never taking my eyes off of her.

"What's with Miss Efficiency?" I asked when I was safely inside Cynthia's office. "She high on some new designer drug?"

"No," Cynthia said, "just the usual thing: money." Cynthia's smile was dazzling. If you could read by Miss Efficiency's newfound smile, you could signal ships at sea with Cynthia's. I leaned in, turning my head to peck her cheek. But she met my lips with hers and kissed me long and hard. There was no hunger in her kiss, only a deep affection that often frightened me.

She broke the kiss. "Good to see you," she said.

"Good to see you. What money?"

Cynthia seemed puzzled.

"You said Miss Efficiency was high on money," I added.

"She has a name, you know. Desirée."

"I had a home economics teacher named Desirée."

"You took home economics?"

"It's a long story."

"I bet."

"What money?"

"I gave her a bonus this morning."

"Must have been some bonus."

"Twenty-five thousand dollars," Cynthia said casually, circling her desk.

"Say what?" I was genuinely amazed.

"It's no big thing."

"Apparently Desirée disagrees."

"Apparently so do you," she said, settling into her chair. "You've received twenty-five thousand dollar bonuses before. I read about it in the paper. That company you helped, August-Crane."

"I helped save August-Crane from a hostile takeover."

"Yes, well . . ."

"How much money did you make on this case, anyway?" I asked, sitting in the large wing chair in front of Cynthia's desk.

Cynthia smiled some more, looked down at the desk blotter, and drew a little circle with her fingernail. "Twenty-seven percent," she said softly.

"Twenty-seven percent of what?"

"Sealed," she replied, shaking her head.

"Does Desirée know the amount?"

"She keeps the books."

"Desirée!" I shouted. The door to Cynthia's office opened a moment later, and Desirée peeked in. "How much did Cynthia—and you—make on the sexual harassment settlement?"

Desirée glanced up at Cynthia and smiled. "Twenty-seven percent," she said.

"Fine, fine, fine," I repeated, admitting defeat.

"You're kinda cute, you know that?" Desirée giggled. "You kids should go home. It's almost closing time," she announced and shut the door.

"The woman has gone goofy," I told Cynthia.

"She'll get over it," she said, putting her feet up on her desk. She was wearing black slacks and a white turtleneck under a black linen jacket. Those were the only colors Cynthia ever wore: black and white. She had hired a woman to choose a wardrobe for her, to devise a "look," and this is what she came up with. She had hired another to do her hair and makeup; another to teach her poise, elocution, and what books to read; and another to decorate her office and home. She was a self-made woman, my Cynthia.

Our eyes locked. She smiled at me and I smiled at her. As is becoming increasingly frequent with us, we found ourselves thinking the same thing at the same time.

"You've come a long way since the psychiatric ward at Lake Memorial," I told her.

"Seems like a long way." She paused a moment and then added, "Sometimes I wonder why I'm not dead."

"Divine intervention," I told her.

"Think so?"

"Either that or the old saying is true: Only the good die young."

"Then I should live forever."

"God, I hope so."

That's when Cynthia went serious on me. It was like someone flipped a light switch. "I'm worried," she said. "I've been worried ever since we accepted the settlement."

"About what?"

"Is my . . . wealth . . . going to affect our relationship?"

"Absolutely."

"It is?" She seemed frightened.

"I expect to be entertained at a much finer class of restaurant for one thing."

"Oh?" she said. "Will you wear a tie?"

"If you're buying, I'll wear a tie."

"And dress pants and shoes instead of jeans and sneakers?"

"You're becoming awfully demanding."

"I can afford it."

"Sure, dress pants and shoes."

"I'm serious."

"So am I," I said, only I wasn't and she was. It's a failing of mine, not taking seriously what others deem terribly important. Her sigh told me that our conversation wasn't going the way she'd hoped, and the hurt look in her eyes . . . I had put it there. The moment called for a show of sincerity, and I wasn't very good at that. But I tried.

"Listen," I told her, "you're good at your job, one of the best in this market, maybe the entire country. And you're paid accordingly. Sure, you could make more money working for one of the bigger law firms, get yourself a corner office, but you'd lose your freedom. Me? I'm also good at my job, one of the best in this market, maybe the entire country. And I'm paid accordingly. Sure, I could make more money working for one of the bigger PI firms, but I'd lose my freedom.

"What I'm trying to say is, you and I are a lot alike—professionally, I mean. We both enjoy what we do, we both care about what we do. The only difference is that the practice of law is more lucrative than my chosen profession, at least for those who do it well. I'm happy doing what I do. I wouldn't be happy doing what you do. Money doesn't enter into it. I'm saying this badly, I know," I said.

"No, you're not," Cynthia told me.

"I don't care about the money; I never have," I added.

"You know how I live. I drive a 1979 Monza, for God's sake. It's not the money, it's the caring that matters to me. If you became just an empty suit chasing bucks, that would make a difference. Getting rich? Who cares? Well, I care; I'm really happy for you. It's great. It's just that . . . "

I paused. "If the money doesn't change you, it won't change us. OK?"

"OK," she said. She seemed relieved. "Anyway, what I said last night about being filthy, stinking rich isn't exactly true, what with taxes. . . . "

"And bonuses," I volunteered.

"Yeah, and bonuses. I'm not so much rich as I am really, really, really well off."

"So instead of being stinking rich, you're merely smelly rich."

"Exactly."

"Not going to retire?"

"Not until I can afford to support myself in a style to which I intend to become accustomed."

"That brings me to why I'm here. I'd like to talk to you about a client."

Cynthia came around the desk, knelt next to my chair, took my hand, and kissed my index finger. "Let's talk later."

"This is important," I told her.

"Later," she repeated, standing and pulling my hand. "I want to go to bed with you. We're ten minutes away from my house. Let's go."

"Can we eat first? I'm starving. All I've had today is peanuts on the plane."

Cynthia was shocked. "If I live a thousand years I'll never understand men," she told me.

"Fast food. It'll only take a minute. . . . "

CYNTHIA SAT CROSSED-LEGGED on her bed, using a spoon to shovel Kung Pao chicken into her mouth from a white cardboard container, marking her pleasure with a series of "hmm's" and "ahh's."

"I love this stuff," she said. "When I was dancing in Minneapolis, there was this Vietnamese joint across the street. Every day I'd go for a helping. I couldn't get enough of it. It was better than mace, too. Whenever the patrons got a little too close, put their grubby paws on me, I'd give 'em one of these. . . ." She opened her mouth and exhaled sharply. "As long as the guy didn't have a sinus condition, I had no problems."

Cynthia was wearing my Christmas present to her, a silver silk nightgown trimmed with white lace that I'd bought out of the Victoria's Secret catalog. She looked as delicious in it as the model, making me want to shout, "My girl! This is my girl!" But I was afraid she would disapprove.

"Now, aren't you glad you waited to eat?" she asked.

"Man does not live by bread alone," I answered from the love seat where I lounged, propped up against a few pillows, eating sweet-and-sour beef from an identical container. I was wearing the same clothes I'd put on that morning in Florida, having been sent into the cold, dark night in search of take-out after Cynthia had had her way with me.

Between bites, Cynthia said, "So, tell me about this client of yours."

I did, leaving nothing out, even describing Mrs. Gustafson's ancient hands.

"'By hook or by crook'?" she asked. "Your father isn't encouraging you to commit a criminal act, is he?"

"Amazing, isn't it? This is the same man who took a belt to me for stealing a stick of Chum Gum from the corner store when I was a kid, then made me go back to the store and apologize."

"What does he expect you to do? Shove a gun into Field's ribs and make him an offer he can't refuse?"

"That's almost exactly what I asked him."

"What'd he say?"

"Didn't say anything, just shrugged."

"Shrugged?"

"'What's that mean?' I asked him."

"And?"

"He shrugged again."

"Eloquent man."

I took another bite of the sweet-and-sour, speaking through it. "My Dad is interested in results. 'Give me solutions, not problems,' he tells his employees. He's not much interested in how I go about it, just as long as I get the job done."

"I know what I'd suggest if he wasn't your father."

"What's that?"

"Tell him to go to hell."

"I almost did."

"Why didn't you?"

"When I was in high school, I convinced him to send me on a senior class trip, a six-day cruise to the Bahamas. Only it wasn't a class trip, it was just a bunch of us who decided it'd be fun to get out of the country during spring break."

"He ever learn the truth?"

"He knew the truth before we left."

"And he let you go, anyway?"

"He admired my audacity," I said. "He said I reminded him of himself."

"Really? If I'd tried to pull something like that, my grandfather would have whipped out that belt you mentioned." She stopped eating for a moment and stared wistfully at some invisible spot above my head.

Cynthia had never met her father, and her alcoholic mother abandoned her when she was just six. Six years later, Cynthia's grandparents did the same, dying within a few months of each other. Cynthia became a ward of the state, a number on a piece of paper that was often mislaid. She wandered aimlessly, unloved and unloving, between halfway houses, foster homes, and the street. Drugs and alcohol were her only friends, and to keep them—although she never admitted to it, and I never asked—I suspect she hooked. Finally, she quit on herself and swallowed a bottle of furniture polish. But she did not die. To her surprise and disappointment, she woke in a county hospital, her arms in restraints, not an angel in sight. Since she didn't have insurance, the hospital quit on her, too, placing her in a security ward with a few dozen major-league crazies. And there, profoundly lost, amid chaos and catastrophic emotional and mental suffering that most of us couldn't possibly imagine, she found sanity.

She was "scared straight," if you will; certainly she started thinking straight for the first time in years. She devised a plan, one she has lived by to this very day. It was really quite simple. Since she so thoroughly detested Cyndi Grey—that's how she spelled her name, dotting the "i" with a heart—she would replace her with someone more to her liking. She would reinvent herself, starting with her name: Cynthia Grey, don't even think of calling her Cyndi.

Cynthia couldn't wait to get out of the hospital; she attempted several daring if not well-thought out escapes that, of course, only put her back in restraints. But once she convinced the staff that she was no longer trying to leave, they were happy to release her. Immediately, Cynthia set about earning her high school general equivalency diploma, at the same time taking the twelve-step cure. Then she entered a three-plus-three program at the University of Minnesota—three years of college, three years of law school—finishing tenth in her class. To pay for her education, she danced on tabletops for twenty bucks a pop at a strip joint in downtown Minneapolis under the name Alette, which Cynthia understood to mean "take wing."

CYNTHIA TOOK ANOTHER bite of her chicken and then announced, "If I ever have children, I'm sending them on a cruise to the Bahamas when they graduate from high school."

I had nothing to say to that.

"So," she said, waving her spoon at me, "how are you going to help your father help Mrs. Gustafson?"

"I was hoping you'd have a suggestion."

"Litigation is expensive and time consuming," she reminded me, picking at her meal with the spoon, searching for more chicken.

"So I've been told."

"Perhaps we can avoid it. That is, if you want my help."

"Yes, please."

"Tomorrow morning I'll give this Levering Field a call and arrange a face-to-face. . . ."

"'Face-to-face'? Is that lawyer talk?"

Cynthia frowned at me and continued, "Just because something's unethical doesn't make it illegal, so I don't think invoking the attorney general will frighten him. And he's not subject to the same rules of conduct as a stockbroker, so we can't bring our case before an arbitrator. But, we can always threaten him with an investor fraud suit, see if he wants to be reasonable."

"Think he will?"

"A man in his position, the last thing he wants is a civil suit. Word gets out, it could kill his business—especially if he's sued by a high-profile attorney with access to the media."

"Like you?"

"Kinda makes you want to treat me with more respect, doesn't it?"

I set the remains of my meal on a table and moved slowly toward the bed. Cynthia set her chicken aside when she saw me coming.

"Respect, admiration, affection, desire . . ." I said.

"Love?"

"There's that word again." Our faces were inches apart.

"Funny how it keeps popping up in conversation."

"I worship the ground you walk on," I told her.

"That'll do," she said, kissing me ever so gently. "For now."

THREE

Levering Field spoke in the oily manner of a man who sold things he's never seen. He appeared to us in the lobby of his Minneapolis office like he had just stepped out of his own brochure—the one on the table in the reception area that pictured him explaining retirement plans to a small group of transfixed seniors. His face was tanned and handsome with a thin mustache that was meant to convey maturity and trustworthiness; his smile had a practiced quality.

Counting the watch and rings, I estimated that the ensemble he wore cost more than my car had new—hell, his suit alone was probably worth a couple of house payments, and this wasn't even a big day for him. He probably wore five hundred dollar sports jackets when he cleaned the garage.

He took Cynthia's hand in both of his and gushed how pleased he was to meet her and how much he admired her. Then he took my hand; his grip was firm but not too firm. "Holland Taylor, the famed private eye," he said. "Welcome."

OK, maybe Cynthia was famous, at least for a few days.

But me? Not a chance. He must have checked me out after Cynthia had called last week.

I gave him a hard look. While I examined him, he examined me, moving practiced eyes over my Kuppenheimer sports jacket, faded jeans, and white Nikes. His lips formed a slight, almost imperceptible grin, as if he had calculated my entire net worth, right down to the two quarters and a nickel in my pants pocket, and was unimpressed. His grin broadened into a full-fledged smile when he appraised Cynthia. But then, she looked like the GNP of Argentina.

"We can conduct our business in my office," he said, leading the way. "My own attorney should be here directly."

"Fine," Cynthia said, all business.

"Miss Portia," Field said, speaking to his secretary, "when my attorney arrives, send her straight in; otherwise, no interruptions, please."

"Of course," Miss Portia said without looking up. A young woman, she had an unhealthy pallor—she looked as though she had taken a bath in whitewash. Her long, golden hair was rolled up like a wave above her forehead. She wore no lipstick, no rouge, no mascara, no makeup whatsoever. She might have been pretty if she worked at it; all the natural resources were there: attractive blond hair, neat smile, and bright if not warm eyes. As it was, she looked incomplete.

"You should buy that young lady a sunlamp," I told Field behind his closed office door. "She looks like a ghost."

"Yeah, but the bitch is an animal in bed," he said and laughed. The laugh died quickly when his brain caught up with his mouth, and he realized Cynthia was listening to every word.

Field ushered us deeper into his huge office. It was very carefully organized to reflect both success and power. The carpet was deep; you could not hear the sound of your own footsteps. The furniture was dark and highly polished. Three walls were filled with works of French Impressionists—Edgar Degas, Georges Seurat, Cézanne, Monet. The frames were painted with gold leaf, and small lamps arched away from the wall, lighting each painting, giving the impression that these reproductions were as valuable as the originals. The fourth wall consisted entirely of glass and had a southern exposure and maximum sunlight. Positioned in front of the glass was Field's desk. Only slightly larger and the Seventh Fleet could have used it for an aircraft carrier. On top of the desk was a computer terminal, phone, notepad, pencil, and a photograph of an attractive young woman of maybe sixteen. Strategically placed before the desk were two chairs, the legs of both had been sawed off so that anyone sitting in them would be looking up at Field and into the sun. He beckoned us to sit.

Expressionlessly, Cynthia tapped the arm of one of the chairs. "I prefer to sit there," she said, motioning with her head at the glass coffee table in the corner. The two sides of the table facing the office were open; the two sides facing the wall were bordered by low-slung leather sofas.

"As you wish," Field said, bowing his head slightly, fighting a frown. He moved to the table, indicating that Cynthia take a seat on one of the sofas. Instead, she turned one of the chairs around and moved it to the table, sitting there. She was now perched several inches above Field, who had to look up at her. Point to Cynthia.

"May I offer you anything? Coffee? Spring water?" Field was smiling again when he made the offer, but it had a forced quality and I found myself humming a lyric from a golden oldie by Undisputed Truth: *"A smile is just a frown turned upside down."*

Cynthia made a production out of reading her wristwatch. It was 9:03 in the morning. She sighed deeply, like she had been waiting for hours and said, "Thank you, no." I shook my head no. Cynthia had made me promise to let her do all the talking.

At that moment the door opened, and a woman hurried into the room. She had black hair trimmed to her shoulders and dark eyes. She wore a black mandarin-collared jacket tailored to emphasize her small waist and a black skirt long enough to be considered professional yet short enough to show off her legs. She was a handsome woman, and just looking at her made me smile. I guessed her age at about thirty-five.

"Sorry, I'm late Mr. Field. Traffic," she said in a firm voice. "Mr. Taylor, a pleasure to meet you," she told me, taking my hand, not waiting for introductions. But she wasn't paying attention to me. Her eyes were on Cynthia, and she didn't take long to get to her.

"Cynthia," she said simply.

"Monica," Cynthia replied.

They shook hands and their eyes locked, like samurai warriors about to strike. Cynthia also had dark hair and eyes, a small waist, and killer legs. But she wore white to Monica's black—an ivory, double-breasted blazer over a matching camisole and a pleated skirt that brushed her knee. The two of them together, shaking hands, was like a scene out of an Akira Kurosawa movie—*Ran* or *The Seven Samurai*, maybe. You just knew blood was going to flow.

"Congratulations on your settlement," Monica said.

"Thank you," Cynthia said. "And congratulations to you. I hear you started your own firm."

"Just following in your footsteps," said Monica.

"As always," was Cynthia's reply.

Oh, man. This is going to be fun, I told myself.

"Let's get to it, shall we?" Monica said, turning her back

on Cynthia and finding a place to sit next to Field. "You are accusing my client of a breach of fiduciary responsibility."

"That is a somewhat premature characterization," Cynthia said. "At the present time we are not accusing your client of anything."

"Then I take it this is just a social call."

"I prefer to consider it a reconnaissance in force."

"You always were partial to military metaphors."

"As opposed to the language of appeasement."

Monica absorbed the blow without faltering. "I ask you, then, to please state your intentions as clearly as possible in whatever tongue you're using these days. We can wait if you first want to hire a PR firm."

"That won't be necessary," Cynthia countered. "There is no one here I need to impress."

I admit I was enjoying the spectacle of these two women slugging it out, and I was speculating on how long it would take before they started tearing clothes and wrestling in mud. But Levering Field's attention span seemed considerably shorter than mine. After consulting his watch several times he announced, "Shit, ladies. Let's cut to the chase, huh? I have things to do."

"Let's," echoed Monica—I had yet to learn her last name. Before she could continue, however, Field did what Cynthia made me promise not to: He spoke for his attorney.

"Mrs. Gustafson. I'm sorry for her losses, but that's the way it goes, OK? No use crying crocodile tears over it."

"Mr. Field . . ." Monica interrupted.

"Hey, if I wait on you two, I'll be here until fucking Christmas," he said, then quickly added, "Forgive my French. Look, Cynthia—may I call you Cynthia?—investments sometimes go south, OK? If it was easy, if there was no risk, everyone would do it and everyone would be rich. Mrs. Gustafson knew what she was getting into—"

"She claims she didn't."

"I have a piece of paper with her signature that says she did."

Monica tried to interrupt again. "Mr. Field, would you please . . ."

Field ignored her. "Now, I keep excellent records. My records go beyond what is required. If you look carefully—and a court will, am I right?—if you look carefully, you'll see I dealt fairly with her. I never misled her. She always knew what I was doing. You cannot build a long-term relationship on misinformation, and we were together—it's gotta be like ten years, OK?"

"We're only concerned about the recent investment in Willow Tree, LP," Cynthia said, "not in your previous dealings."

"If that had paid off, she would have made more money than you did on that harassment case. Easy. It was a risk, sure. Didn't work out, fine. That's the way it goes. But she knew about it, she knew what we were getting into. I sent her the information. She didn't respond. That's how we worked together, OK? I sent information, explaining what we were getting into. If she had questions, she called and we did what we had to do, otherwise I went ahead. That's how we did things for ten years. I have records."

"She was lying on her back in a hospital recovering from a stroke when you concocted this scheme," I told him, probably with a little more anger than was necessary.

"I didn't know that, did I?"

"The hell you didn't," I said.

Cynthia shot me a look. It was not pleasant. I tucked my head in, folded my arms, and pretended to be somewhere else.

"That's enough, Mr. Field," Monica insisted.

But Field insisted right back. "Look, I'm paying you by the hour, right? I can't afford to pussyfoot around," he told her and then turned back to Cynthia. "I have records."

"I'm looking forward to subpoenaing them," Cynthia said.

"Subpoena, shit. You can have 'em, lady. I have nothing to hide. Just don't try to strong-arm me, OK? I have a good lawyer sitting here, and she's dying to mount your head on her wall. Am I right, Monica?"

Monica said nothing.

"Now, they tell me you're smart," Field told Cynthia. "They say you're as sharp as a broken beer bottle, OK? Well, I'm a pretty bright fellow, too. For example, I know you can't take me to an arbitrator alleging broker fraud 'cuz I ain't a broker. There aren't any rules of fiduciary responsibility I'm mandated to follow. Which means you're comtemplating a civil court case. Now, don't deny it," he said when Cynthia began to speak. "Well, the average investor fraud case takes five years or more to litigate, and even those who win only recover fifty-to-sixty percent of their losses."

"True," Cynthia agreed. "On the other hand, seventy percent of investor fraud suits that are filed are won by the investors in court or settled to their satisfaction out of court."

"Notice the way I'm trembling with fear?" Field said contemptuously.

Monica clearly wanted to say something to him, but she didn't.

"You want to file on me, I'll keep you in court for six, seven years, maybe go for a world's record for length of litigation," Field added. "And even then I'll win. Because I did nothing wrong. I didn't steal from anybody, and you can't prove that I did. But for argument's sake, let's say I don't win. Let's say you get yourself a bleeding-heart jury that sees it your way. There isn't anything they can give you. No, ma'am. All my assets—my house, my cars, every penny—is in my sixteen-year-old daughter's name. She has everything, I have nothing."

"The court will change that in a hurry," Cynthia said.

"A hurry?" countered Field. "What legal system do you work in? It'll add another year to the process, easy. What are we talking about then, eight years? More? Mrs. Gustafson just celebrated the big eight-five, did she not? And she just suffered a stroke? I'm willing to bet that she's not around to see the end of this. How about you?"

"For Mrs. Gustafson's sake, it was our hope we could avoid a protracted court case," Cynthia admitted.

"You want me to settle? Is that the alternative? I don't think so."

"Perhaps we can convince you to change your mind."

"And how are you going to do that, Cynthia? Wait. Let me guess. You're going to tell me that if I don't settle, you're going to use your media contacts to wreck my business—maybe bring the old lady up from Florida and hold a press conference, put me on the evening news. Is that the plan? Think again." Levering Field nudged Monica with an elbow. "Tell her."

"This is a low-profile litigation," Monica spoke up. "The only reason it would interest the media is because of your involvement in it. You would be the story. And we believe the media's attention to your . . . let's just say, your past . . . would more than offset any negative publicity my client might receive." And then Monica smiled. "I know all your secrets, Cynthia. I know you like a book."

Cynthia's expression did not change. I was ready to drive a spear hand through Monica's throat, but Cynthia remained as calm and businesslike as when she had first entered the office. She'd spent nearly ten—God, fifteen—years carefully remaking herself, creating and nurturing an image as pure and unblemished as the Lincoln Memorial. Now Monica was threatening to tag it like a graffiti artist, and Cynthia did not so much as bat an eyelash.

"Know me like a book?" she asked. "I think not, Monica.

Or you would know better than to underestimate me."
The room went silent for a moment; then Cynthia announ-
ced, "I think we're finished here," and she started to rise.
  "Now, now, there's no reason for petulance," Field said.
  "Pet-u-lance?" I repeated slowly, but Field ignored me.
  "I was merely suggesting what *could* happen, not what
will happen."
  "I'm listening," Cynthia countered.
  "I feel real bad about Mrs. Gustafson, and I would like
to do something for her, but not because of the threat of
litigation. I want to do something because, well, dammit,
because I'm a nice guy."
  Monica rolled her eyes, but neither Field nor Cynthia
seemed to notice, locked on each other the way they were.
  "I'm listening," Cynthia repeated.
  "What I propose is this: I will return to Mrs. Gustafson
all the money I made on the deal. Ten percent, OK? I'll
give you a check right now for twenty-eight thousand
seven hundred dollars; tell her I'm sorry it didn't work
out. Is that satisfactory?"
  "Mr. Field . . ." Monica tried again.
  "What do you say?" Field smiled at Cynthia. Then he
smiled at me. That's when I knew the sonuvabitch could
be had.
  "There was this guy named Raskolnikov," I told Field.
"An asshole, only interested in money—you know the type.
One day he murdered his landlady." I shook my head for
emphasis. "The crime completely ruined his life. Nothing
worked out for him after that. His relationships—everything fell apart. And the guilt? It got so bad, he couldn't live
with it. Eventually, he decided that in order to save himself,
he had to turn himself in and pay restitution."
  "What are you talking about?" Monica wanted to know.
From her expression, I gathered Cynthia was just as curious.

"*Crime and Punishment,*" Field answered. "You know, by Dostoyevsky." Monica's and Cynthia's confused expressions did not change. "Don't you guys read?"

"I bet the same thing happens to you," I continued. "I tell you, Levering . . . can I call you Levering?"

"My friends call me Ring."

"Ahh. I tell you, Ring, you did a terrible thing, ripping off that poor old woman, leaving her penniless. It wouldn't surprise me a bit if your conscience came to bother you so much that one day you just up and called me and offered to give the money back—all two hundred and eighty-seven thousand."

Field laughed. Monica did not. She was on her feet, accusing me of threatening her client, promising legal action if I continued.

"What threat? Did you hear a threat, Ring? I just told the man about a book I read, that's all." I took a business card from my wallet and dropped it on the table. "Call me when you're ready," I told Field.

CYNTHIA WAITED UNTIL we hit the street before asking, "What the fuck did you think you were doing?"

"Ms. Grey," I feigned shock. "What would your elocution master say?"

Cynthia stopped me, maneuvered in front of me, and pointed a finger. "Don't joke. I am not in the mood."

I took her arm. We were on Sixth between Marquette and Nicollet in downtown Minneapolis, heading toward my office in the Butler Square Building.

"He's vulnerable," I told her. "He can be squeezed. And that's what I intend to do—squeeze him like an orange until there's nothing left but pulp."

"You're kidding, right?"

"He overplayed his hand," I said. "That's what my dad would tell you. He had all the cards, and then he overplayed his hand. Why?" When Cynthia did not reply, I continued. "He thinks twenty-eight seven is a generous offer. Maybe it is. The question is, why did he make it?"

Cynthia pulled her arm out of my hand; I guess I was gripping it too tightly. "Maybe he is a nice guy. Maybe it was all a terrible mistake."

"You believe that?"

Cynthia thought carefully before answering, "He wants to stay out of court."

"Why?" I asked.

"Because it's bad for business, why do you think? Monica isn't stupid; she knows what I intend to do next."

"What do you intend to do next?"

"We file suit on behalf of Mrs. Gustafson. Then, using the rules of discovery, we subpeona the records of every single client Levering Field has ever had. Let's say we learn he's defrauded ten, fifteen, twenty other investors. In response, we file a class-action suit on behalf of all of them. Then we'll send a letter to every one of his clients telling them what we're doing, asking them if they want to participate in the suit. We could get hundreds of participants. And even if we don't, the letter will destroy him."

Cynthia smiled at the prospect. "Let's see if he likes going back to making cold calls."

"How long would it take?" I asked Cynthia. When she didn't reply, I asked, "Can you guarantee that Mrs. Gustafson will get her money back? All of it?" When she still didn't answer, I said, "Forget it."

Cynthia stopped, letting me walk several steps ahead. "You're not making any sense!" she shouted.

I turned back to her. "Levering Field is not afraid of you. He has a lawyer who's already painted a bull's-eye on your forehead. He put all of his assets in his kid's name, what do you think that is about? He's not afraid of the legal system. But something else does frighten him. He made the offer because he doesn't want us to discover what it is."

"What difference does it make as long as he settles?"

"For ten cents on the dollar? Or a quarter? Not good enough."

We continued walking, crossing Nicollet, heading west toward Hennepin.

"Why are you so angry?" Cynthia asked.

"I don't like the way he treated you."

Her reaction was swift. "Don't you dare," she said, grabbing my arm, swinging me around. "Don't you dare do this because of me." She backed me against a store window. There was a mannequin on the other side of the glass, smiling.

"I will not have it! No, I most certainly will not!"

My first impulse was to go with a joke, something like, "Gosh you're beautiful when you're angry." I thought better of it. I had taught her a few karate moves, and she was perfectly capable of hurting me. I said nothing.

"Sooner or later someone is going to come after me, using my past as a weapon. I know that. I have always known that. When it happens, I'll deal with it. *I will deal with it!* If you can't, then we should hang it up right here and now because I will not have you going around picking fights to protect my virtue. I will not tolerate it."

Being at a loss for words, I did the only thing I could think to do. I kissed her. Yeah, it's a cliché—probably a sexist cliché—but it always worked for Humphrey Bogart and Erroll Flynn and even John Wayne. People on the street walked by smiling as I kissed her. And when I finished kissing her, she said, "So, are we clear on this?" I kissed her some more. Then I did something I did not think to do at all—but should have done a long time ago. I said, "I love you."

"I'll be damned," she replied.

———————————

A FEW MINUTES later we were walking arm in arm toward my office. We stopped for a traffic light, and I said, "Tell me about Monica."

"Monica Adler," she said without hesitation. "We were classmates at the U. And friends, I suppose. I didn't have many friends in those days. Truth is, I still don't. I guess I confided more to her than I should have, certainly more than I've told anyone else. Except you." Cynthia hugged my arm with that admission, then continued her story.

"We were pitted against each other in moot court when we were L-threes. Both our teams reached the quarter finals. Her team had a stronger case than we did, so when we won the coin toss, my partner and I chose to argue off-brief, meaning we decided to take her side in the case, and she was forced to take our side; the idea is that the school wants to make sure that their lawyers can argue both sides of a case. She wasn't prepared to argue off-brief, and we cleaned her clock. It was her own fault, hers and her partner's. They should have been ready. But the way she saw it, she and I were supposed to be friends, and I made her look bad.

"Later, when we were graduated, I was ranked tenth in the class. She was eleventh. Rankings in law school are like your precious NBA draft: It affects where you end up and the amount of money you can command. I had always planned to start my own shop, so it wasn't a big deal to me. But Monica, she wanted one of the old firms that had the word 'prestige' practically stamped on its letterhead. Dropping out of the top ten lost her the opportunity to work for some of them and reduced the amount of money she could earn from the others. She blamed me for that, too. She couldn't understand why I didn't take a dive for her during finals."

"Now she wants a piece of you, prove who's the fastest gun in town," I suggested.

"Just another tough-talkin' sodbuster lookin' ta make a name for herself. Lord, listen to me. I'm beginning to talk like you."

I nodded but said nothing. In the back of my mind I was plotting my assault on Levering Field, and wondering if there was a way I could get Monica Adler at the same time.

I invited Cynthia to dinner when we reached her car, which was parked in the lot across from my building. She declined. She was meeting with a group of potential clients. They wanted to file a suit claiming emotional distress against the family clinic where they had been patients—the clinic had employed a doctor who had recently died of AIDS.

"What are you going to do?" she asked me. She wasn't referring to my dinner plans.

"You don't want to know."

"Dammit, Taylor," she muttered, opening her car door, sliding in, "I'm not a criminal attorney."

Never do anything out of anger. Who told me that? Dad, of course. My high school hockey coach. An instructor at the academy. My Sensi at Dragons, he was a great one: *"When anger goes out, withdraw hand; when hand goes out, withdraw anger."* Something like that. He was right, too. They all were. So I went to my office, popped a Dr Pepper, put my feet on my desk, and looked out the window, forcing myself to stop being angry. It wasn't easy.

Guys like Levering Field infuriate me. He's a part of that growing class of people who have no conception of the pain they cause others through their carelessness, indifference, neglect; who refuse to accept responsibility for their actions. Our streets are literally teeming with them, too. Individuals who cry, "Don't blame me, it's not my fault" at every mishap. A guy falls from the top rung of a ladder the label says not to stand on, he sues the manufacturer. Woman smokes for forty years and dies of lung cancer, the family blames the tobacco company. Man embezzles a million bucks from a charity, claims he's not responsible because he's suffering from brain atrophy that makes him impulsive. I remember serving paper on a couple that had owned an advertising agency in St. Paul. They had ripped off their suppliers to the tune of $1.2 million before locking their doors and walking away. They were packing for a trip to Epcot Center when I'd found them, absolutely mystified that anyone would be upset. It wasn't their fault they never paid their debts. Blame the economy.

Well, Levering Field wasn't going to get away with it. I was going to crush him like a grape, core him like an apple. I found myself chuckling at the images—for some reason I thought of him as produce. How to go about peeling him like a banana wasn't an issue, either. I had conceived my plan on the spot, marveling at its simplicity. The immense risk did not occur to me until much later.

But I did not want to be angry when I went after him. Angry people make mistakes.

I emptied the pop can and tossed it at my waste basket. It clanged on the metal rim, then fell in. Two points. I pushed myself out of the chair and went back to the refrigerator. Before serving myself another can, however, I ran my finger along the top of the refrigerator and regarded the grit and grime it had collected. I decided the place needed a good scrubbing.

Retrieving a roll of paper towels and a jug of liquid cleaner with a spray nozzle from the bottom drawer of my desk, I started to clean. I clean a lot. Cynthia often ridicules my "neat freak" ways, but she's not one to talk—she hires a woman to clean her house every week. Besides, cleaning is good therapy; it relaxes me.

I dusted my hockey stick, the one Wayne Gretzky broke against the North Stars back when he'd played for Edmonton. I dusted my framed "homer hanky" that, like a lot of people who won't admit now, I waved like a damn fool when the Minnesota Twins won the 1987 World Series. And I carefully dusted the framed photograph of me and Kirby Puckett. He's wearing his baseball uniform; I'm wearing a stupid grin. He had written on the photograph: *To a good guy, best wishes, Kirby Puckett.* People who see it invariably ask, "Do you really know Kirby?" I always cross two fingers and hold them up. "We're like that," I say. Truth is, I met Kirby Puckett twice, once at Camera Day when the photo was taken and the second time outside the players' entrance to the Metrodome, where I begged him to sign it. He seemed like a nice guy.

Next to it is another photograph in which I look even more ridiculous. It was taken for the Minneapolis newspaper and shows me dressed in a trench coat and fedora and leaning on my personal computer. HAVE PC—WILL TRAVEL, reads the headline of the accompanying article. The story was all about how detectives find missing witnesses, untangle insurance frauds, search for hidden assets, screen potential employees, and investigate business rivals by scouring computerized databases—and how I used my PC to discover damaging information about the key officers of a Chicago-based high-tech firm attempting a hostile takeover of August-Crane, a much revered local firm.

It had been simple enough. I merely followed the social security numbers of Datatron's CEO, CFO, and president until I uncovered several hidden bank accounts in Nevada and Nassau where the three men had quite illegally squirreled away nearly fifty million bucks. I turned the information over to August-Crane, which in turn gave it to the

FBI, SEC and IRS, who fell on Datatron like the wrath of God. The takeover was aborted, the officers were indicted, Datatron was forced into Chapter Seven, and John Crane personally handed me a bonus check for twenty-five thousand dollars. Even Steve VanderTop had been impressed.

Yeah, Steve. I paused in front of the photograph. *If I'm going after Levering Field, I'll need his help,* I told myself.

THE MAIL ARRIVED while I was cleaning. I sorted the batch: bill, junk, bill, junk, bill, junk, junk, junk, junk—hey, a check. It was from Sullivan, Shea, Rock, and Engler. Forty-eight hundred bucks and a note from David Shea: "Without the eleventh-hour information you uncovered, the plaintiff would have ripped off our client for half a million. Thanks for saving our ass. If you ever need a reference, I'm the guy to call. Thanks again."

That was nice of him, I told myself as I did the paperwork, recording the check in my ledger, then folding it and stuffing it in my wallet. Of course ten percent of the five hundred thousand would have been nicer. Or five percent. Or even two and a half. Still, when I left my office, I wasn't angry anymore. Money will do that. Something else. You have a pocketful of money, you start thinking about getting more.

FOUR

STEVE VANDERTOP HAD lived much of his third decade in poverty. And it had made him happy to do so.

Five dollars for food for a week, nights spent sleeping in his car because he didn't have an apartment, clothes from the Salvation Army: these indignities hadn't bothered him a bit. He'd embraced them. Unlike the rest of us who live two paychecks away from homelessness, Steve had enjoyed the precariousness of his lifestyle. It hadn't been poverty to him, it was "the simple life." He'd had his friends, an extended social circle that included nearly anyone except those who have actually known real poverty. He'd had his freedom. And he'd had his philosophy, which, loosely translated, proclaimed: I'm going to live my life now!

Of course, it had helped that he was a VanderTop—one of *the* VanderTops of North Oaks. When times became really tough, his family could always be counted on to provide a square meal, a change of clothes, a Jeep, a membership in a health club. . . . Steve's nourishment for the day might have consisted of a half loaf of French bread off the day-old shelf, but thanks to Mom and Dad, in the evening he'd be going to see the San Francisco Ballet at Northrop Auditorium and then catch "the artist formerly known as Prince" at Glam Slam. The way Steve saw it, he had done his family a favor by mooching off of them.

"It made my parents feel better to give me things," he once told me. "They hated to think their son was living like a dog. Besides, they never really expected me to pay my own way."

However, two separate events during his twenty-fifth year dramatically altered Steve's plan to live blissfully and irresponsibly among the privileged poor—at least until he received his inheritance. His parents gave him a personal computer for his birthday. And he discovered Sara.

STEVE—AND SARA—lived in a warehouse across the tracks from downtown Minneapolis, about twenty minutes walking time from my office. A sign above the front door announced that twenty-seven thousand square feet were available to lease on the first floor. To gain entry, I had to identify myself through an intercom.

"Hey, Taylor, come on up," Steve said happily, buzzing me in.

The elevator was little more than a large metal box with thick pads covering the walls—the kind of quilted blankets movers use to keep furniture from banging the side of their trucks. It shuddered and shook, and when the doors finally opened on the third floor, I literally jumped out, half expecting the box to fall, surprised when it did not.

Steve's place was behind a large steel door that slid sideways on a metal track when you released a spring. It did not have a lock. I pounded on the door, and he yelled, "C'mon in!" The door squealed painfully when it opened.

Steve's loft was decorated in early industrial: Metal beams supported steel girders overhead, huge factory windows made up an entire wall, the wood floor was stained and warped. It was about the size of a junior high school gymnasium; if it wasn't for the beams, there would have been more than enough room for a full-court basketball game.

The only area enclosed behind walls was the bathroom. Steve's kitchen, bedroom, guest bedroom, library, and living room were arranged like galleries in a furniture store, with only empty space separating them. His possessions now included computers, stereo system, big screen TV, aquarium, pool table, golf clubs, and a ten speed. Also in plain sight were their clothes, which hung on racks bought at a department store's going-out-of-business sale. A red silk dress cut down to there hung on the end of one rack. Sara's, I presumed.

Steve was sitting in front of a computer screen, his back to me, long delicate fingers flying over a keyboard. Actually there was a bank of four screens, but only one was on. There was a lot of other equipment, too: hard disk drives, printers, modems, and systems I was not literate enough to identify.

"How the hell are ya, Taylor?" he said, turning his head slightly—one eye on me, one on the screen. "I haven't seen you in ages. Where you been keeping yourself?"

"Here and there," I said.

Steve gave the computer screen his full attention again. He was wearing a University of Minnesota sweatshirt and jeans torn at the knees, no socks or shoes. Thick, silken hair fell in a golden sheet over his shoulders—he usually wore his hair in a ponytail to keep it out of his eyes as he bent to the keyboard, but today he kept brushing it back with his hand. I knew women who would kill to have his hair, as well as his eyebrows and lashes.

"Give me a minute, I'm almost done with this," he said. "Why don't you put on some tunes?"

I took his advice and wandered to his CD/stereo system. He had a huge selection of jazz recordings, half on CDs, half on vinyl. "Nice," I said soft and low, picking up an ancient record.

"What?" he called from across the room.

"Coleman Hawkins with the Mound City Blue Blowers, nineteen twenty-nine," I called back. "Hawkins on tenor sax, Glenn Miller on trombone, Gene Krupa on drums, Pops Foster on bass—oh, man, Pee Wee Russell on clarinet . . ."

"Put it on," Steve urged. I did, as carefully as I could, what with the way my hands trembled with anticipation. I set the needle ever so gently on the rim of the record and was immediately surrounded by sound coming from a dozen speakers. It was an original recording with all the pops, clicks, rumbles, and surface noise you'd expect, but none of it could detract from the pure power and soulful majesty of Hawkins's sax or Russell's clarinet. You just don't get that kind of beauty with fully equalized, digitally mastered CDs, I don't care what the tech heads say.

I continued to search Steve's collection as I listened. Jack Teagarden, Red Nichols, Earl Hines, Duke Ellington, Bix Beiderbecke: all original recordings. I stepped back. The things money could buy. . . .

"Where did you get these?" I called to Steve across the room.

"What? Oh, the Victors. Old guy in New York had a huge collection; some Verve, some Blue Note. He died, left his collection to his son. Son moved to Duluth. Then he died, and his wife sold the records at a garage sale."

I was appalled at the idea and looked it.

"Yeah. Me, too," Steve said, recognizing my expression. "Anyway, a woman from Stillwater bought the collection. She was impressed by the dates, not the names—thought they were antiques. She sold them on consignment at an antique mall on Lake Street. A buddy of mine who knew I liked jazz told me about it. I hustled down and bought up all the old Victors from before 1930, before the label merged with RCA. I was just in time, too. While I was writing the check, another guy came in and bought everything that was left."

"Can I ask how much you paid?"

Steve grinned. "A lot less than if the woman had known what she was selling. Hey, if you like that, I have *Jazz at the Philharmonic* from 1946; Charlie Parker, Lester Young, Willee Smith. . . ."

"Isn't that the first Verve release?"

"Yeah," Steve said. "What became the Verve label, anyway. Back then it was called Clef."

I found it and put it on, listening to "Oh, Lady be Good" by the Gershwins. That's how Steve and I met, listening to jazz. We had seats side by side at a Sonny Rollins concert. The next day we bumped into each other at the Electric Fetus, a record store in Minneapolis.

By then Steve had become thoroughly infatuated with the Orwellian world of computers, by the notion that the most intimate information about any individual or company could be revealed to him with the stroke of a key. Phone records, utility records, credit card charges, arrest records, IRS returns, medical records: He delighted in obtaining all this data and more. He learned to intercept electronic mail, invade voice mail and smoke a PC in minutes—computers yielded their secrets to him like spinsters confessing to a priest. He began to think of himself as the Garry Kasparov of computer wizards, for a time even using the chess master's name as a handle. When he was on his game, no program could beat him.

Steve slowly abandoned his bohemian ways—not as a repudiation of his privileged poor philosophy and certainly not because of any newfound maturity. As he had often told me, "I can't do nine to five, man. No way." He simply discovered that using his computer skills to collect isolated bits of information gave him more pleasure than just about anything else. And the primary employers of such skills—especially on a freelance basis—were big businesses. Big businesses did not hire flakes.

Besides, he liked the money; Sara had expensive tastes. So he started his own business. VanderTop Intelligence, Inc. "The timely collection, analysis, and dissemination of data for a company about its competitors" was the service he sold—at least over the counter.

He finished his program and came to where I was standing by his music collection, putting a Chet Baker reissue on the CD player. He sat on the floor and asked to what he owed the pleasure of my company.

"I need a hacker," I told him.

"I am not a hacker," he replied. "I am an intelligence research professional."

"What's the difference?"

"About a hundred and fifty bucks an hour."

"Does that include industrial espionage?"

"No, that's extra."

"How much extra?"

"What have you got in mind, Taylor?" he asked.

"There's this guy named Levering Field—"

"What kind of name is that?" Steve wanted to know.

I didn't answer. Instead I told him about Mrs. Gustafson and what Field had done to her, I told him about my meeting with Field that morning, and I told him what I wanted done.

"I want his electricity turned off. I want him to get calls from his mortgage company asking what happened to his last three house payments. I want stores to confiscate his credit cards and cut them in half. I want his checking account to be suddenly overdrawn. I want to take this guy apart piece by piece until he cries uncle."

Steve was lying on the floor now, his legs crossed at the ankles, his hands supporting his head, golden hair fanned about him—he looked like a saint in one of those early Christian paintings, a nimbus around his head.

"What you're suggesting is illegal to the max," he told me. He was staring at the steel girders that held up his ceiling.

"I know."

"Why come to me? Why not do it yourself?"

"I'm not good enough," I answered. "We didn't cover these things when I was your pupil."

I was just starting my PI firm when Steve and I had met in the record store. After exchanging occupations, I told him I needed to learn how to use a computer, needed to learn how to compile dossiers for clients by dragging databases for information. Steve had been happy to instruct me. He'd done his job well. But not that well.

"Do you realize what you're asking, Taylor?"

"I do."

"This isn't waste retrieval, you know; sortin' through some guys trash. Illegal use of a telephone access device, computer fraud. We're talkin' serious time, man. Federal time."

"I know."

"Gig like this, can't leave no fingerprints. Gotta go in like the CIA."

"Those amateurs?"

"And credit card companies, banks? Shit, man, they've got firewalls you can't knock down with sledgehammers; strong passwords, cryptographic programs—some of them employ a posse, computer security experts whose only job is to track down anyone who even attempts a break-in. . . ." Steve smiled. "Sounds like fun. Count me in."

"No, no, no," I told him. "Think about it first."

"Nothing to think about," he said, rising off the floor. "I appreciate the challenge. Besides, the motive is pure."

What was I going to do, argue with him?

"One rule," I said. "No permanent damage. I don't want to do anything to Field that we can't undo after he pays off."

"Not a problem."

"What's it going to cost me?"

"Gratis, man. No charge."

"Cut it out."

"Hey, I'm serious."

"You're going to risk going to federal prison for nothing?"

"It's not the money, Taylor," Steve said. "It's the game, man. To pull this off is gonna take some killer apps. I can't wait. When do we start?"

"Need anything besides the man's name?"

"Nope."

"Then we can start now."

"Cool," he said, looking at his watch. Then he wandered over to the clothes rack, removed the red dress, held it in front of him by the hanger. "What do you think?"

"Little flashy for my taste," I told him.

Steve returned the dress and started searching the rack. "We'll start after lunch," he said without looking at me. "You can buy."

"Is Sara going?"

Steve took a woman's suit from the rack and examined it. "You have a problem with that?"

"I was just wondering if I should take out a loan."

Steve grinned, laying the suit across his bed. "She *is* a pricey vixen," he said.

STEVE WAS TESTING me. I had always known he was a cross-dresser. I figured it out the day he showed up at my office wearing a sweater and skirt. But this was the first time he dressed in front of me, showed me the process. I figured he wanted to know if I was willing to risk embarrassment for him if he was willing to risk federal prison for me.

He shaved twice, first with an electric razor and then with a straight edge. Then he put on a seven-hundred-dollar pair of breast prostheses from Denmark, attaching them to his chest with Velcro and adhesive anchors. After that he slipped on a white lace bra, pantyhose, and a white lace half slip. Not once did Steve look at me, not once did I look away—although I admit I wanted to. I had enjoyed watching Laura get dressed, especially when she was going all out for a night on the town. The same with Cynthia. It gave me a pleasure I felt deep in my lower extremities. But watching Steve become Sara made me feel creepy.

Sara began to emerge almost immediately. The way Steve carried himself, tilted his head, relaxed his posture, used his hands, became, well, feminine. His voice changed, too. It did not become higher, as you might expect, but deeper, throatier, and softer. I swear to God he sounded just like Lauren Bacall.

"There is a reason why I enjoy your company, Taylor," Sara said as she smoothed into her skin a healthy dab of Nye Coverette foundation, the same foundation used by actors, concealing the red blotches from shaving and Steve's inevitable stubble. "In the four, five years we've known each other, you never once asked, 'What went wrong?'"

"Did something go wrong?"

Sara smiled. "There are those who think so."

"Mom and Dad?"

"Mom and Dad and the rest of the VanderTop clan do not know about me," Sara confessed. "Every time I see my father, he asks when I'm going to get a haircut. Can you imagine what he would say if I showed up wearing a Donna Karan original?"

Sara applied a Q-tip's worth of Nye Coverette stage cream to each side of her nose, and magically it was narrower.

"Very few people know about me," Sara continued. "It's not because I feel ashamed or humiliated. It's because I don't want to deal with *their* shame and humiliation. The American Psychiatric Association's *Diagnostic Statistical Manual* lists transvestitism as a paraphilia or fetish. It claims people like myself derive abhorrent sexual excitement from cross-dressing. That is not true. I simply like to dress like a woman. Is that wrong?"

"It's not for me to say," I answered.

Sara turned and looked at me for the first time. "Yes, it is for you to say."

I gave it a beat, then answered, "No, it is not wrong." It wasn't hard to do. I had expected the question and planned my answer the moment Steve started performing for me, doing a striptease in reverse. If Sara had caught me by surprise, I might have answered differently. Or maybe not. Truth is, except for an uneasiness I felt in Sara's presence, I didn't much give a damn. I try not to pass judgment on other people's lives unless I'm paid for it.

Sara turned back to her vanity and started applying black eyeliner on the lid of first her right, then her left eye.

"I started cross-dressing when I was a kid," she said, then turned to me. "I thought you might want to know but were too polite to ask."

I shrugged.

Sara continued. "I was about twelve. Mom caught me trying on my sister's miniskirt and sent me to a psychiatrist. The idea that I was nuts scared the hell outta me, so after that I worked real hard at being a macho boy: went out for hockey, picked a few fights, drank beer behind the Burger King. It must have worked, too, because I didn't think much about cross-dressing until years later when I realized I was the only guy I knew who looked at the Victoria's Secret catalog for the clothes. I would take binoculars to the Vikings game and scan the crowd. My buddies thought I was scoping out chicks. What I was really doing was looking at women to see what they were wearing, how they did their hair. I'd be in a club and I'd watch a woman walk by. My date would get all hot and bothered. 'Why are you looking at other women?' she'd want to know. I'd say I was just admiring her dress, or her shoes. My date would accuse me of lying, but I wasn't.

"Anyway, after Mom and Dad gave me my first computer, I began to surf the Internet and I found a news group devoted to cross-dressers. I started lurking, reading the messages they posted. After a while I realized I was one of them.

"Eventually, I found myself," Sara added. "It didn't happen right away. I purged over and over again, throwing out all my clothes, every tube of lipstick, vowing never to cross-dress again. But like Popeye says, 'I yam what I yam.' And over time I became comfortable with it. It also became fun. A challenge. I began going out to 'ladies' night' at the local bars to see if people could read me."

"Could they?" I asked.

"At first, sure. But not so much after I became competent with makeup and clothes. A few of the more observant women will know I'm a man. Men almost never do. But kids? The younger ones always seem to figure it out instantly; I'll be damned if I know how."

Sara pushed herself away from the vanity and returned to the suit she had tossed on the bed. She picked it up by the hanger and examined it carefully.

"I'm not gay, I'm not a transsexual—very few cross-dressers are," Sara said. "I'm not a drag queen or a female impersonator. I'm just a guy who likes to dress in women's clothing. What do you think of this?" she asked, holding the suit up for me to see.

"I like it."

"You don't think the skirt is too short?"

"No, it's fine."

"I used to wear a lot of short skirts," Sara told me. "But then I started to think, Hey, I'm not a teenager anymore."

Sara pulled on a floral print skirt, roses on a peach background. The solid peach jacket was shaped-to-the-body and cut to her hips. The shoulders were padded, the collar was rounded and six covered buttons closed the jacket from her waist to her throat. Sara tousled her hair, then returned to the vanity for pearl drop earrings and a pair of strappy sandals with two-inch heels. With the earrings firmly attached to her lobes and the sandals on her feet, she moved to a full-length mirror. She turned this way and that, smoothing the skirt, adjusting the jacket, admiring herself. Then she turned to me.

"What do you think?" she asked.

I couldn't answer. My mouth was hanging open in disbelief. Backlit by the huge factory windows, beatified by the light shining through her golden hair, Sara resembled an actress in a beer commercial, the one where all the men stop and stare when she walks into the room. And the sight left me feeling both dizzy and slightly nauseous, like I had just ridden the double Ferris wheel at the Minnesota State Fair on an empty stomach. I couldn't get past the idea that if I had not witnessed the metamorphosis myself, I would be just like the other dolts she deceived on ladies' night, buying her drinks and claiming I had been looking for a woman like her all my life.

While Sara hunted for a suitable handbag, I stood at the steel door, waiting. She stopped at her computer setup, opened a drawer, and withdrew a black cellular telephone.

"Here," she said, handing me the phone. "If you want to talk to me or make any other calls you don't want traced, use this. If it rings, don't answer it. If I want to speak with you, I'll let it ring three times, hang up, wait exactly sixty seconds, then call again."

I took the phone, examined it, and slid it into my jacket pocket.

"How . . . ?" I asked.

Sara looped the strap of her bag over her shoulder and stepped through the doorway. "I commandeered a few cellular phone circuits that I use on special occasions."

"Sara," I said, "you scare me."

"You don't know the half of it, darling. . . ."

SARA TOOK IT easy on me, ordering the lobster salad instead of the lobster. Several men swiveled in their chairs as she walked past, gave her the once-over as we ate, and smiled at her. I wondered if they could read her, wondered if they could read me. After lunch we parted on the sidewalk just outside the restaurant's door. I offered Sara my hand, but she hugged my shoulder instead. I don't know what I would have done if she had kissed me.

"I'll see you later," she said smiling, fluttering her fingers in good-bye.

When I turned, I found a cabbie leaning against his blue and white, watching us. He nodded with approval.

"What the hell are you looking at?!" I wanted to know.

FIVE

I RETURNED TO my office, made a pot of French almond roast with the Mr. Coffee that sits on top of the small refrigerator I keep stocked with Summit Ale and Dr Pepper, and poured a healthy cup. It was one-thirty by the time I powered up my PC and began the tedious chore of dragging Levering Field's name through the various data banks that were available to me, compiling a dossier that would help in my assault on him.

Turned out he'd attended the same high school as my wife—Irondale in New Brighton. So had his wife, Amanda, only her last name was Meyer back then. He'd been cocaptain of the football team; she, homecoming queen. Figures. They graduated the year before my wife enrolled; he went on to the University of Minnesota, and she attended the all-female College of St. Catherine in St. Paul. They were married two years after receiving their degrees. Two years later they had a child, Emily Elizabeth. She was sixteen now.

I kept searching: employment history, credit history (thirteen credit cards? Wow!), residences (they went from a $90,000 house to a $450,000 house in one jump), criminal record (none), medical records, school records (she was summa cum laude and a Phi Beta Kappa; he was lucky to have graduated), reading habits (she was a member of the Book-of-the-Month Club and The Literary Guild; he had subscriptions to *The Wall Street Journal, Forbes,* and *Business Week*).

It was pushing four when I called it a day. By then I knew more about Levering and Amanda Field than I did about myself—more than enough information to proceed. God knew what Sara could add. I went back to the Mr. Coffee, warmed my cup, and while I sipped, I gazed out the window.

Down on Hennepin Avenue a school bus was unloading senior citizens into an asphalt parking lot. The lot was all that was left of "Block E," formerly the most notorious chunk of real estate in Minneapolis, a place of disreputable businesses, rough-and-tumble bars, peep shows, and sex-oriented bookstores and theaters that accounted for nearly twenty-five percent of all the crime in the city. It'd had everything: pimps, prostitutes, drug dealers, strung-out addicts, and tourists, plenty of tourists, driving by with windows rolled up and car doors locked, trying to catch a glimpse of the dark side, *"seeking out the poorer quarters where the ragged people go,"* as Paul Simon might sing.

Block E had been a blight on the fair name of Minneapolis, the City Council claimed. Besides, they reckoned they were losing a shitload of convention business. So they did what any self-respecting, civic-minded governmental body would do. They bought all the buildings facing Hennepin Avenue between Sixth and Seventh Streets and took a wrecking ball to them. Block E was reduced to a pile of rubble. And the businesses that had thrived there? They relocated to other parts of Minneapolis and her suburbs, redistributing sin throughout the greater metropolitan area, giving every neighborhood its fair share.

Oh, well. I drained the coffee cup. That's when I noticed the two window washers working out of a gondola suspended over the side of a building—Levering Field's building.

"Let the games, begin," I said, smiling.

WE WERE ON the roof. The window washers were stepping out of the gondola, securing their equipment. They were surprised to see me up there; they rarely get visitors fifty floors above the earth. I flashed them a phony badge and ID card I had made up. "Parker, IRS," I announced.

They looked at each other, then at me.

"We didn't do anything," one of them said. The other shook his head.

"I didn't say you did."

"Then, what do you want?"

"Gentlemen, let me buy you a beer."

We retired to a pub down the street. I sprung for three Summit Ales, my favorite beer, brewed in St. Paul, my hometown.

"This is good," the one named Sid announced. He had never tasted it before, usually going with a less expensive brand.

"What'd I say?" asked the window washer named Bob. "Top-of-the-line brew. I buy it all the time when I go to the Saints baseball games."

"You a St. Paul Saints fan?" I asked.

"Damn right. Seen every home game since they started the Northern League. Got season tickets right behind home plate, about halfway up. You like your baseball, you gotta go with the minor leagues; forget those spoiled brats in the bigs."

As much as I loved the Show, it was hard to argue with him. Especially since the strike. I changed the subject.

"Tell me, gentlemen, how much money do you make a year?"

Again they looked at each other, then back at me.

"I made twenty-seven thousand last year," Sid confessed.

"Twenty-seven thousand?" I was genuinely surprised.

"I made about the same," Sid added, on the defensive now. "People think we make a lot of money, because we work high. But we only get thirteen dollars an hour."

Thirteen dollars an hour? You couldn't get me up there for less than a thousand. "Gentlemen, you are grossly underpaid," I told them.

"Then why pick on us?" asked Bob. "We're just little guys. Why don't you pick on some big guys for a change?"

"Yeah," Sid added.

I put my hands up, showing that they were empty—the universal sign for peace.

"That's why I'm here. There's a millionaire named Levering Field with an office on the thirty-fourth floor of the building you're working on. We want to put some pressure on him, send him a message."

"Yeah?" Sid asked.

"How would you two like to make five hundred dollars doing a small job for your government, two-fifty each?"

THE NEXT MORNING Levering Field found the word REPENT painted on the outside of his office window. Of course, from his side of the glass it was spelled TNEPER, but what the hell.

THE MIDDLE-AGED WOMAN behind the counter read the ad back to me:

PROFESSIONAL

Corporate SWM 45 offers emotionally
mature, affectionate, attractive, sensu-
ous woman a relationship of mutual

<blockquote>
respect and physical pleasure. I am
kind, handsome, financially secure, and
extremely generous.
#11789B
</blockquote>

"Sounds good," I admitted.

"The first twenty words are twenty-five cents each, the rest are fifty-five," the woman explained. "That comes to nine dollars and forty-five cents. Now, Mr. Field, we can hold the responses in a PO box here for you to retrieve, or we can forward them to your home for the cost of mailing."

"Send them to my house," I said, giving her Levering Field's address.

"YEAH, THIS IS Levering Field," I said, speaking through Sara's cell phone. "Levering, yeah ... L E V E R I N G ... Huh? ... Problem is I got mice all over the fucking place. When can you send out an exterminator? ... No, I can't hang around my house all day, I work for a living. ... Saturday's good. ... No, I don't mind paying extra as long as I get rid of these goddamn rodents. ... See you Saturday, then."

LEVERING FIELD LIVED two blocks from Eastcliff, the residence of the president of the University of Minnesota, located in a posh neighborhood on the St. Paul side of the Mississippi River. His was a tall redbrick house on a corner; the front door faced one street, his garage the other. Ivy grew on the brick. The lawn was green but spotty; it hadn't recovered yet from the winter. On a thin stake pounded into the lawn was a sign. I read it carefully with a pair of Bushnell 7X25 binoculars I keep in the glove compartment of my car. The sign said THIS PROPERTY IS PROTECTED BY TOTAL SECURITY, INC. I cursed. Unlike most home security firms, these guys actually knew what they were doing. Oh, well. I hadn't planned on B and E anyway. Instead, I sat in my car across the street with a universal remote garage door opener, working the code, trying to find the right combination that would open Field's door and set off the burglar alarms.

As I worked the switches, I caught a glimpse of a St. Paul Police Department squad car in my rearview mirror. It was approaching fast from behind. I was seized with panic for a moment, but started to breathe again when the squad sped past me, pulling into Field's driveway. The car contained a single officer and a woman. The officer opened the back door, and the woman slid out. She was young, I figured about sixteen, and very attractive beneath her grunge-style clothes—dark eyes, auburn hair. I looked at her through the binoculars. It was the teenager in the picture on Field's desk. My research had told me her name was Emily.

Immediately, the back door of the house opened, and another woman ran out, rushing to the car. She was an older version of the teenager—same height, same color hair, but prettier by my way of thinking. I assumed she was Levering's wife, Emily's mother, Amanda.

"What happened? Are you all right?" she asked the teenager. I read the words off her lips more than heard them. Emily pushed past her and went into the house, slamming the door behind her. That I heard loud and clear.

Amanda turned to the officer. She kept shaking her head as he spoke, finally holding it in both hands and turning away. The officer laid a hand on her shoulder and spoke some more. She nodded, smiled, offered her hand in thanks. The officer shook it, then retreated to his squad car. I ducked down when he backed out of the driveway and drove off. Amanda returned to the house. The sky was darkening, and she turned on several lights. I watched her move from one window to the next, then she disappeared. Finally, a light on the top floor was lit, but it was behind a translucent curtain that I could not see beyond.

I continued to work the code until I hit upon the correct combination. The garage door opened slowly, rose halfway, then stopped. I pressed the button a half dozen times, but the door would not budge. Then I noticed the lights in the house were off.

"Sara," I said aloud. "You're beautiful."

NIGHT HAD FALLEN completely when I reached my home in Roseville. I turned on my inside garage light to see by and rummaged through the clutter that had accumulated on my work shelf. It took a few minutes to find what I was searching for—a Havahart trap. I wiped away the cobwebs as best I could with a rag and left the trap on my picnic table. I unlocked the back door of my house and went inside. A moment later I returned with a handful of apple chunks I stole from my pet rabbit, Ogilvy. I put the fruit inside the trap and set it in the center of my backyard.

Usually at this time of year my yard would have been covered with snow. But the Twin Cities was currently experiencing its warmest March in decades. Temperatures were hovering around the mid-fifties, and all the snow had melted. Still, only a visitor would mistake it for an early spring. The natives fully realized we could be back to freezing temperatures in no time; few of us were confident enough to put away our snow blowers.

I went into the house, cooked up some New England clam chowder, fed Ogilvy—carrots, not chowder—and watched hockey on ESPN2. I debated calling my father, giving him a status report, letting him know how much he was in to me for expenses, but decided against it. He could wait.

SIX

THE NEXT MORNING I called a buddy who works out of the Ramsey County Sheriff's Department to ask him if he could get Levering Field's license plate number and the make and model of his car from DMV. I could have done it myself, but it would have taken twenty-four hours, and I didn't care to wait. He called me back with the information fifteen minutes later, and I made a note to send him twenty-five bucks—in cash, of course.

I took the chance that Field had a contract with the parking ramp beneath his building. He did. I found his BMW on the third level between two pillars. He'd probably picked the spot so no one could ding his doors. I drove beyond the BMW to the first empty stall, parked, opened my trunk, and withdrew the live trap. The squirrel inside the trap was not happy.

I carried the trap to the BMW as nonchalantly as possible and ducked down behind the pillar on the passenger side. I used a rubber wedge and a "slim jim" to pop the lock. Opening the door, I freed the squirrel in the back seat and closed and relocked the door. I was back in my car and heading for the exit in three minutes flat.

I WAS ON Sixth Street, heading east toward the I-94 entrance ramp when the cell phone startled me by ringing. It rang three times then stopped. One minute later it rang again.

"Yes?" I said tentatively

"Hi, Taylor, it's Sara."

"Sara, my love," I said before I realized I was saying it.

"How are you this fine day?"

"Swell, thank you. And yourself?"

"Great. Hey, you turned off Field's electricity. That was wonderful."

"That was easy," she said. "The power company's computer is about as secure as a box of Cheerios. Field's power should be back up by now, though."

"Are you going back in?" I asked.

"No way. They might be waiting for me. Anything we do is a good idea—but only once."

"I hear you."

"So what have you been up to?" she asked.

I told her. The squirrel pleased her no end.

"Buy me lunch and I'll give you a lot more ammunition," she told me after she had finished laughing.

"Where and when?"

She named a café in the Nicollet Mall in downtown Minneapolis that had an outside terrace. "Noon," she said. "If the weather holds."

THE GIRL BEHIND the customer service counter giggled when she spoke, as if embarrassed to hear the sound of her own voice. "You want this ad to start running tomorrow?"

"That's correct," I answered. "Tomorrow and every day for a week. How much is it?"

She counted the words carefully, consulted a rate card, then named the price. I paid in cash, declining a receipt.

"OK, look it over one more time to make sure it's correct." She giggled again.

> For sale by owner, prestigious brick residence near river, 4BR, 3 baths, 4,000 sq ft + lg gourmet kitchen, elegant dining area, 2 massive fireplaces, dramatic master suite & bath, wet bar, spa, sauna, 2 car garage, extras. MUST SELL BY NEXT WEEK. Will accept best offer, call day or night.

"Perfect," I confirmed.

"And this is your correct phone number, Mr. Field?" she asked, showing it to me.

"Yep."

"Thank you and good luck," she said, still giggling.

SARA WAS WEARING a pink double-breasted blazer over a matching sweater, pleated trousers, and white gloves. She looked cold sitting at an outdoor table, a light breeze mussing her hair. The DJ on KBEM, the jazz station I listen to, said it was fifty-eight degrees, but I didn't believe him. I was wearing a heavy brown-leather jacket zipped up over a wool sweater, and I was freezing.

"Sure you wouldn't rather eat inside?" I asked after apologizing for being late.

"No, I like it out here," she insisted, watching two men watching her as they walked past. That's when I realized why she had chosen that particular restaurant—she wanted to be seen.

Sara ordered grilled salmon and white wine. I went with a club sandwich and a Summit Ale. After the waitress departed, I asked Sara what she had for me. She slid a file folder across the table. Inside the file folder was a list of credit card numbers; one of them was circled. I asked her why.

"Because it's in the name of a twenty-two-year-old college freshman named Crystalin Wolters."

"Crystalin?"

Sara nodded, taking a sip of wine.

"Who's Crystalin?"

"Background is on the next page," Sara informed me. I perused it quickly:

> Crystalin Jean Wolters, 22, eyes green, hair blond, height 5-9, weight 135, no corrective lenses; address 127 Cathedral Hill Apartments, St. Paul; owner red Porsche 911; speeding tickets September: 95 in 55 zone paid $150 fine, November: 110 in 55 zone $500 fine, March: 105 in 55 zone, pending; freshman Macalester College, St. Paul, MN; previous occupation: waitress Dixieland Barbecue, quit September; no current employment; parents: John & Sybil Wolters, St. Cloud, MN; John, construction worker, Sybil, grocery clerk; no marriage license filed her name Ramsey, Hennepin, Scott, Dakota, Washington counties . . .

"Apartment on Cathedral Hill? Porsche? Think she's paying for all this with what she earned from tips?" I asked.

"The credit card," Sara said in reply. "It's in Crystalin's name, for her exclusive use. But all the bills are sent to Levering Field—at his office, not his home."

"Ahhh."

"What do you want to do?"

I gave it a moment's thought, then said, "Cancel the card. Can you make it look like it was on Field's orders?"

"Sure."

"Good. When she calls the company, that's what they'll tell her."

"What about the cards in Field's name?"

"How often can you spoof the system?"

"I only want to go in once; gain root status, mess with Field's cards, get out—no sniffers, no back doors, no fingerprints. Man, I gotta tell ya," Sara said excitedly, using Steve's voice, "this is really juicy, but it's scarier 'n shit."

"Then don't take any chances. Leave his cards alone for now. I have a use for them, anyway."

Sara nodded her agreement, then added, "I'm trying for his bank accounts now."

"Don't take any chances," I repeated.

"Not to worry, I'm using cutouts."

"Cutouts?"

"The telephone company keeps records of all local phone calls—"

"MURs," I volunteered.

"Message unit records, right. Any local call you make is recorded on your personal MUR; the cops can check it to see who you called. Well, you know that."

"Uh-huh."

"Anyway, with a cutout, every time I make a call, the record of the call is assigned to a random telephone number—my calls are listed on somebody else's MUR."

"What about a direct trace?"

"I set up a special number last night, goes all around the world—Rome, Singapore, Nova Scotia—through a half dozen long-distance telephone companies, a few local exchanges, three cellular-phone companies. I own the telephone companies, man."

I believed her.

"When I go in, I watch the line carefully. Someone tries a trace, I'll know and break the connection before they can complete it. No way they can find me if I'm quick enough."

"You are a marvel."

Sara smiled. It was not the smile of an elegant, sophisticated woman receiving a compliment. It was the smile of a mischievous boy planning his next prank.

"Be careful," I stressed yet again. Sara was too cocky, and it made me nervous.

FREDDIE CAME OUT of nowhere. Before I even knew he was there, he was sitting at our table. "Hiya, Taylor, how you been?" he said without looking at me. He was looking at Sara, staring into her hazel eyes. He took her gloved hand. "I'm Sidney Poitier Fredricks," he announced.

"Sara VanderTop," Sara replied quickly.

Freddie kissed the back of the glove. "It is my great pleasure," he said. Sara smiled and withdrew her hand, holding it like she had no intention of ever washing it again.

"I'm an old friend of Taylor's," Freddie added.

"No, he's not," I corrected him.

Freddie was the only black private investigator I knew. He was also one mean sonuvabitch. I didn't trust him as far as I could throw the Hubert H. Humphrey Metrodome, and while I didn't mind sharing a booth with him in a crowded bar if we met by accident, we certainly were not friends.

"He's just saying that because I intruded on his party without asking," Freddie claimed. "But when I saw you from across the street, I couldn't resist."

Sara smiled. "I'm glad," she said.

Oh, man . . .

"I bet you work out, a figure like yours," Freddie said.

"Every day at the Y," Sara said.

"That's funny. I go to the Y a lot, but I've never seen you there," Freddie replied, grinning.

"Different branches, perhaps," said Sara, smiling even more brightly in return.

"Perhaps."

I cleared my throat, and they both turned to me.

"Now Taylor, here, he's into martial arts; can break a man's back forty different ways," Freddie said. "Ain't that right, Taylor?"

"Forty-one."

"Yeah, but who's countin'?" Freddie asked, eyeing the remains on my plate. "You gonna eat those fries?" Freddie shoved a handful into his mouth and continued flirting with Sara while he chewed. Smooth, man, smooth.

The waitress arrived, bused the plates, and asked if we wanted coffee. Sara said she did.

"Cream or sugar?" the waitress asked.

"I like my coffee the way I like my men: strong and black."

Freddie smiled broadly and said real low, "Ooooh, mama."

"All right, that's enough," I announced. "Cut it out, the both of you."

Sara chuckled, pushed away from the table, and excused herself. I watched as she made her way to the ladies' room. So did Freddie.

"Very nice," he whistled low.

"Go away, Freddie," I told him. He ignored my suggestion.

"You humpin' her, man?" he asked.

"Excuse me?!"

"Oh, sorry, don't want to hurt your delicate sensibilities." Freddie smiled again. There was ketchup on his lip. "Are you and the lady having relations? Hmmm?"

"Strictly business, Freddie."

"You ain't lookin' for her husband, are you?"

"No."

"And you ain't slippin' it to her, right?"

"Freddie!"

"So there's no reason why I can't make a play." Freddie pulled the lapels of his jacket. "I like white women," he said.

I didn't say anything.

"You got a problem with that, Taylor? You got a problem with a black man and a white woman bein' together? I never pegged you for no bigot."

"A couple months ago you whipped my head with a pistol and left me for dead in an alley," I reminded him.

"So? Couple days later you shoved a Colt Commander into my mouth—my own gun, man—and threatened to blow my fuckin' head off. I don't take it personal, why should you?"

"Freddie . . ."

"What?" he asked as Sara made her way back to the table.

"Help yourself."

Sara did not sit when she returned. Instead, she announced she had to return to her office.

"Is it downtown?" Freddie asked.

"In the warehouse district," Sara replied.

"Not the best part of the city," said Freddie. "I should walk with you, keep you safe."

"I'd like that," Sara agreed, then looked at me.

I shook my head. "You live dangerously," I told her.

She smiled. "What's a little danger?"

ACCORDING TO MY research, despite his apparent wealth, Levering Field had never donated so much as a nickel to any charitable or nonprofit organization: no United Way, no American Cancer Association, no Save the Whales. I helped him make up for it, pledging a total of fifty thousand dollars to a wide array of groups, everyone from the Corporation for Public Broadcasting to the American

Nazi Party. They could send a pledge envelope or a representative to pick up the check, it was all the same to me, and of course they could use Field's name in their newsletters.

I was contemplating further mischief when I heard a no-nonsense rapping on my office door.

"Who is it," I sang out sweetly in a high falsetto.

"Monica Adler," a voice shot back.

"Are you armed?"

"What?"

"Nothing. Come in."

Monica Adler pushed the door open and stood there like a gunslinger about to make a play. She regarded me carefully for a moment from the doorframe, then marched to my desk, tossing a piece of paper on the blotter before she came to a stop.

"What's this?" I asked, without touching the paper.

"It is a temporary restraining order issued by the Ramsey County Court. You are forbidden to contact Mr. Levering Field in any fashion or to come within five hundred feet of his person, his family, his home, and his office. Is that understood?"

"Sure. Want some coffee?"

"What?"

"Coffee. French almond. I grind my own beans."

"Did you hear what I just said?"

"Perfectly. And I want to give you my personal assurance that I will strictly adhere to the court's request. Now, about that coffee . . ."

Monica glanced down at the paper, picked it up again, and held it out for me to take. "Are you Holland Taylor?" she asked, serving me properly this time.

"Yes, I am," I said, taking the paper and tossing it back on the desk. Monica's eyes followed it to the blotter, then turned on me. I shrugged. "I just had lunch with a guy who pistol-whipped me couple of months ago. I don't hold grudges."

Clearly Monica had expected some kind of confrontation, would even have welcomed it—why else deliver the restraining order personally when she could have hired it done? Instead, I was being hospitable, offering her a beverage, and now she was confused. No doubt she figured I was up to something, so she accepted my offer while she tried to determine what it was.

She smiled with pleasure when she sipped from my mug—I make dynamite coffee—then wiped the smile from her face, not wanting to give me the satisfaction.

"So, how is the Ring man these days?" I asked when I was sitting snug behind my desk and she was sitting in front of it.

"You should know," Monica told me.

"But I don't know," I claimed. From her expression, Monica did not believe me.

"He's angry," Monica said.

"Why is that?" Monica did not answer the question, so I did. "Let me guess. He got a flat tire, a couple of crank calls, and he's holding me responsible. He remembers what I said, and now everything that goes wrong in his life he figures is punishment because he ripped off poor Mrs. Gustafson. A guilty conscience will do that."

Monica set the coffee mug carefully on my desk and said, "You and I both know there's been a lot more going on than just flat tires and crank calls."

"Such as?"

"Such as death threats in the middle of the night."

Monica's answer shook me, and I took a long pull from my own coffee mug before I was ready to reply. I chose my words carefully: "That is something I would never do."

"Oh? Why not?" Monica asked, retrieving her mug,

leaning forward, on the offensive now. "You've killed before. How many times? Four?"

"Four," I agreed.

"Of course, the review board let you get away with it. What was it they said? 'You were acting within the scope of your employment'?"

"Close enough," I replied. She was fighting dirty now, hitting me where it hurt. I was sorry I had offered her the coffee.

"I know all about you, Taylor." Monica was leaning across my desk now, her hands supporting her weight, her face only inches from mine. "You've been skating on thin ice with the Public Safety Commission for years. You keep it up and I'll personally see that your license is revoked."

A trick my father taught me years ago: When someone is giving you the business, threatening you, trying to put the fear of God into you and you want to get the upper hand, ask something innocuous that will throw them off track and break their concentration.

"Would you like to have dinner with me tonight?" I asked.

Monica stopped speaking. A quizzical expression crossed her face.

"You obviously think I'm this terrible person stalking innocent victims in the night, and I'm not," I added. "I'd like to prove it to you."

She pushed herself upright, took a step backward.

"I'm just an average guy trying to help a little old lady get her money back from a thief."

"'Average' is the last word I would use to describe you," Monica said after her brain reset.

"See, I knew you liked me."

"I didn't say—"

"How 'bout I pick you up at seven-thirty?"

"Mr. Taylor, I certainly will not have dinner with you."

"Some other time, then," I said, glad she turned me down. Cynthia would never have understood.

Monica made her way to my door, stopping only long enough to say, "Remember what I told you."

"About what?" I asked.

The slamming door was her answer.

DEATH THREATS? I hadn't made any death threats.

I picked up the folded paper. The burden of proof is pretty low; still, you have to give the court some evidence of actual menace before it'll be moved to issue a restraining order. No doubt Mr. Field embellished his story just a tad in his affidavit—if he'd had any real evidence, this would have been an arrest warrant.

Death threats. I wondered what other crimes he'd accused me of, accusations that now are part of a court record somewhere.

Man, I hate liars. Don't you?

THE PHONE RANG five times.

"Twin City Florists," a woman answered.

"Hi, my name is Levering Field," I told her, shifting the cell phone from one ear to the other. "I would like to have two bouquets of a dozen roses each delivered this afternoon. No, make that three bouquets of a dozen roses—one white, one yellow, one red. Send the white roses to Amanda Field. . . ." I gave the florist Amanda's address. "The yellow roses go to Ms. Crystalin Wolters. . . ." I spelled that name and recited the address. "And the red roses go to Monica Adler. Just a moment . . ." I had to look up the address of her law office.

After I gave the florist Levering's credit card number and expiration date, she asked me if I wanted cards included with those bouquets. I most certainly did.

"For Amanda Field write: For Crystalin, the only woman

I will ever love."

"Sir?"

"You heard me correctly."

"Yes, sir."

"For Crystalin Wolters, write: For my darling wife, nothing will ever make us part."

"Yes, sir."

"For Ms. Adler write: For the best attorney in North America. Sign them all: Love Ring."

"Mr. Field?"

"Yes?"

"Is Ms. Adler a divorce lawyer?"

"You're very perceptive," I told the florist. "From now on you're going to get all my business."

I DROVE PAST Eastcliff, turned east then west, and parked a block away from Levering's home where I could clearly see both his front door and garage. I wondered vaguely how much the house would fetch if it really were on the market, then asked aloud the question I always ask when confronted by ostentatious displays of wealth: "Why wasn't I born rich instead of just good looking?"

I couldn't tell you exactly what I was looking for. But I saw plenty, starting with a silver '73 Cadillac that had seen way better days—the rocker panels were rusted, and the rear passenger taillight was missing. The Caddy stopped in front of Levering's door. A young black man slid out from behind the wheel, glanced up at the house, then gave his horn two long blasts. He was wearing an Oakland Raiders warm-up jacket—the preferred attire of hoodlums everywhere. He sounded his horn a few more times. A moment later, the front door opened, and Emily skipped out. The girl's mother was behind her. She shouted something, but the daughter ignored her. The young man settled inside the car, slamming his door. Emily was soon sitting next to him and the car sped away. Amanda watched from the front stoop as the car turned left and sped out of sight, cradling her head with both hands as she had when the cops brought her daughter home. She went back into her house and I wrote down the license plate of the kid's Caddy on a notepad I carry, asking myself the same question Freddie had asked earlier: "You got a problem with a black man and a white woman bein' together?"

AT FOUR-THIRTY by my watch, a blue van with TWIN CITY FLORIST painted in gold on both sides came to a stop in front of the Fields' residence. A young man carrying an oblong box made his way to the door and rang the bell. Amanda answered and smiled. The delivery man handed her the package and left without waiting for a tip. Amanda went inside, shutting the door behind her. A few minutes later she emerged from the back door, carrying the box over her shoulder with both hands.

She walked purposefully to the garbage can next to the garage and kicked the lid off with her foot. Then she smashed the box onto the rim of the can. Over and over again she brought the box down hard, like it was something she was trying to kill; white rose petals and bits of green stem flew around her. She kept swinging the box until it broke in two, and then she threw both halves into the can. She collapsed to her knees, holding the rim. Watching through the binoculars, I saw her chest heave and her shoulders shake. I felt about as big as a period at the end of a sentence.

I DIDN'T LEAVE. The sadist in me wanted to see what would happen when Levering rolled up. But ten minutes after Amanda staggered back into her house, she was on the move again, with a fresh coat of lipstick and a determined look on her face. She drove a dark-green Pontiac

Grand Am. I gave her a half-block head start.

I wondered if she intended to confront Levering in his lair, but instead of driving west to Minneapolis, she went south, catching I-494 and staying with it until she was in Bloomington. I followed her as she took an exit near the Mall of America. Was she going shopping? No. She turned off, drove past a hotel that served both the mall and the Minneapolis–St. Paul International Airport, pulled into the driveway of a small office complex. The words ADOLPH POINT were carved into a monument at the mouth of the driveway. Amanda found an empty space in the first row of the parking lot and hurried inside the building. I watched from the back row.

Fifteen minutes later she emerged from the office building—with a man. The man had his arm draped over her shoulder. She leaned into him as they walked; he kept looking around as if he was afraid of being noticed. I suspected he wasn't Amanda's big brother.

That suspicion was soon confirmed. After giving her a hug and helping Amanda into her car, he moved quickly to his own, a Buick Regal. The two cars left together. They didn't go far. They both pulled into the hotel's parking lot. Amanda and her companion were walking arm in arm when they went through the hotel's front doors.

I actually said aloud, "Have a good time, Amanda." But that didn't make me feel any better about what I had done to her.

"ARE YOU FAMILIAR with Minnesota's stalking laws?" Cynthia asked from my kitchen table.

"Vaguely," I answered.

"I'll get copies," she volunteered. "We'll review them tomorrow. Carefully."

"Are you trying to tell me something?"

Cynthia shook her head. No, not her.

I stirred my beef Stroganoff mixture while the egg noodles boiled. Cynthia sat at the table, paging through the latest edition of *The Sporting News*. I watched her from the stove. She shook her head over an article. Something about Albert Belle's contract.

I wondered if Cynthia knew she was beautiful. Certainly her clothes were beautiful; her makeup, her poise, her manners, her speech—she had paid enough for them. But when she looked in the mirror each day, did she see the pure physical beauty that existed beneath all that, or had the years on the street, the years spent dancing naked before leering imbeciles, stripped away her ability to judge her own value?

I asked her, "Do you know you're beautiful?"

Cynthia fidgeted in her chair. "Where did that come from?"

"Just answer the question, Counselor: Do you know that you're beautiful?"

"So I've been told."

"Objection, hearsay. The court requires the witness to answer according to her own knowledge."

"Taylor, what are you doing?"

"Just answer the question, please. Do you know that you are beautiful?"

"I guess."

"You guess?"

"What do you want me to say?"

"Do you know—"

"Yes, I suppose I do. Lately I've come to think I'm beautiful. Is that all right?"

"Yes, it is. That's good. I'm glad."

Cynthia set my magazine aside—she didn't like sports, anyway. She regarded me carefully, watching as I drained the noodles in a colander.

"I'm still angry," she announced.

"I know," I said.

I poured the noodles into a glass bowl, then poured the Stroganoff mixture over the top and tossed. People who have eaten what I set in front of them will tell you I'm a helluva cook. Don't you believe it. A good cook can improvise, can create from scratch. Me? Without my recipe books I couldn't scramble eggs. Don't tell my mom.

Cynthia helped herself to a plate of the Stroganoff, ate a forkful, and promptly requested ketchup. Talk about angry.

"It's not that bad," I said, not referring to the food.

"I think what you are doing is horrid. What you did to that poor woman . . ."

"I'm sorry about that," I said in self-defense. "But not the rest."

"Sometimes I don't understand you. I would never have guessed that you would . . . stalk . . . a man."

I frowned.

"That's the correct word," Cynthia insisted. "That's what you're doing. And it's terrible."

"Is it?"

"You're telling me you don't agree?"

"Like I said, I'm sorry about Amanda but not the rest. You see, I know something about Levering's life right now. I know how his stomach churns and his head throbs. I know how he fears every phone call and jumps at every knock on his door. I know how he's unable to eat, unable to sleep at night; how he's reluctant to rise in the morning. I know all this and the thought of it makes me happy."

"What kind of man are you?"

"The kind of man you call when you want to get two hundred and eighty-seven thousand dollars from a thief."

SEVEN

T HE PHONE CAUGHT me on the way out. Levering Field was on the other end. He was angry. I know because he told me so. And because his voice crackled like the electric sounds of a welder's torch.

"Enough!" he yelled. "I have had enough!"

"Enough of what?" I answered innocently, aware that he was probably recording the conversation.

"You know fucking well," Levering insisted.

"Should we be talking? Your lawyer served me with a restraining order yesterday that said I'm not supposed to have any contact with you."

"You listen to me, you little prick—"

"Hey, hey, hey! Be civil or I'm going to hang up."

"You stay away from me and my family."

"I swear to God, Mr. Field, I don't know what you're talking about. I've never gone near you, and I didn't even know you had a family."

"You liar!"

"Listen, if things are not going well for you, don't blame me. Blame your bad karma"—it was probably the first time I've ever used that word. "Nasty things happen to nasty people."

"Once more, Taylor. One more time, goddamn it—"

"Frankly, Ring, I'm disappointed," I told him. "I just never thought a man could have as much money as you do and not be smart. As for your threats, you're doing it all wrong, man. You want to scare someone, you have to be scary. Tell you what. Rent *Kiss Of Death* at the video store—the original black and white, not the remake—and pay close attention to Richard Widmark's performance. Chilling . . ."

"You sonuvabitch!"

"See, what he'd do is he'd giggle. There's this great scene where he ties a crippled woman to a wheelchair and throws her down a flight of stairs; giggles all the way through it. . . ."

"Fuck you!"

"You should try that. Giggling, I mean. Worked for Widmark, made him a star. Maybe it'll work for you. It has to be better than the patter you have going now—"

Levering slammed the phone down, nearly puncturing my ear drum.

I stared at the now dead receiver, outraged. "Some people have no telephone manners."

Since I had the phone in my hand, I dialed my friend in the Ramsey County Sheriff's Department again. Yes, he'd received the twenty-five bucks I sent him; was there anything else he could do for me?

"Now that you've mentioned it, could you run a plate off a silver '73 Caddy for me? Usual fee?"

Five minutes later I learned that the Caddy belonged to a Kareem Olds, 19, who lived in the lower apartment of a duplex on Collins Street in St. Paul. "That's Railroad Island," said the deputy, who was familar with the 150-year-old, decidedly blue-collar neighborhood on the east side of St. Paul, surrounded, like a moat, by railroad tracks. For another twenty-five, the deputy was happy to

91

run Olds's vitals through the NCIC. No wants, no warrants, no arrests, no convictions.

I PARKED ON Selby Avenue in St. Paul, not far from the hotel where F. Scott Fitzgerald used to hang out and a bar where August Wilson wrote some of his plays. It's the area the real estate types call Cathedral Hill, named after the magnificent church that looms above downtown St. Paul—the biggest, grandest church in the Midwest, some say. It was designed by the French architect Masqueray and has a definite Notre Dame feel to it.

However, the nickname changes, along with the property values, just a few blocks west as you pass Western and head toward Dale. The cops call this neighborhood simply "the Hill." To the media it's known as "Crack Street."

I had spent a lot of time on the Hill, mostly trying to take it back from the dealers who ply their trade there. It was a losing battle. It did not matter that we walked day and night patrols throughout the area or that neighbors would walk with us, pointing out the stash pads and crack houses, cheering when we hit them, taking personal pride in our soaring arrest rates. Cocaine distribution is an example of a free-market economy in its purest form, and as long as people want to buy, someone will sell. That's why I begged my superiors to ignore the dealers for a time and instead concentrate on the lily-white suburbanites who cruised the Hill in their Honda Civics and Ford Tauruses—destroy the demand and let's see what happens, I pleaded. Unfortunately, my experiment was never attempted. Of course, punching out a prosecuting attorney didn't help my argument much.

I had been undercover for seven months, setting up busts, pretending to be all kinds of people. For some reason one suspect got antsy and decided to move. He'd loaded all of his goods into a large suitcase: two kilograms of powder, thirteen pounds of crack—we're talking sixty thousand hits—a half dozen nickel bags of grass, fifty-eight thousand dollars in cash, and a Colt Python and holster. Then he threw a going-away party for himself. We crashed the door as he and his friends were toasting themselves with champagne, the suitcase lying open on the living room floor. Only the prosecutor wouldn't file. He'd said there was a chance the constructive possession rules would have resulted in a dismissal—I couldn't prove which suspect actually owned the suitcase.

The prosecutors are always doing that, refusing to file charges unless they have a lock. Over sixty percent of all drug cases are dismissed before charges are brought. Sure, of the forty percent that are actually filed, nearly all result in convictions, but that only proves my point: Most prosecutors simply will not risk screwing up their conviction rates, an admittedly important part of their performance-review process.

So I hit him. Call it anger, frustration, stupidity: I hammered his collar bone, cracking it, and walked away. For a long time I thought I had lost my job along with my temper. Hell, he might even have filed charges. He certainly had had the right. Instead, I was transferred to Homicide. I was ecstatic. Laura was not. The word "homicide" conjured frightening images to her. As it turned out, after Narcotics, Homicide proved positively restful.

FROM WHERE I was parked, I could see the comings and goings of all the residents of Crystalin Wolters's apartment building, located at the high end of Selby, close to the Cathedral. I had only a cursory description of Crystalin. But she drove a Porsche, and there was only one in the lot. I watched that, using the small, collapsible 3X binoculars I sometimes carry in my jacket pocket.

At about eight-thirty a young woman with Crystalin's hair color exited the building's glass doors and walked purposefully to the Porsche, glancing at her watch as she went. Sixty seconds later she was on Selby, heading west. I followed. She turned left, then right, then left, then right again. We were on Fort Road now, heading toward the airport.

Fort Road used to be called West Seventh Street. As West Seventh Street it had as dreary a reputation as Block E in Minneapolis. But the St. Paul City Council did not have the same resources as the City of Lakes, so instead of taking a wrecking ball to it, they simply changed its name, hoping that would solve everything.

And politicians wonder why so few of us bother to vote.

Crystalin pulled into the parking lot of a restaurant that advertised eggs, ham, hash browns, toast, and coffee for $3.99. I wondered if she was meeting Levering for a cheap breakfast. But she wasn't. She sat alone in a booth, ordering quickly, not waiting for anyone. I was lucky again because the place was jammed with customers. Crystalin thought nothing of it when I asked if I could share her booth.

She was a buxom, green-eyed blond, bursting with energy and rosy-cheeked health. She looked like she'd come straight from the factory—no nicks or scratches. She had a little voice; when it dropped down at the end of her sentences you sometimes lost it completely. Her smile came quickly and stayed long.

We both ordered the special. While we ate, she asked what I did for a living.

"Public relations," I lied. "How about you?"

"I'm a student at Macalester College."

"Really, what's your major?"

"I haven't decided, yet."

"Hmm."

Then we praised the glorious spring weather and lamented that no way it was going to last; the TV meteorologists were already gleefully predicting the impending arrival of several storm fronts. That was about as deep as our conversation got. Still, Crystalin seemed quite articulate, which did not surprise me at all. Most men—and women, too—they see an attractive woman, they naturally assume she's as dumb as Sheetrock. Especially if the woman's young and blond to boot. Not me. With few exceptions, the attractive women I've known over the years were all quite intelligent. Or was that the other way around?

In any case, Crystalin was pleasant enough, with a touch of little-girl shyness that was rather endearing—not at all the personality you'd expect from a gold digger, from an adulteress. The way she played with her golden hair while she spoke reminded me of a woman I pursued in college named Susan—one of those that got away. Because of Susan I actually regretted what I did to Crystalin. Just as she drove her car from the parking lot, I used the cell phone to call the St. Paul Police Department, dialing the direct line—911 is taped and the reels are stored forever.

"Someone just stole my girlfriend's Porsche," I told the officer. "Me? My name is Levering Field. L E V E R I N G . . ."

KBEM'S NEWS GUY warned us that we had already reached the day's high, that temperatures were now falling like a melon off the top of the IDS Tower. Heavy snow was predicted by nightfall. Like nearly everyone else in the Twin Cities, I was not surprised by the report, but I cursed it just the same.

I drove to my office, brewed a pot of coffee, sat behind my desk and realized I had nothing to do. So I decided to visit Dragons, my dojo, for a workout. I don't study a particular art, but rather a combination of judo, karate, and aikido. I'm not interested in earning a belt, although they tell me I could if I applied myself. Nor am I one of those diehards who believes in the spirituality of hand-to-hand combat. I'm interested solely in survival. I barely passed the minimum height requirement for a police officer—probably wouldn't have if the doctor hadn't laughed at all my jokes—and in my business if you don't have size, you better have skills because screaming "Quit it, you big meannie!" isn't going to do it.

I've been taking instruction for nearly fifteen years. True, in a gym anyone above my weight class would probably kick my ass. But on the street, without a referee, without a nice, soft mat to fall on, size and strength don't matter nearly as much as what you're willing to do. And given the proper motivation, I'm willing to do anything.

My Gi was in a locker at Dragons with my other equipment, so I grabbed my jacket and walked out the door, locking it behind me. I walked down Sixth Street and across Hennepin to where a bearded man in ragged clothes carried a baby on his shoulder and yelled, "Minneapolis, you should be ashamed of yourself!" at whoever came within shouting distance. He never made it clear just why Minneapolis should be ashamed, and no one bothered to ask. Instead, we marched past him, trying to avoid eye contact, hoping he would go away. On the same corner a popcorn vendor shook his head. He wanted the man to go away, too. The guy was killing business.

Dragons was on the third floor of an ancient building without elevators that once belonged to a now-bankrupt dance company. I ran up the steps. An hour later I limped down. I had thrown a front snap kick at my instructor. He deflected the blow with his left forearm, stepped forward, grabbed my right shoulder with his left hand, brought his right leg behind my left leg, swept up, and flung me to the mat. Then, to emphasize his point, he shot a right fist inside my upper thigh, just to the left of my groin. It was your basic Inner Rear Sweeping Throw/Groin Attack, and why the hell wasn't I looking for it, he wanted to know. I couldn't believe I was paying for this.

The bearded man and his baby were gone when I hobbled back to Sixth and Hennepin, but the popcorn vendor was still there, so I popped for a seventy-five-cent bag, heavy on the salt. Yes, I know salt is bad for you. So is worrying about it. I finished the popcorn by the time I reached my office, tossing the crumpled bag into the wastebasket from fifteen feet. It danced on the rim and dropped in. Two.

Well, that had killed a couple of hours.

I decided to reorganize my filing system. When I got to the Cs, I had a brainstorm. Well, a squall, anyway. I used the cell phone to dial a 1-900 sex number. The breathlessness of the voice that answered made me fear for the woman's health—I figured she was having an asthma attack. I gave her Levering's credit card number and told her to just start talking.

"What do you want to talk about?" she said in a way that made me think of only one thing.

"Surprise me," I told her.

She did.

But by the time I finished with the Fs, I had become bored listening to her. I hung up, leaving Levering with a thirty-six minute phone bill at—what? Four ninety-nine a minute?

I called Cynthia, wanting to ask her to lunch, but Desirée informed me that Ms. Grey was unavailable. She wasn't nearly as pleasant as the last time we'd spoken.

I went downstairs, bought a submarine sandwich from the convenience store, returned to my office, and choked down half. I put a CD on the music machine, a reissue of the Bill Evans album *You Must Believe In Spring*. He does a nice cover of "Suicide Is Painless," the old Johnny Mandel song that was the theme for *M*A*S*H*. Only I didn't hear it all. I fell asleep.

IT WAS FOUR P.M. when I awoke. The sky was dark and ominous, and from the way the people on the street leaned forward, holding tenaciously to their hats, I guessed a stiff wind was blowing.

I dialed Cynthia's number again. While her phone rang, I took her photograph off my desk and held it with both hands, using my shoulder to rest the receiver against my ear. I wanted to see her face and hear her voice at the same time.

After I got past Desirée, I asked Cynthia if she wanted to meet for dinner, but she had a meeting. She could come to my house afterward, I suggested. But she said she wanted to sleep in her bed tonight. Alone. She had said the same thing the night before.

"How long are you going to stay angry at me?" I asked.

"How long are you going to stalk Levering Field?"

"Shouldn't be much longer. I think he's ready to break. . . . Hello? Hello?"

I WENT TO a restaurant on First Avenue that's owned by a local TV sportscaster. Good food, lots of TV monitors. SportsCenter was on ESPN. The boys were interviewing Minnesota's Tom Kelly. T. K. was saying he liked what he saw in spring training, and he expects the Twins to be competitive this year if the starting pitching holds up. But then, he always says that.

I sat at the bar, ordered a Leinenkugel's Red after I was informed the restaurant didn't carry Summit Ale. The lager was served in a twenty-two ounce glass. After consuming ten ounces, I decided to order dinner. They told me the special was good—orange roughy grilled in a lemon-dill sauce. They were right. I was just finishing it up when she walked in.

It was hard to miss her. For one thing, she was wearing a lustrous white cotton corset dress, loosely laced in front, that was held up by remarkably thin spaghetti straps. For another, she wore no coat, despite the fact that the temperature had dropped to nothing, the wind was howling, and snow was blowing. In fact, snow was melting off her white pumps and dripped from her ankle-length hem as she stood near the hostess station, searching the room for a familiar face.

She began to slowly move through the restaurant, paying particular attention to the faces of the men who sat alone. I watched her with great interest—something about the laces tied in a lazy bow between her breasts. You knew she was a Cosmopolitan girl, what with all the cleavage she gave away.

I was distracted by the bar der who bused my plate and encouraged me to order another Leinie's. When I looked up, she was gone. Nuts. Oh, well. I sipped the beer and returned my attention to the TV. ESPN2 was broadcasting a hockey game featuring the much-hated Chicago Blackhawks—at least I hate them. I used to follow the Minnesota North Stars pretty closely until they were moved to Dallas by an owner embarrassed over allegations that he sexually harassed his secretaries. Now my favorite team is who ever is playing the Blackhawks. Tonight it was the Boston Bruins. The Bruins were on a power play but having a hard time setting up in the Chicago zone.

And then she was at my side.

"Is this seat taken?" she asked.

At first I didn't hear her. That damn Wurlitzer the Blackhawks fans crank up every time their team scores a goal was ringing through the restaurant. The Blackhawks had scored short handed, the bastards.

"Excuse me?" I asked.

She motioned to the empty stool next to mine. "Is this seat taken?" she repeated.

"No," I said, gesturing for her to take it. She did, but not very far. If anything, she moved it closer to me.

"Some weather we're having," she said, smiling coyly.

"It's not so bad if you're dressed for it," I suggested.

She put her hands over the cups of the corset and squeezed her breasts together. They bounced when she released them, a not altogether unpleasant sight. I watched them carefully. Since meeting Sara, I take nothing for granted.

"I was betting the weather would hold for at least one more day," she said. "I lost."

"Sure."

"Bailey's on the rocks," she told the bartender when he came around. Then she asked me, "Are you married?"

"No."

"Divorced?"

"No."

"Gay?"

"Nope."

"A good-looking guy like you, who's your age, who's not married or divorced, you might think he was gay. No offense."

"None taken." The gay reference didn't bother me at all. But I was curious. "How old do you think I am?"

She shrugged, drained her glass and ordered another Bailey's. "I like older men," she said.

I took no comfort in that. "Older than what?" I asked.

"Older than me."

"How old are you?"

"Old enough."

"I bet."

"Let's go someplace," she suggested, downing her second Bailey's.

100

"With or without my VISA card?"

She turned on me like I had just called her a whore, which, I suppose, I had. "What's that supposed to mean?" I didn't answer, and she ordered a third Bailey's. She was drinking them like they were chocolate milk.

"I'm not a pro," she told me and I believed her. But she was definitely something. I've always thought of myself as a Harrison Ford–Mel Gibson kind of guy, only good looking. But in my entire life, not once has a beautiful woman tried to pick me up in a bar. Or anywhere else for that matter. So why was I lucky tonight? The ring on her right hand gave me part of an answer. It carried the emblem of Macalester College.

"What's your name?" I asked her.

"Why?"

I offered my hand. "I'm Holland Taylor."

She hesitated, took my hand, hesitated some more, then said, "Melanie."

I nodded. "That's a pretty ring you're wearing. May I see it?"

"This?" she asked, holding her class ring out for me to get a good look at it.

"Could you take it off?"

Again she hesitated, then slipped it off her finger. I held it up to the light. Her name was engraved inside—and it wasn't Melanie.

"Pretty," I repeated, returning the ring.

"Let's go someplace where we can . . . talk," she said.

"We're talking now."

"You know what I mean?"

"Yes, I do."

"What do you think?" she asked.

"I think I'd like to know you better first. Tell me what you do for a living."

The woman was clearly frustrated. She wanted me to

leave the restaurant with her, and the reason had nothing to do with the laces of her corset. But she went along with my request, feeding me a cockamamy story about answering phones and taking appointments for a doctor. She couldn't answer telephones for five minutes—her personality began and ended with her cleavage. At first her voice was clear, controlled, but after her fourth Bailey's it began to slur and words like "fuck" and "shit" began creeping into her sentences. A lot of people, the more they drink in public, the lewder, cheaper, and dumber they become.

Finally, she wrapped her arms around my neck and kissed me hard. "Let's go," she whispered.

"Let's," I agreed, anxious to meet whoever was outside, holding her coat. Cotton dress and pumps in Minnesota! In March! Who was she kidding?

I paid the tab, including her drinks, and ushered her to the door. We stood just inside while I zipped my jacket to my throat. Snow was blowing hard and I wished I had brought my gloves.

"Where to, Piper?" I asked.

"My car is in the alley across the street. Hey, wait a minute. I didn't say my name was Piper."

"Sure you did. Piper Lindquist."

· "I did?"

I pushed her out the door. We stopped to let a snowplow pass before crossing the street. There was a car parked deep in the alley. It was running. Two men were in it. When we dashed across the street they got out, crossed their arms, and waited next to the car. They were big.

"It's him," Piper said as we entered the alley.

Both men were young. College-age kids. They looked like they played the defensive line, but that didn't bother me. Macalester hadn't won a football game since Reagan was president—assuming, of course, that they were smart enough to get into Macalester, a fairly prestigious school, after all.

I walked up to the man standing next to the driver's door. He dropped his arms as I approached.

"Hi," I said brightly. "Are you a friend of Piper's?"

Before he could reply, before he could move, I kicked him in the groin real hard. He went down, his mouth twisted with agony, a soundless scream deep in his throat, like a child crying without oxygen. He caught his breath and the pain spilled out, then he lost it and was quiet again until his lungs filled with air. All in all, I found his performance quite satisfying, his hands between his knees, his knees drawn up tightly against his stomach, rolling side to side in the snow.

His partner hesitated for about five seconds, then came around the car in a hurry. He threw a punch at my face, but he started too soon. I ducked under it and his momentum carried him toward me. He collided with a ridge hand I threw at his solar plexus. He was already falling, his feet slipping badly on the snow, when I stepped behind him, locked a claw hand over his throat, and flipped him on his back.

I could have finished him, could have finished them both, probably should have, but what the hell. They weren't pros. They were just a couple of kids looking to score a few quick bucks.

"Motherfucker!" shouted the youngster I had tossed to the ground.

"Hey, watch your language," I told him. He tried to get up. I advised him not to do that.

"Fuck you," he said.

I hit him with your basic forefist—but I slipped, and it went high. A sharp, piercing pain raced through my fingers, wrist, elbow and shoulder blade before dissipating through my upper right quadrant. You'd think someone with my experience would be more careful than to hit the hardest part of someone—the braincase—with his hand. That's what hammers are for.

"Dammit!" I cried, shaking the pain from my fingers. Now I was mad. "Go on, get up you dumb sonuvabitch! G'ahead. Christ!"

The football player didn't move.

I turned on Piper. She was weeping quietly, clouds of breath coming from her mouth with each sob as she shivered in her cotton dress, snow melting on her bare shoulders.

"So, does Levering hold paper on you, too?" I asked.

She didn't answer.

"Who hired you?"

"*Nobodyyyyyyy!*" she wailed, her voice bouncing off the alley's stone walls.

"Crystalin?" I shouted at her.

She shook her head.

"Yeah, right."

I turned back to the kids laying in the snow. They looked like they would recover.

"Fellas," I said. "You don't want to do this for a living. The money is lousy, there's no health plan, no retirement fund, you have to work nights—and besides, you're not very good at it. Think about it."

"Fuck you, asshole," said the youngster who had hurt my hand with his head.

I went into a guard position, careful of my footing, and snapped a front kick to his forehead. I tried hard to maintain my balance on my back foot but slipped and fell on my ass anyway. No one laughed, but I was embarrassed just the same. I got up, brushed the snow off and said, "Let that be a lesson to you."

OGILVY, MY GRAY-AND-WHITE mini lop-eared rabbit, nibbled popcorn from the bowl on my left. I soaked my throbbing hand in another bowl filled with water and ice on my right, occasionally flexing the fingers. The knuckles were swollen but not broken. I sat on the floor between the bowls, my back against the sofa, watching the second game of the TNT NBA doubleheader. The Celtics were playing the Lakers. It was a good game, the Lakers leading by a field goal at the half. But it was a far cry from the days when Larry Bird, Kevin McHale and Robert Parrish were matched against Magic Johnson, James Worthy, and Kareem Abdul-Jabaar. I dozed off. The ringing telephone brought me back. It was nine-thirty, and I wanted it to be Cynthia. I answered in the kitchen.

"Hello," I said hopefully.

The threat wasn't particularly imaginative, just your basic I'm-going-to-kill-you-you're-dead-there's-nowhere-you-can-hide crap; nothing I haven't heard before. I listened closely, trying to place the voice, but couldn't. Definitely not Cynthia. I hung up without comment. My caller ID flashed: PAY PHONE and UNAVAILABLE where the number should have been—to cut down on the drug trade, Ma Bell has fixed it so that you can call out but not in to most pay telephones.

LA jumped on Boston early in the third quarter, taking an eighteen-point lead. The fourth quarter was merely a formality, a matter of final statistics. I emptied the ice water in the sink and tossed what was left of the popcorn. I lay on the sofa; Ogilvy lay on my chest. I fell asleep.

Again I woke to the sound of the telephone. TNT was broadcasting an old John Wayne movie. The Duke was inexplicably dressed like some kind of Mongol warrior with bad facial hair. *Who the hell are you supposed to be?* I wondered. *Genghis Khan?* Well, yes, as it turned out, he was. Go figure.

I answered the phone.

"Hello?"

"I'm gonna kill you, motherfucker."

EIGHT

Minnesotans love snow. We love to work in it and play in it; we build two week festivals around its coming and going. We particularly delight in blizzards. Not the little stuff, snowfalls of three inches or less. Nuisance snow, we call that, useful only to groom ski trails and conceal exhaust-stained drifts along the freeways. But the big stuff, six inches or more, always brings a smile. And heavy, wet snow—heart attack snow—man, we love it. We love the threat of it, the excess of it, the endless work of it. It feeds our collective ego the way doing penance nurtures Catholics, reaffirming our long-held sense of superiority over souls who live in more temperate climes. It amuses us that two inches of snow in Washington, D.C., can shut down the government. Five inches can put New York, the city that never sleeps, into deep hibernation. But ten inches in the Twin Cities isn't even a decent excuse for coming late to work.

The weather guy said nine inches of snow had fallen overnight at the Minneapolis–St. Paul International Airport. In my driveway it measured closer to a foot. Schools didn't close. The government didn't take a holiday. The mail still got through. Which is why we tend to smile knowingly whenever critics ridicule our state for its climate. Unlike them, we can take it.

I cleared my driveway with an ancient snowblower my father-in-law bought for me at an estate sale. My driveway is long, two hundred feet from the street to my garage set well behind my house, with another one hundred fifty feet curving like a horseshoe around a towering willow in front of the house. The job took over an hour, and I enjoyed every minute of it.

My house is a two-story colonial built three hundred yards from a large boulder fixed with a metal plate denoting the forty-fifth parallel. That means I live midway between the equator and the North Pole.

It was constructed in 1926 by a well-to-do businessman who had wanted to escape the rat race that was St. Paul. In those days, Roseville was all farm country. Now it's one of the Twin Cities's oldest suburbs, with scores of look-alike split levels and ranch houses, all with attached garages.

Laura and I had found the house while looking for something else. It had hardwood floors, beamed ceilings, arched doorways, stucco walls inside and out, a fireplace in the living room, two corner china cabinets in the dining room, French doors leading to a three-season porch, a wood-paneled family room, three bedrooms, two-and-a-half baths, a completely modern kitchen, detached two-car garage, a huge dual-level yard with a wooden swing hanging from an apple tree, and an owner who was desperate to move to Southern California where a house like this can fetch a half million dollars easy, maybe more. We couldn't afford it, even at Minnesota prices, even with two incomes, even with the interest rates being low. To our astonishment the owner cut twenty percent off his asking price.

"Are you going to have kids?" he'd asked. We told him one was already on the way, and we were hoping for at least two more. He smiled. "I was raised in this house," he said. "Kids belong in this house."

Mortgage insurance paid off the house after Laura and Jennifer were killed, and now I stand to make a bundle if I sell it. Don't think I hadn't thought about it, either. But where would I go? To some balsa-wood apartment? To a condo or a town house with a yard the size of a postage stamp?

Still, the man had been right. Kids do belong in this house.

THE CELL PHONE rang just as I stepped out of the shower. I followed Sara's instructions, waited, and answered when it rang again. Steve's voice sounded excited.

"I hacked Levering's bank," he told me gleefully. "No kidding, I did it! God Almighty!"

Steve was having some fun.

"Man's got a ton of dough just sittin' there," Steve added. "Over seven hundred grand. And it's all liquid. He has it in a brokerage account—stocks, bonds, mutual funds. Gives him unlimited check-writing capability. He could come up with the two eighty-seven in cash in like a minute. Only here's the thing. It's all in his daughter's name. What is it? Emily, yeah. Emily Elizabeth Field, age sixteen."

"Is that a problem?" I asked.

"For the IRS maybe, but not for Levering. Listen, I buried a sniffer in the bank's mainframe. Anytime they access Levering's account, my computer will know."

"Be—"

"Careful?" Steve finished for me. "That's my middle name. What's going on on your end?" I told him. He was taken aback. "I didn't think there would be, you know, violence."

"We're trying to take a quarter of a million bucks off this guy," I reminded him.

"I know but I didn't think . . . What will he do next?"

"I HAD AN interesting phone call last night regarding you," Freddie told me. He was sitting in my visitor's chair, his feet on my desk, drinking my Summit Ale like he owned the place. I was drinking coffee from the mug the SPPD gave me when I joined Homicide. It was blue and gold with an inscription that read: THOU SHALT NOT KILL SAITH THE LORD. AND WE WORK FOR HIM.

"So you said," I reminded him. Why else would I let him put his feet on my furniture and drink my beer?

"Guy wanted me to do you."

"Do me?"

"Do you dead in any way that suited my fancy."

"Uh-huh," I grunted, taking a sip of the coffee, trying to act oh so cool and indifferent—not at all like a man whose life was suddenly in jeopardy. Freddie didn't buy it. He caught me flexing the still sore knuckles of my right hand.

"What happened to your hand?" he asked.

"I hit a wall," I told him.

"Gotta watch that temper," he advised me. "Hitting walls with your gun hand—only bad relief pitchers do that."

"I'll be more careful in the future," I assured him, taking a sip of coffee. I was scared, oh Lordy, Lordy, Lordy. But I didn't want Freddie to know. Call it professional pride. Or male ego if you prefer.

"Want to know who put out the contract?" Freddie asked.

"As a matter of fact—"

"Can't say."

"Ahhh."

"Said we didn't need to meet. Said he would put ten thousand dollars cash in a locker at City Center and send me the key. If I picked it up, we had a contract."

"And if you just took the money, gambled it away down at Treasure Island?"

"Said he knew me but I didn't know him. Or anyone he might send to chat with me."

"Kinda makes you think he's done this sort of thing before."

"Kinda."

Freddie drained his bottle. "Want another?" I asked. He nodded, handing me the empty.

"You take the job?" I asked as nonchalantly as possible, taking a second bottle of Summit Ale from the refrigerator.

Freddie smiled brightly. "For ten thousand dollars? Hell, no."

I handed him the beer and sat behind my desk again as Freddie took a swig.

"What I said," he continued, "I said a man like Holland Taylor, he deserves the best. I told 'im make it twenty thousand and we can talk. Only he wouldn't go for it. Says he could get a hitter from Chicago for ten."

"In Chicago, you can hire a killer for five thousand," I suggested.

Freddie snorted. "Whaddya know about hired killers, Taylor? You don't know shit about hired killers." He tapped his chest. "I know fuckin' hired killers."

"I was a homicide cop, remember?"

"Shit, man. You made your living bustin' husbands for offing their wives. I'm talkin' *real* killers. I'm talkin' professionals. Guy in Omaha, very cool, uses nothin' but hollow points, one shot per customer, fifty Gs a pop, seventy-five if there was a deadline—that kind of professional I'm talkin' about."

"Are you a professional, Freddie?"

The big man eyed me carefully, then smiled. "Not for no ten grand I ain't."

"But maybe for twenty?"

"What? You don't think I'm worth twenty? Fuck, Taylor, don't go dissin' me, now."

"I'm just saying, you knock on my door, I tell you to come in, you pump a few rounds into me, hop the next Greyhound out of town, who's to know? Five minutes work, ten thousand dollars. Who do you know makes that kind of money who isn't playing pro ball?"

Freddie looked embarrassed. He took his feet off my desk, tried to get comfortable in the chair, and said, "I didn't want the contract, anyway."

We stared at each other for a few moments. It occurred to me that I knew nothing about the man except the caliber of gun he carried.

"You ain't nervous are you?" he asked at last.

I shrugged my reply.

"A guy puts a contract out on me, I'm shittin' bricks."

"Let's see who he sends, first."

"Just hope it ain't no fuckin' amateur with a street sweeper, cuttin' down a dozen civilians to get to you."

"Wouldn't want anyone else to get hurt," I said.

"What I say." Freddie smiled again. "Let me know how it works out."

"Hey," I stopped him. "You working these days?"

"You hirin'?"

"Could be."

"Whaddya want me to do? Provide air cover?"

"Something like that."

He shook his head. "I did my good deed for the day."

I nodded, yawned, stretched, glanced at my watch. It was eleven-thirty, a typical day in the life of your average PI. "Well, least I can do is buy you lunch."

"Where?" Freddie asked.

"You pick it. Some place expensive."

"Want to get the good last meal, huh?"

"That's it," I said, moving through the door with the big black man at my side, hoping he wouldn't see through my facade. It wasn't the meal, it was the company I craved. Freddie and his 9mm Colt Commander.

WE WERE WAITING at the hostess station of Sir Walter's along with a small knot of people, mostly businessmen. Sir Walter's was one of our better restaurants, with a decidedly English motif. Fortunately the food they served was strictly American with a nod toward Kansas City. They claimed to serve a steak so tender that you could cut it with a spoon—although who eats steak with a spoon I wouldn't know. While we waited three people came in. Grandpa, Dad, and little Billy. Little Billy was talking up a storm, mostly to his grandfather, until he saw Freddie and bam! It was like someone hit his mute button. He stared up at Freddie. Freddie smiled down at him.

"How you doin', man?" Freddie asked.

The boy nodded but said nothing.

The hostess told us, "Your table will be ready in a moment," then guided away the party waiting in front of us.

"I ain't eatin' with no niggers," a voice said in a stage whisper, meant to be heard.

I pivoted and caught Dad smiling. Grandpa was shocked. Little Billy stared at his father, unsure. Freddie did not move.

"You hear me, boy?" Dad added.

Freddie turned slowly. He was smiling. He looked down at little Billy and said, "I bet you'd rather have a hamburger, anyway, huh?"

The boy nodded.

"There's a McDonald's just down the street. Two blocks."

The hostess returned, sensed something was wrong, and tried to get past it. "This way," she said, her eyes locked on Freddie. We followed her.

"I want to go to McDonald's," we heard little Billy whine. Apparently Dad agreed; the trio didn't follow us into the dining room.

"Why didn't you bounce his ass?" I asked Freddie after the hostess seated us.

Freddie didn't answer.

"I would have," I assured him.

"'Cuz you're white," he said. "White guys bang each other, the cops come, sort it out, everybody goes home with a lecture on good citizenship. Black man hits a white man, he's cuffed, thrown into the back seat of a squad car, spends thirty-six hours in the joint. No one asks for his side of the story, no one asks was he provoked, no one gives a shit.

"Least this asshole calls me nigger to my face," he continued. "Man, I get called nigger a hundred times a day by people who never say a word." Freddie smiled at the expression on my face. "You don't know what I'm talking about," he said. "You think you do, but you don't. It's a white man's world, Taylor. But bein' white, you got no idea what that really means."

Freddie had a beer while we waited for our steaks. I had iced tea—I like to be sober when people shoot at me.

"Who I feel sorry for is the kid," Freddie added. "You gotta know he's gonna grow up stupid just 'cuz his old man's stupid. Won't know nothin' about African-Americans."

"You aren't, you know."

"What?"

"African-American."

"Fuckin' fooled me," Freddie said.

"What I mean is, you were born in this country, right?"

"Yeah."

"And so were your parents?"

"What of it?"

"Then you're an American, period. Not a hyphenated-American, just a plain, ordinary American."

"Who you calling ordinary?"

"You want to be a hyphenated-American, go to another country and become a citizen there. Go to Morocco. You can become a Moroccan-American."

Freddie looked at me like I was nuts.

"It needed to be said," I told him.

"Why would I want to live in fucking Morocco?"

"Never mind . . ."

Our steaks arrived. A few bites into them, Freddie said, "You're really naive about some things."

"What things?"

"African-Americans, Chinese-Americans, Hispanic-Americans, all the other hyphenateds. You think if we dropped the hyphens and acted like everyone else, acted like white guys, then we'd all be one big happy family. Ain't no way that's true. It's not how we act that makes us different, it's how we're treated."

I wanted to say something but couldn't think what. In any case, before I had a chance to speak, Levering Field walked into the dining room with two men and his secretary, Miss Portia—she of the golden mane and pale skin.

"I don't believe it," I said.

"You think you know more about racism than—"

"No, no, no," I corrected, turning my head away from Levering as he passed. "That guy walking past, with the charcoal suit, red tie . . ."

"Yeah?"

"That's Levering Field."

"Who's he?"

"The guy who wanted you to kill me."

Freddie's eyes narrowed as he watched Levering and his party settle in at a table about forty yards from us, his back to me, my back to him.

"Sure?"

"Not absolutely. It would be nice if you could recognize his voice."

"Got a working bee?"

"What?"

"Have you got fifty bucks?"

I pulled out my money clip. I had about eighty-five. No fifties.

"Give me a twenty."

I handed Freddie the bill.

He left the table, went to the arch leading from the foyer to the dining room, then walked directly to Levering's table.

"Excuse me, sir," he said, standing at Levering's elbow, holding out the twenty. "I believe you dropped this."

Levering said something in reply.

"Are you sure?"

Levering checked his wallet.

"My mistake," Freddie said, heading back to the hostess station. Levering lowered his head, spoke to his companions, threw his head back and laughed. The others chuckled nervously, glancing around to see if anyone else had heard the joke.

"Not him," Freddie said, returning to the table.

"You sure? He could have disguised his voice on the phone."

"Voice wasn't disguised on the phone," Freddie insisted. "The caller spoke plain."

I was actually disappointed to hear that. Still, that didn't mean Levering hadn't ordered the contract, only that he didn't make the call.

Instead of sliding the twenty into my money clip, I
shoved it into my jacket pocket. The cellular telephone
was there. In my other pocket I carried the tiny 3X binoculars. I had a thought.

"Want to have some fun?" I asked Freddie.

"Always."

I turned in my seat and looked at Levering over my
shoulder. The angle was good.

"Take these," I said, handing the binoculars to Freddie.
"Train them on Field. Can you see his right hand clearly?"

He could.

"Waiters, waitresses, they always serve from the right."

"They did when I was waiting tables."

"You waited tables?"

"When I was a kid, before I joined the Air Force,"
Freddie told me.

"Terrible job," I suggested.

"Not so bad in a good place. Tips were nice."

"I worked in a car wash," I volunteered.

"Talk about your shitty jobs," Freddie said.

I retrieved the cell phone from my pocket and started
punching numbers.

"Who you callin'?"

"Sara."

Freddie was annoyed. "Why didn't you tell me she was
married?"

The telephone was ringing.

"How do you know she's married?" I asked.

"I'm a fuckin' detective, remember? Her old man's
name is on the mailbox. And when I did a credit search, I
found out her credit cards are in her and her old man's
name."

"You didn't ask if she was married," I reminded him.
"You asked me if I was looking for her husband."

"You knew what I meant."

Steve answered the phone.

"Steve, this is Taylor," I said.

"That's the fucker," Freddie said.

I told Steve what I wanted. He told me it could be done, but it was dangerous. I told him to forget it, then. But he wouldn't. The challenge appealed to him. The problem was guessing which credit card Levering would use. I would supply the information, I told him.

"Let's try it," Steve said.

I set the phone on the table but did not turn it off.

"What?" Freddie wanted to know.

"We're going to sit here until Levering goes for the check," I said. "You're going to watch with the glasses and tell me which credit card he uses. I'm going to tell Steve, and he's going to cancel the card. He's going to program the credit company's computer to tell the restaurant that the card should be destroyed and Levering should be detained for the police."

"The fuck you say! How?"

"He's going to hack their system."

"I hate computers," Freddie said, focusing the binoculars on the target. "But I like the plan."

So we waited. Levering and his party took their own sweet time. I had two desserts and so much tea, my back teeth were floating. Freddie regaled me with the plots of movies he'd seen recently, mostly shoot-em-ups. The plots were all the same, only the special effects changed.

"Read a book," I told him.

"Man, this is the video age," he replied. "Ain't nobody reads anymore."

Finally, the check arrived. It was tucked inside a red leather folder. Levering didn't even look at it. Instead, he reached for his wallet, took out a card and slipped it into the folder.

"It's gold," Freddie said.

"Gold," I repeated for Steve.

"I'm on it," he said.

I kept my ear to the receiver. A moment later, the waitress took Levering's folder and moved to the hostess station. She spoke briefly with the hostess and then disappeared behind a partition.

"How long does this take?" Freddie asked.

Ninety seconds by my watch. The waitress returned to the hostess station, the credit card in her hand. She spoke to the hostess, then both of them disappeared behind the partition. I glanced at Levering. He kept looking toward the front of the restaurant, impatient. The hostess returned to her station, the waitress at her side. A few minutes later, two Minneapolis police officers entered the restaurant.

"We got him!" I practically yelled into the phone.

"Yes!" Steve exclaimed in reply.

"Now change it back."

"What?"

"Change it back, change it back. It's all just a terrible misunderstanding."

"I hear you," Steve replied.

The hostess kept the police in the foyer and went herself to Levering's table. A big smile on her face, she asked Levering to accompany her. Levering resisted. Finally, he muttered, "Sonuvabitch!" loud enough for us to hear and followed the hostess out. The cops were waiting for him.

"Oh shit! Goddamn it!" Steve yelled, and then the cell phone went dead.

"Steve, Steve," I repeated into the unit.

"What?"

"Something's gone wrong," I told Freddie. "Let's get out of here."

I signaled for the check. Our waitress was happy to give it. I paid in cash and left a big tip. Freddie insisted.

Levering was gesturing wildly. The other two men in his party stood by, bewildered. Miss Portia looked even paler than usual. The hostess, her face red, threw up her hands and disappeared behind the partition. Levering continued to talk, speaking to his party now. The hostess returned. Her face a deeper crimson. She handed Levering his card.

"I'm sorry, sir. The machine must have made a mistake," she said as we approached.

"Mistake?! Mistake?! You embarrass me in front of my clients, and you call it a mistake?!" Levering yelled.

"Having problems, Ring?" I asked as I brushed past.

He didn't realize who I was at first. When he did, his expression became pained, like I had just kicked him in the shin. I smiled at him as Freddie and I exited. I heard Levering scream my name on the other side of the closed door.

"What happened?" I asked when Steve answered the phone.

"They almost got me, the credit card posse." he confessed. "They traced me to Madrid. Christ, Madrid! I had maybe ten, fifteen seconds to spare."

"Are you safe?"

"No problem. But, man, those guys are good. Wow . . ."

"Wow, nothing," I told him. "That's it, we're done. No more credit card companies, no more banks."

"The bank is safe," Steve insisted.

"I don't care. Enough. We hurt him enough. I don't want you taking any more chances."

Steve was quiet for a moment. Then he said, "Screw it. Why don't we stop messing around and just cancel all of his credit cards?"

"Steve, you're out of control."

"And you know what?" he added. "Levering has cable,

but he only gets basic programming. No premium channels, no pay per view, no adults-only movies. Couple of key strokes and we could greatly expand his viewing choices. What do you think?"

"God, Steve . . ."

"And since we're at it . . ."

I told Steve I didn't want to hear anymore, told him I had created a monster.

He chuckled into the phone and said, "This is fun."

THE SUN WAS out, and the snow was melting fast. By the time I reached my driveway, the foot of snow that had fallen the night before had been reduced to half that.

I parked in the garage and went into the house. After feeding Ogilvy and changing his litter, I went upstairs to my bedroom. I knelt before my waterbed, took a deep breath, then unlocked a drawer built into the pedestal, sliding it out. The drawer contained all my guns.

I looked without touching: Two identical Beretta 9mm parabellums, one in a holster. A Smith & Wesson 9mm parabellum, modified and silenced for the U.S. Navy SEALS—they call it the "hush puppy" because it was originally intended to kill enemy watch dogs. A Charter Arms .38 special wheel gun. A four-and-a-half-inch long .25 Beretta that could literally fit in the palm of your hand. A Ruger .22 target pistol. A cut-down Mossberg twelve-gauge shotgun with pistol grip called "the persuader." A .45 caliber Ingram Model 10 submachine gun with three thirty-round clips.

I took a deep breath and slipped the 9mm Beretta out of its holster. A little over two pounds fully loaded, it felt heavy in my hand. I hadn't lifted it for quite some time now, since I used it to kill a man who had tried to kill me. One Review Board member thought it was excessive force, shooting a man four times in the chest. But they let me off just the same, saying I "acted within the course and scope of my employment." One witness even testified I had saved his life. Maybe so. But I lost a lot of sleep over the "subject"—as the review board referred to the deceased. Him and the other three subjects I've killed "within the course and scope of my employment." It wasn't until I stopped carrying, vowed never again to kill a man, that I have been able to go more than a few nights' sleep without waking drenched in sweat.

I slipped the Beretta back into the holster and closed and locked the drawer.

NINE

Paranoia is a terrible disease, and I had it bad. It was barely nine A.M., and my nerves had already been assaulted by a jogger who crossed my path when I was pulling out of my driveway, by a guy in a Jeep Cherokee who pulled next to me at a stoplight, by a man who bumped my shoulder in the parking lot outside the Butler Square Building, and, finally, by a young woman who made me hold the elevator, who rode the car alone with me, and who asked, "Isn't this your floor?" when the doors opened and I made no effort to get off. If I had been carrying my gun, I would have shot all four of them.

I was out of breath by the time I reached my office, locking the door behind me. "This is no way to live," I told myself aloud, then jumped two feet when the telephone rang. It was Monica Adler.

"We can't go on like this," she told me after identifying herself.

I wholeheartedly agreed but wasn't about to admit it. "What are you talking about?" I asked, wary of tape recorders and bugs. "Go on like—?"

"Taylor, I don't want to hear it," she said, interrupting me. "I'm tired. Mr. Field is tired. We want to end this."

"End what?" I asked, not trusting her for a minute.

Monica sighed deeply. "If it is convenient, I would like to discuss your differences with Mr. Field over lunch today."

I thought about it for a moment, then said, "I don't know what differences you're referring to, but I'm not one to pass up a free lunch."

"Swell," Monica said. "Noon. The St. Paul Grill."

"Fine," I said.

"Fine," she repeated and hung up.

The problem with working alone is that you have no colleague to turn to, no one of whom you can ask, "What do you think?"

I'VE ALWAYS LIKED Rice Park, especially in the fall when its many assorted trees are shedding their leaves. I like sitting at the base of its enormous fountain, just gazing at the beautiful buildings that surround it: the St. Paul Public Library and Minnesota Club to the South, the opulent Ordway Theater to the West, the Landmark Center with its ancient elegance to the North, the St. Paul Hotel, which houses the St. Paul Grill, to the East.

The last time I had been in the park was in February with Cynthia. We had come to admire the entries in the St. Paul Winter Carnival ice sculpture contest. It had been about eight degrees then. It was fifty-eight when I parked my Monza at the meters in front of the Ordway. The ground was still wet with melting snow, but the benches scattered throughout the park were dry, and so was the ledge surrounding the now-dormant fountain. The dry spots were nearly all occupied by brown baggers, some of them in short sleeves.

I waited as several cars passed me, most of them disappearing into the maze of downtown streets. One car circled the park twice, then found a space on the east side near the entrance to the St. Paul Hotel. A man got out; his hands were empty. He went inside the hotel.

I didn't see anyone carrying a sniper rifle, so I left the car and made my way across the park, following a path around the fountain. I ignored the intersection, crowded with people queued up for the dogs and sausages a street vendor hawked, deciding to cross in the middle of the street. I waited between two parked vehicles for the traffic to clear. My hand was resting on the quarter panel of a new Ford Explorer, just above the headlight. And then *WHOOM!* the headlight was gone. Splinters of glass and metal cut into my thigh and the palm of my hand, but I didn't feel the pain just then. What I felt was astonishment. It turned quickly to panic.

Fifty feet away on the other side of the street, a tall man wearing a dark-blue parka was drawing a bead on me with a handgun the size of a baby howitzer. He fired again. *WHOOM!* A tongue of flame licked four feet from the muzzle. I dived backward onto the boulevard. The bullet zipped past my ear, sounding like a high, inside fastball. I didn't see where it hit. I was on my feet, slipping in the snow and slush, moving fast along the line of parked cars, trying to keep the cars between me and the shooter. I heard a third shot but didn't see where that hit, either. The fourth caught the three-inch trunk of a baby red maple on the boulevard directly in front of me. It cut the tree down, leaving a four-foot high jagged post growing out of the ground.

I had never seen a gun like this.

I slid between two cars, glancing behind me. Half the brown baggers were running, the others were hugging the wet ground. Not as many people were screaming as you might expect and I was loudest.

The shooter was on the sidewalk now, coming fast. He was carrying his gun low; it must have weighed a ton. I was squatting between the cars. My strategy was simple: Hit the street and run like hell. A van was approaching. I was going to use it for cover, cut in front of it, hope the driver didn't run me down. But I never got out of the starting block. The shooter pinned me down, putting two rounds *through* the car I was hiding behind. I fell back.

That's when I heard a series of explosions. *Bang! Bang! Bang! Bang!* They sounded tinny and distant compared to the deafening blasts that were still echoing in my ears. I looked up.

The shooter was down, half on the sidewalk, half on the grass, his gun two feet in front of his outstretched hand. Blood formed a growing pool under his unmoving body.

I rose from my cover slowly.

Freddie stood above the shooter, his Colt Commander gripped in two hands, the muzzle pointing at the shooter's head. I walked to him as the air bleated with the sound of a half dozen sirens.

Freddie was breathing hard when I reached him, like he had just run a marathon. Police were filling the streets, guns drawn. I gently nudged him. Freddie looked at me, an odd expression in his eyes, an even odder smile across his lips. He deactivated the Colt and let it rest against his thigh. The cops were approaching cautiously, yelling, telling him to drop the weapon. Freddie tossed the Colt onto the grass like it was a candy wrapper, still staring down at the body; a nervous officer picked it up by the barrel.

I told Freddie softly, "Anyone asks, you're working bodyguard for me."

Freddie nodded. To my utter astonishment, he chuckled. "Motherfuckin' eh!" he said, his smile broad. "Did you see that fuckin' gun?"

My HANDS WERE trembling, and I couldn't make them stop. I put them in my pockets, but that made my legs shake, so I took them out again, hoping no one noticed. Freddie sat next to me on the park bench, immensely pissed. His hands were cuffed behind his back, wrists facing outward.

"Fuckin' racist cops," he muttered.

"Why?"

"They didn't cuff you."

"I didn't shoot anybody," I reminded him.

A moment later he asked, "You OK?"

"Hell, no, I'm not OK," I answered him loudly. He gestured with his head at the bloodstain on my thigh. "Oh," I said, gently rubbing my leg. The stain covered an area the size of a softball. My jeans were torn in several places within the circle, the largest rip about three-quarters of an inch. "I think I have some glass in there. Hurts like a sonuvabitch."

"Can we have some medical attention over here?" Freddie shouted.

An officer standing about ten yards behind us, watching us, his hands behind his back, shrugged and went right on watching. Freddie cursed him.

I tore my jeans another inch and with thumb and forefinger pulled a quarter-inch shard from my thigh, examining it carefully like I expected to see the manufacturer's name stamped on it, then flicked it away.

"Tell me something," I asked Freddie.

"Huh?"

"Why'd you do it?"

Freddie didn't hesitate. He answered like he was waiting for the question. "Man was lookin' to send you to the promised land."

"No. I mean, why were you watching my back? You said you didn't want the job."

"Yeah, well, I had a change of heart."

"Why?" I asked again.

"Why not?"

"Fuck, Freddie . . ."

"Shit, Taylor . . ."

Anne Scalasi was angry. By the time she arrived, the medical examiner had already examined the body and was telling the wagon boys to load it up. Forensics had taken their photographs, the scene had been searched for physical evidence, and the homicide detectives were nearly finished taking statements from the brown baggers. Annie hated to be late for a killing.

She was speaking with McGaney and Casper, a salt-and-pepper team from Homicide, who had directed the investigation until she arrived. She asked brief questions, they provided long answers. McGaney held up a plastic bag containing Freddie's Colt Commander and another containing the shooter's cannon. He gestured toward us. Anne went ballistic.

"Separate the goddamn suspects!" she shouted. "It's SOP, dammit!" She was striding quickly across the park to where we sat.

"Hi, Annie," I said.

"Hi, Annie," Freddie repeated.

Anne took Freddie by the lapels of his jacket and literally pulled his massive frame off the bench, up to her. She leaned in close. Her eyes were cold; her words were like icy fingers wrapped around your heart.

"In polite society, it is considered inappropriate to use an individual's first name unless you've been properly introduced."

She released his jacket, and Freddie fell back onto the bench.

"Anne, this is Sidney Fredricks," I said. "Freddie, this is Lieutenant Anne Scalasi, chief of Homicide, St. Paul Police Department."

"Pleased to meet you," Freddie said.

"Get this asshole outta here," Anne shouted to Casper and McGaney behind her back. They hustled him out fast.

Anne sat next to me. She sighed deeply. "I'm in a bad mood," she said.

"Not something I did, I hope."

The look in Anne's eyes—man, I wasn't going to wait for questions before supplying answers. "Yesterday, Freddie learned that a contract had been put out on my life. He doesn't know who or why. I hired him to watch my back. This morning an attorney named Monica Adler invited me to lunch at the St. Paul Grill. When I arrived—" I aimed my chin at the wagon that was just pulling away—"this guy started shooting at me. Freddie killed him."

"That's real good, Taylor," Anne said. "Now, what *aren't* you telling me?"

I shrugged. The soul of innocence.

"Martin!" Anne shouted. McGaney hurried over. "Check the St. Paul Grill. See if reservations were made for a woman named Monica Adler. If she's there, bring her out."

McGaney took off.

"Casper!" Anne shouted again.

"Yes, Loo?" he answered after hustling over.

"What did the suspect say?"

Casper read from his notebook. "Yesterday, he heard that a contract had been put out on Taylor's life. He doesn't know who or why. Taylor hired him to watch his back. This morning an attorney named Monica Adler invited Taylor to lunch at the St. Paul Grill. When Taylor arrived, the assailant started shooting at him. The suspect killed the assailant."

Anne closed her eyes, leaned back, and rested her head on the bench. "You guys have to separate the suspects before questioning," she said quietly.

"Sorry," Casper told her. Then he added, "Shooter's name was Tom Storey. ID says he's from Chicago. We ran him through NCIC. Mary Jane says the printout is taller than he was."

"What are the highlights?" Anne asked.

Again, Casper consulted his notebook. "He was on the FBI's detainer list—two capital murders, one in Detroit, one in Washington, D.C."

"A capital in the capital," I said.

Anne looked at me and shook her head.

"Had to be said," I told her.

"What are you working on?" Anne asked.

"Nothing," I answered.

"Try again," Anne urged me.

"I'm not working," I told her.

"I don't believe you."

"I don't care."

Anne leaned in close. Her words came like an Arctic blast. "You will," she said.

"I'M AN ATTORNEY," Monica Adler announced when she was brought before Anne Scalasi.

"So?" Anne asked.

Monica didn't have anything to say to that.

"Did you invite Mr. Taylor to lunch at the St. Paul Grill?"

Monica hesitated, then answered, "Yes."

"Did you specify the time?"

"Noon," Monica answered carefully.

"For what purpose?"

"A legal matter, involving one of my clients."

"Your client's name?"

"I'm not at liberty to say," Monica insisted.

"Sure you are," Anne told her.

Monica did not reply.

"Did your client know about your lunch date with Taylor?"

Monica remained quiet.

"Did he know what time you were meeting Taylor?"

Monica looked away.

"All right," Anne said, rising to her feet. "You, you, and you," she said, pointing to Freddie, Monica, and me. "Downtown."

"We are downtown," I reminded her.

She stared me in the eye while adding, "Separate vehicles, separate interrogation rooms."

I RODE WITH Anne. She was in the front passenger seat. A uniform was driving. I was in the rear, my hands cuffed together behind my back.

"How are the kids?" I asked, referring to her two daughters and son.

"Kids are good," she said. "My son wants to know when you're going to take him to another basketball game."

"First chance I get," I replied.

Anne had been married to a St. Paul patrolman who rolled with the Midway Team. They divorced a few months back, and he hadn't spent much time with his kids since. I don't think it was because he didn't like his kids; I think he was bitter. He was a five-year veteran when he married Anne. She was a schoolteacher. Fourteen years later, she was a lieutenant, chief of Homicide, and the highest ranking female officer in the State of Minnesota. And he was still a patrolman.

What's more, I think he felt cheated. He had supported

Anne every step of her career, encouraging her when she was down, helping her cram for tests, taking care of the kids when she was in Quantico being trained by the FBI to hunt serial killers and rapists. I guess he thought he'd be getting something out of it besides the satisfaction of seeing his wife reach the top of her profession. Something for himself. It might have been different if Anne had stayed with the Minnesota Bureau of Criminal Apprehension instead of joining the St. Paul PD. The differences in their ranks would not have been as pronounced, and he wouldn't have had to listen to fellow officers who wondered aloud if he saluted her in bed. But, hell, he'd encouraged her to make that move, too.

Understand, I never liked the guy. In all the years I knew him, he never once called me by name. It was always "Detective." But I guess I can't blame him for that, either. I was Anne's partner in homicide for over four years—I had a lot more of her time than he did.

"How's the old man?" I asked.

"Ex-old man," Anne corrected me. "I haven't heard from him for a while. He was supposed to take the kids last weekend, but he never showed."

"Sorry," I said.

Anne looked out the side window. Then she asked, "How's Cynthia?"

"She's pissed off at me."

"Why should she be different from the rest of us?"

"YOU EVER SEE a gun like that?" I asked Anne. We were alone in an interrogation room. It was early evening.

"Sure," she said. "Desert Eagle. Fifty caliber. The Israelis make it for a company here in Minnesota. Located in Fridley, I think. Schwarzenegger and Stallone wave 'em around in all their movies. Makes a helluva noise. A lot of ranges won't allow them, especially indoors."

"My ears are still ringing," I admitted.

Back in the old days—1800, say—you wanted to shoot someone, you'd get out your custom-made dueling pistols, and you and your guy would have a slug of brandy and go at it. Everything was accomplished elegantly and subtly and courageously—there was actually some courage involved, even though standing in an open field letting someone shoot at you was dumber than tarpaper. But big, goddamn fifty-caliber handguns? Jesus Christ!

"Damn thing must be as heavy as Liz Taylor's jewelry case," I speculated.

"Four pounds," Anne said, then added, "Everybody goes home tonight. The assistant county attorney says to cut you loose."

"Nice of him," I said.

"It's only temporary," Anne warned me. "After the grand jury hears that lame story of yours, I have no doubt you and Fredricks will be back."

She pulled out a worn black pocket calendar and dropped it in front of me. "We found this on Storey's body," she said. "Looks like he was a gambler. Not a very good one, either. Almost every single day has a notation for how much he wagered, how much he won or lost—mostly lost. The last couple days are the most telling."

She opened the calendar and quickly found her place. I read over her shoulder, surprised she didn't shoo me away. Muscle memory, I guessed; when we worked together I was always reading over her shoulder.

MONDAY—Paid Mike $150. Still owe 6G. $100 on 6ers. 479

TUESDAY—6ers lost, fucking pussies. $50 on Rangers. $50 on Devils. 821

WEDNESDAY—Won 1, lost 1. $500 on Celtics. 901

THURSDAY—Lost ass again. Owe Mike $6,500. He has deal. Guy in Minneapolis has job. Pays 10G. I keep 4, pay Mike 6, call it even. Leave Friday. 476

Anne said, "Friday is blank."

"Looks like he lost his ass again," I said.

"What do you think these numbers represent?" she asked, pointing at the three digits following each notation.

"Daily lottery," I guessed. "Illinois Pick Three, probably. Looks like he was keeping track."

"Maybe," Anne said, not willing to commit. She closed the calendar.

"Chicago PD helping you find this Mike?" I asked.

"So they say."

"Think it'll do any good?"

Anne shrugged then smiled. "Are you going to tell me what you're working on now?"

"Like I said before, I have no paying clients," I assured her.

"That doesn't answer my question," she told me.

When I didn't say anything more, Anne sighed heavily. It was her I-don't-believe-a-word-that-you're-telling-me-but-I'm-going-to-let-it-slide-for-now sigh. Then she added, "Interesting company you've been keeping," she said.

"Freddie?"

"He's having a wonderful time; was positively gleeful when he told the assistant county attorney how he pumped four rounds into the victim. 'Saved Taylor's worthless fuckin' life.' Must have said it twenty times."

"He's a helluva guy," I admitted. "They should carve his face on a mountain."

"He's an asshole," Anne told me, then watched my face to see how I would react. I wasn't sure myself. A few hours ago I would have agreed with her. But now? I said nothing.

"We confiscated his gun," Anne added.

"Probably a wise precaution. Wouldn't want him saving my life again."

"Shouldn't be a problem. Just don't have lunch with Monica Adler."

"I won't."

"Or Levering Field," Anne oh so casually tossed out.

"Hmm? What?"

"Levering Field. Surely you remember Mr. Field. The Ramsey County court was moved to issue a restraining order forbidding you to have any contact with him."

"And I haven't," I lied.

"Monica Adler is his attorney."

"You don't say?"

Anne did not reply. She looked away, preferring not to look me in the eye when she said without emotion, "I would cry if something happened to you, Taylor. I would be so upset, I'd have to recuse myself from the case and let Casper and McGaney work it. You wouldn't want that, would you?"

"No," I admitted. Especially the part about her crying.

THE SIGNS AROUND Como Lake were identical and spaced about one hundred feet apart. They demanded that pet owners pick up after their animals. Apparently, pet owners in St. Paul take such signs seriously. It took me over an hour to find enough dog droppings to fill a grocery bag a quarter full. Then I double-bagged the droppings so the fire would burn longer. Leaving it on Levering Field's doorstep, I lit the bag, rang the doorbell and dashed to my Monza. I reached it, hid behind it, just as Levering's front door opened and he stepped out. He

looked at the bag, hesitated a moment, then stomped on
it.

"Aww, shit!" he yelled.

I THOUGHT IT all was just so damn funny that I had to
tell Cynthia, describing the expression on Levering's face
in exquisite detail. "When it comes to pranks, you just
can't beat the classics," I told her. But Cynthia was not
amused; I should have guessed. Instead she chose to
linger over what had happened earlier in the day.

"It scares me, what you do for a living," she said.

"Scares me, too," I said. "That's what makes it interesting."

She just stared, her eyes wide. I could not identify the
emotions she was working through. Anger? Frustration?
A tear formed, but she brushed it away quickly. Sorrow?
Why sorrow?

"It's what I do," I said.

"You can do other things," she replied, her voice strong
and clear.

"But not as well."

"Quit joking."

"I'm not. Truly I'm not."

TEN

LEVERING FIELD NEVER actually said "uncle." Or "I give." Or even "I'm sorry." What he said was, "Come to my house at eleven o'clock, and I'll have your money."

"All of it?" I asked.

"All of it," he said, and hung up.

"I'll be damned," I said to the receiver.

I took my time shaving, showering, getting dressed—at least I thought I did. Truth is, I was so jazzed that I managed the job in fifteen minutes flat. It was barely eight when I finished. I'm not a breakfast person, and there isn't anything on TV on Saturday mornings worth watching—even ESPN is disappointing, broadcasting nothing but fishing shows. I decided to pass the time in my office. Only there wasn't much to do once I got there, either. I made coffee, read the *St. Paul Pioneer Press* and *Minneapolis Star Tribune* newspapers, and waited. I thought about calling my dad but decided he could keep until I had the cash in my hand.

Of course, the thought that I might be walking into another trap never entered my mind. That's why I took the Beretta 9mm, the one with the holster, out of my drawer and hung it on my belt just behind my right hip. I also considered calling Freddie, then decided against it. Levering didn't make me half as nervous as Freddie did. Besides, a hit at Levering's own home? I just couldn't see it.

At ten-thirty I left my office, reclaimed my car from the lot and drove to my house, taking the entrance ramp to I-94. I accelerated hard off the ramp. My Chevy Monza surged forward and then, inexplicably, began to coast. All the red lights on my dashboard flared at the same time. I pressed the accelerator, but there was no power. I slipped in the clutch, turned the ignition. Nothing. I drifted to the shoulder of the freeway, slowed to about fifteen, and tried to pop the clutch. Nothing. I stopped the car just past the Riverside Avenue exit.

I raised the hood and looked underneath. I don't know what I expected to find. A big switch stuck in the off position, I suppose. I fiddled with a few wires, went back behind the wheel, turned the key. Zip.

I cursed the Monza. She had served me without fail for eighteen years and an astonishing one hundred ninety-four thousand miles come hell or hard winters, but what has she done for me lately? Then I cursed myself when I realized I had left Sara's cell phone in my office.

I-94 was at the bottom of a steep man-made valley cut through Minneapolis. There was nothing for me to do but climb one side of the valley, vault the fence at the top, and follow the service road to a Perkins restaurant.

When I walked into the restaurant, the hostess saw the mud on my shoes, knees, and hands and clearly breathed a sigh of relief when I went to the public telephone. My first call was to Park Service, a garage I frequent on Como Avenue. I explained my situation to Nick, the owner, and requested a tow. He said a wrecker would be rolling in minutes. My next call was to Levering Field's home. The phone rang six times before it was answered by a machine. As requested, I recited my name, the time, and delivered a message: Car trouble; I'll be there as soon as possible.

When I returned to my Monza, a representative of the Minnesota Highway Patrol was placing a citation under my windshield wiper—it is an offense to park on the freeway. I attempted to explain the difference between parking and breaking down, but he ignored my argument. I told him I had already called for a tow and would be out of his way in ten minutes. He thought that was swell. Then I told him I was an ex-cop. He smiled at that, took the citation from the windshield and pressed it into my hand. He told me to have a nice day.

The patrolman went back to his unit, I sat inside the Monza, and we waited separately for the wrecker. It arrived ten minutes later. Ten minutes after that I was loaded up, and we were heading east again, along I-94 to Highway 280. I gave the patrolman a one-finger wave when he passed us at the exit.

Another ten minutes later and we were at Park Service. I called Levering Field yet again, getting his answering machine once more. I asked Nick, if I could borrow his loaner. He said sure, directing me to a maroon American Motors Ambassador that he had bought at auction from the Minnesota Department of Transportation. It had a sluggish transmission and about one gallon of gas, but it was clean. I stopped at an Amoco station and filled it up, using my credit card.

It was eleven-forty-five when I arrived at Levering Field's home.

I'LL TELL YOU the difference between St. Paul and Minneapolis. In St. Paul, someone knocks on your door, you open it. In Minneapolis, you peek through the spy hole and shout, "What do you want?" But Levering's front door was unlocked and open about a foot. Hell, they don't do that even in the suburbs. I slipped the Beretta out of my holster, gripped it with two hands, nudged the door open further, and slipped inside.

I stood for a long time in the entryway, listening intently. There was no sound except my breath coming fast. Nothing moved. Not me. Not the stiff on the floor.

It was too bad about the blood. Levering was a nifty dresser; it was the only thing about him that I admired. Take the charcoal number he wore now. Silk. Hand stitched. Impeccable. But the blood that seeped from the bullet hole in the back of his head soaked the collar and shoulders. Have you ever tried to remove blood stains from silk? I shook my head in disgust. That suit must have cost—what? Twenty-five hundred bucks? Maybe more. Now it was just an expensive dust rag. As for Levering . . . I bent to the body and placed two fingers across his carotid artery. It was a wasted gesture. Judging from where the bullet was lodged in back of his skull, he was probably dead before he hit the floor.

Levering was stretched out in his living room, his mouth full of carpet, his left hand reaching toward the second floor staircase just beyond the front door. The room was neat, no sign of a struggle. No sign of the money, either. I squatted next to Levering's body, wondering why these things always happen to me, when I heard her.

"Ohmigod! Ohmigod! Ohmigod!" the woman's voice screamed. I looked up to see Levering's sixteen-year-old daughter, Emily. She was standing just inside the entryway, a half dozen shopping bags gripped in her hands. She dropped the bags and screamed some more.

"You killed my father! You killed my father!"

I straightened up, slipping the Beretta into the holster on my hip.

"It sure looks that way," I admitted.

THE 911 OPERATOR wanted me to stay on the line after I reported the murder, but I had nothing more to say to her. I wished her a nice day and hung up. The first squad car arrived exactly eighty-seven seconds later by my watch. It carried only one officer. He sprang from the unit like he was landing on Omaha Beach. Twenty minutes later Levering Field's house looked like an invasion site. I counted no less than eight blue and whites and four unmarked cars, grille lights flashing, light bars going full.

The St. Paul Police Department's lab guys were already inside, dusting everything, shooting videotape of every square inch of the crime scene. Outside, the crews from four different TV news stations recorded the comings and goings at the Fields' residence from the other side of the yellow tape that kept them on the sidewalk. Occasionally, they pointed their cameras at me. Why not? I was the only one leaning against an SPPD cruiser with handcuffs on, palms facing outward, uncomfortable as hell. One of the newshounds jumped up and down and waved and yelled, "Hey, pal!" I gave his camera a nice smile. Wait until Mom hears about this.

Anne rode the hammer into the driveway and was out of the car before the siren's whine had died away. She had already been late for one shooting this week; damned if she'd miss a second. She saw me leaning against the car and stopped. I smiled at her. She did not smile back. A moment later she was inside.

Uniforms with nothing better to do were loitering outside the door, around the squad cars, and along the perimeter of the crime scene, standing inside the bright yellow tape like they were something special. They all snapped to when Anne arrived. One ambitious team started noting the license plate numbers of all the vehicles parked anywhere near the scene. The officer who had cuffed me was on his radio, checking to see if any citations for parking or moving violations had been issued in the area that morning. Suddenly, everyone wanted to help. Anne does that to people.

THEN AMANDA LEVERING arrived, holding unsteadily to the arm of a man who never took his eyes off her, and went into the house. I recognized him immediately. It was the man she had met after I sent her the flowers.

Amanda was in the house for less than fifteen minutes. When she emerged, she was holding the hand of her daughter, the man following behind. They all stopped to get a good look at me. This time I did not smile.

THE MEDICAL EXAMINER followed the stretcher out. He was wearing a black sports jacket over his medical blues, a stethoscope hanging out of his pocket. A body bag lay on the stretcher. The color matched the ME's coat. He was still wearing his rubber gloves.

I watched as they loaded the body into the ambulance. The ME retreated to his station wagon. Both vehicles left, an officer holding the yellow tape high to let them creep underneath it.

ANNE CROSSED THE lawn slowly, McGaney following at her heels. She was carrying my Beretta in a plastic bag.

"I thought you stopped carrying," she said when she reached my side.

"It hasn't been fired," I assured her.

"Have you been informed of your rights?" she asked, handing the bag to McGaney.

"C'mon Annie. Cut me some slack."

"Excuse me? What did you say?"

"Nothing."

"You said something. What was it?"

"Nothing, nothing. I didn't say anything."

Annie wouldn't let it go. "Did you hear him say something?" she asked McGaney.

"He wants you to cut him some slack," McGaney answered.

"Book him," Anne said.

"'Book him'?" I repeated. "Who are you, Steve McGarrett?"

Anne took a backward step, an odd expression on her face, one I had not seen before. Then her right hand came up. I turned away from it, but it caught me high on my right cheekbone just below the eye, sending a shiver of pain up through the top of my head and then down. I hunched, waiting for a second blow that did not come. After a moment, I turned toward her.

The knuckles on Anne's right hand were red and already swelling. I knew she was hurt, but she refused to acknowledge the pain, refused to even flex her fingers. Instead she let her hand rest at her side, motionless. If my hands hadn't been shackled behind by back, I would have resisted the impulse to rub my throbbing cheek for the same reason.

"Take him in," Anne told McGaney softly.

"What charge?" I demanded to know.

Anne's reply came in a hiss between clenched teeth. "Suspicion of murder, you dumb sonuvabitch."

THE Q & A WAS conducted by McGaney and Casper, but I knew Anne was watching from behind the one-way mirror. I could feel her.

McGaney was trying hard to put me at ease, reminding me that I used to be a cop, and us cops, well, we stick together, so you know this interrogation—not interrogation really, just, you know, a few simple questions—was only a formality. That was as far as I let him get.

"Listen closely," I said. "I'm only going to tell you this once." And then to Casper, "You should take notes."

Very slowly, very carefully, giving as many names, times, and other details as I could remember, I recited the events of my day, starting with Levering Field's telephone call that morning. I told the detectives about my car, about the highway patrolman, about the calls I made from Perkins, about my call from the garage, about my visit to the Amoco station. I told them to interview the witnesses, to subpoena the MURs from all the locations; told them to cross check my movements against the ME's postmortem interval. And that's all I told them. When they pressed me for more information, I recited my constitutional rights and claimed I had no more to say—with or without an attorney present. They weren't happy about it, but what could they do?

I WAS TWO days in the Ramsey County Adult Detention Center. It was crowded. The joint, located on a white sandstone bluff overlooking the Mississippi River in downtown St. Paul, was originally built to house one hundred thirty-four prisoners. There were two hundred fifty-three the weekend I was there.

They put me in a triangular cell featuring an aluminum toilet, aluminum wash basin, mirror, and two bunks attached to the wall. I had the top bunk, my cellmate the lower. I was allowed to wear my own clothes while he was dressed in jail green and slippers—a trustee doing time for kiting checks.

"What are you in for?" he asked first thing.

"Suspicion of murder," I told him.

He avoided me after that, which took a hell of an effort considering the size of the cell.

The cell was just one of ten that opened up into a common area where meals were served, where the population could get together and debate the pros and cons of the judicial system, where they could make calls from the telephones anchored to the wall, use exercise equipment, and watch TV. There were dozens of such areas in the center, each with fewer prisoners than your average elementary school classroom.

From ten P.M. until five A.M. I was locked in my cell. The rest of the time I watched cable—mostly CNN; channel selection was controlled by the deputies. I admit to being nervous; jail would frighten anyone. But if you really want scary, try watching CNN World News for forty-eight hours straight. It'll curl your hair.

IT WAS LATE Monday afternoon before they took me back to the Ramsey County Annex on the third floor of the St. Paul Police Department building. I did not complain about the delay. I didn't complain about anything.

The assistant Ramsey County attorney was pouring coffee when I arrived, led through the door by county deputies. He nodded, and one of my escorts unlocked the cuffs that pinned my hands behind my back.

"Have a seat," the ACA said. "Coffee?"

"Sure," I replied, sitting in a metal chair at the end of a long table. At the other end was a video camera pointed directly at me.

The ACA poured six ounces of coffee into a paper cup and set it in front of me. "Everything OK in jail? No problems?"

"It was very quiet," I lied. "Very relaxing."

He moved to the other end of the table, near the camera, and paged through a file folder.

"Is that camera on?" I asked.

"No," he said, then looked at me hopefully. "You want to make a statement?"

"I already made a statement," I answered.

"So I read," he replied, going back to the folder. "Even though you haven't been charged yet, a public defender has been assigned to your case until you can secure counsel of your own."

"I don't need a lawyer," I announced as the door to the interrogation room swung open.

"Yes, you do," Cynthia Grey said, following Anne Scalasi into the room.

"What are you doing here?"

"Shut the fuck up," Cynthia told me, jabbing her finger in my face. "Not one goddamn word." I was shocked. Cynthia's elocution instructor had strictly forbidden the use of obscenities.

Anne rounded the table and handed the ACA the file she was carrying. Her hand and wrist were wrapped in an ace bandage.

The ACA read the file carefully, looked me in the eye, then read it again. "Your movements between ten-forty-five and eleven-forty-five Saturday morning are well documented," he said.

"How 'bout Levering Field's movements?" I asked. Cynthia dug her long fingernails into my hand, making me yelp.

It didn't appear as if the ACA was going to answer, so Anne did.

"He was seen entering his home by a neighbor at approximately ten-fifty; they waved at each other."

"And?" I asked, moving my hand away from Cynthia's fingernails.

This time the ACA answered. "The ME estimates that the victim was killed about two hours before he examined the body—rigor had developed in the small muscles, but nowhere else."

"When did the ME examine the body?" I asked.

"One hour after you called 911," the ACA admitted.

It didn't take a genius to figure it out. I called around noon, which means Levering was killed sometime after eleven. Between eleven and noon I was enjoying my well-documented adventures in motoring.

Cynthia was on her feet. "Are you prepared to charge my client?"

The ACA shook his head.

"Then I'm taking my client home," she announced.

"We have a great many questions for your client," the ACA countered.

"Not today," said Cynthia. "My client will be available to answer all your questions at a later date. But he has just spent two days in jail for a crime he did not commit. He's going home to eat, to sleep, to take a shower . . ."

"Not necessarily in that order, I hope," Anne said.

Cynthia ignored her and said to the ACA, "Contact my office, and we will arrange a mutually convenient time to meet."

The ACA said, "Soon."

Cynthia nodded and turned to the door. I followed. Stopped. Turned back.

"What happened to the money?" I asked Anne.

"What money?"

ELEVEN

"WHAT ARE YOU doing here?" I again asked Cynthia when we were outside, walking along Cedar Street toward the World Trade Center.

"Anne called me," she answered, then repeated herself more loudly. "Anne called me. You didn't. Why didn't you call me?"

"I figured you knew where I was; there were reporters all over the place."

"Sure, that's what I do. If I want to know where the man I love is, I watch the evening news, read the newspapers to see if he's been arrested."

"Man you love?"

"Goddamn you, Taylor! You should have called," Cynthia insisted.

"Next time I will," I promised.

"Next time? You intend to make a habit out of this?"

"'Man I love.' You said 'the man I love'."

"Don't change the subject!"

We were at the corner of Cedar and Seventh, in the shadow of the Minnesota Public Radio building. I took Cynthia's arm and turned her toward me.

"Am I the man you love?" I asked.

Suddenly I felt a sharp pain down low. It made me gasp. My first thought was that Cynthia had kneed me in the groin. "I don't believe it," I said aloud, the pain shooting up from my groin into my voice. I doubled over, covered my groin with my hands. They came away bloody. Cynthia was calling my name, hands on my shoulders, helping to lower me to the ground. It wasn't hard. I was folding like an accordion. I stared at the blood on my hands. How unusual. I looked for the source. There was a hole in my thigh, about five inches down from my groin. Whew, that's a relief. I was smiling. Cynthia's face hovered over me. She lifted my head and slid her purse underneath. She was talking. I didn't hear what she said; she was too far away. But her voice was calm and warm. I said something to her. Damn if I can remember what. . . .

REMEMBER THE TV show *Emergency*, where all the paramedics talked like Jack Webb? Well, they do, you know. Just like him. In clipped, short sentences.

There were four of them. One was applying pressure to my wound, wrapping it with sterile gauze. Another was calling out vital signs: "Systolic one-twenty, weak and thready." A third was setting up an IV, shoving a needle into my right arm. "Ringers lactate." Something like that. The fourth was talking on a telephone, talking to his girlfriend, telling her something about a superficial femoral artery. Probably a new-wave rock band I don't know. I couldn't see their faces, they were miles away on all sides of me, except for the one sliding the needle into my arm. He was far away, too, but right above me.

"Do you know who you are?" he asked.

"Huh?"

"What's your name? Do you know who you are?"

"I am Ra, the sun god, supreme deity of ancient worlds. So watch it."

I laughed. See, I hadn't known I was Ra. Up until that moment, I thought I was someone else. I closed my eyes and drifted off, confident that tomorrow morning I would rise in the east and live forever.

THERE WERE VOICES all around me talking at once, maybe a thousand voices.

"How many units has he taken?"

"This is his third."

"BP is ninety."

"I have no pedal pulse."

"What's his blood pressure?"

"Ninety."

"Weak popliteal."

"What do you think?"

"We have to reestablish circulation."

"Angiogram?"

"No, we'll go right ahead and operate."

"Where am I?"

"You're in the emergency room at St. Paul Ramsey Medical Center."

"Why don't we just send him to room ten and let them evaluate up there?"

"He's awake."

"Might be best."

"Do you know who you are?"

"Can you move your feet?"

"I'm not sure."

"Move your leg for me."

"Leg?"

"Are you allergic to penicillin?"

"Who should we notify?"

"Mom? Dad?"

"Let's get him out of here."

THEY WERE WAITING for me in room ten, the emergency operating room located on the third floor of St. Paul Ramsey Medical Center—three surgery residents, a scrub nurse, circulating nurse, anesthesiologist, anesthetist nurse. The one in charge—a woman—said, "Put him on the table." And they did. She said she wanted a chest X-ray and pictures of my leg, and they started arranging that. Then she said she wanted a second IV, and they put a needle into my other arm.

A resident started asking me the same questions as the guys in the ER. I wasn't as lightheaded; whatever they were pumping into me was doing the trick, and I understood the questions and answered them as accurately as possible. I told him the lights were too bright, they hurt my eyes, but nobody did anything about them.

Someone was rattling off my vitals again; someone else was playing with my feet. "Wiggle your toes," he said, and I did, but I couldn't feel them. "Can you feel this?" he asked and poked my foot. I did, but it was like being stabbed with a Q-tip. He stood there, a needle in his hand, and told the boss, "No pedal pulse, the artery is blown."

"No kidding, Dick Tracy," said the woman as she examined my wound.

"Hey, that's funny," I said.

She ignored me.

"We're going to have to repair the vessel," she announced then told a nurse, "Tell the lab to draw blood for CBC, lytes, and type, and cross for four units of packed cells." The nurse repeated the order just like she knew what the doctor was talking about.

"Hey? Hey Dick? Dick Tracy?"

The doctor bent over me, put a soft hand on my forehead, brushing the hair out of my eyes.

"Am I in trouble?"

She smiled. "Not anymore," she said.

The anesthesiologist moved past her to the second IV, shot a syringe full of something into it. A few seconds later I was out.

I OPENED MY eyes. The room was dark. People were lying on beds on both sides of me. A steady *peep, peep, peep* echoed in my ears. A nurse was hovering close by, reading white numbers off a black TV monitor. I closed my eyes.

I COULD SEE only gray sky through my window. I tried to raise myself up to get a better view, but a flock of flashing red lights beat me down. I closed my eyes, wincing at the assault. When I opened them again, the sky had turned blue. A deep breath brought me the unmistakable scent of lilac—lilac, like the bushes that surrounded my home. I turned and found Anne Scalasi sitting in a chair, watching me. She smiled.

"Hi," she said.

"Hi," I answered. My voice sounded funny, like I hadn't heard it before.

"I can only stay a little while," she said.

I nodded.

"Did you see who shot you?"

I shook my head.

"Cynthia?" I asked.

"She's OK, she's fine. They wouldn't let her in ICU because she's not family. My badge bought me fifteen minutes."

I nodded some more. So tired. I closed my eyes. Ahh, yes. Lilac . . .

———————

I WAS IN a room, alone except for two nurses. I was the one in bed. I licked my lips and said something about being thirsty. One of the nurses wet my lips with a cloth.

"Not what I had in mind," I told her.

She removed the blanket and asked me to move my leg. I did. Wiggle my toes. I did. She noted my small successes on a chart. "You have good color," she said.

"Thank you."

"Are you in pain?"

"Yeah."

She set the chart down and went to a cabinet where she fixed a shot.

"What is that?"

"Morphine," she said. "A small shot to relieve discomfort."

"How come I have bandages on both my legs? You guys didn't cut on the wrong leg?"

The nurse replaced my blanket. "The doctor will come by later to explain everything."

Fine, I told myself, closing my eyes.

I wasn't happy about being in a hospital. Hospitals are dangerous places. Sick people stay in hospitals; sick people with contagious diseases. And people in hospitals made mistakes—oh, man, do they make mistakes—with blood and diagnoses and test results and charts that are all screwed up. I heard of a guy in Florida whose right foot was amputated when they were supposed to cut off the left. I reached under the blanket and ran my hands over the bandages on both legs. As far as I was concerned, all hospitals were made-for-TV movies just waiting to happen.

And doctors? Don't get me started on doctors. They might appear pleasant and charming at first meeting, but give them time. I have yet to meet one who doesn't eventually turn into an arrogant, see-all-know-all asshole. The way most doctors figure it, the MD following their names endows them with a deep knowledge on all subjects great and small, knowledge that is far superior than that possessed by us lowly, unlettered patients.

I was lying there, feeling sorry for myself, when the doctor came in. She blew in the way most doctors enter a hospital room: without knocking. She was the doctor, I was the patient; her patient, like Ogilvy was my rabbit. My privacy didn't mean shit to her.

She said, "How are you feeling today?" but did not wait for an answer, didn't seem to notice when I didn't answer. Instead, she unwrapped my legs, both of them, spending most of her time with the left—the one with the bullet hole. It was swollen and discolored. I had to turn away for a moment. But she was pleased. "No bleeding," she noted.

"Want the good news or the bad news first?" she asked me, leaving the nurse to rebandage my legs.

"The bad news."

"You've been shot in the leg."

"So I've been told. What's the good news?"

"There are no permanent injuries. At least none you can't walk away from."

"Very good news."

"I told you in the OR you weren't in trouble."

"That was you?"

"That was me."

"What's your name?"

"Dr. Stephanie Sampsell."

I offered her my hand, "Pleased to meet you," careful to avoid calling her "Doctor." "I'm Holland Taylor."

"Pleasure," she said, shaking my hand. "Call me Sam."

I decided right then and there that I wouldn't.

When the nurse finished her task and left the room, Stephanie found a perch on the edge of my bed.

"I have a few questions," I told her.

"I figured," she said.

"Why do I have bandages on both legs?"

"I operated on both legs."

"Uh-huh."

Stephanie smiled. It was a good smile. "What happened was this," she said. "The bullet—"

"I want the bullet," I interrupted her.

"The police have it," she said.

"Even better," I replied.

"The bullet entered your upper thigh and partially transected your superficial femoral artery—that's a major artery, by the way. You came dangerously close to bleeding to death."

I had nothing to say to that. Instead, I said, "'Partially transected'?"

"The bullet didn't sever the artery. One wall, one side of the artery was torn away. To repair it, we had to cut away the damaged part of the artery and splice in an undamaged vein. Question is, where do we get six inches of undamaged vein."

"My right leg?"

"Yep," the doctor replied. "We took a length of saphenous vein from the inner part of your right thigh. Don't worry about it," she added when she saw the concerned expression on my face, "you don't need it. The saphenous is a superficial vein; it's usually stripped out of people with varicose veins. Anyway, we took six inches and used it to resect the artery above and below the injury. Simple."

"What happens now?"

"Your blood pressure is a little high for me, so we'll keep you in intensive care for a while longer, until it drops to about one-twenty over eighty. Then we'll move you into a semiprivate room. You heal, you go home."

"Just like that?"

"In a couple of days you'll lose the IV, and we'll put you on pain pills. By then you should be ready for therapy—leg lifts, exercises. You should be out of here in a week and walking normally in four more."

"Good news again."

Stephanie smiled some more. "That's why I get to use MD behind my name."

Yeah, right.

She went to the door, promising to look in on me from time to time. Before she left, I told her, "Next time you enter my room, knock first."

Stephanie seemed genuinely surprised by my demand. The surprise lasted maybe two seconds; then it turned to indignation, her mouth twisting into an "or what?" expression. But she let it go and left the room.

CYNTHIA GREY SMELLED sweet. I took a good pull on her perfume after she kissed my mouth and laid her head on my chest. But it wasn't a scent I could place, so I asked her, "What is that you're wearing?"

"Calyx," she answered. "Like it?"

"Absolutely," I said, noting that it was not a scent found in nature.

"So, how are you doing?" I asked. It was the first chance I'd had to see Cynthia since I was shot. My blood pressure had finally met Stephanie's criteria, and I was transferred from ICU to a semiprivate room, which turned out to be all private since the other bed went unoccupied. No cable, unfortunately, just local stations. Hell, I was better off in jail.

"I'm fine," she said, then quickly added, "They told me you would be all right, that there wouldn't be any permanent damage."

"I'll be dancing at First Avenue in a week."

Cynthia smiled. I hated the music at First Avenue and she knew it.

She gave me a pile of magazines she had collected—*The Sporting News, Sports Illustrated, Inside Sports, Hockey Digest, Golf Digest,* and *Vanity Fair*, which had Nicole Kidman on the cover. I like Nicole a lot, but I put that magazine on the bottom just the same.

"Tammy is taking care of Ogilvy," she told me. I nodded. Tammy Mandt was the little girl next door who had given me the rabbit in the first place. She'd made me a present of it after my wife and daughter were killed—"So you won't be lonely," Tammy had said. Then Cynthia told me, "I was so frightened. I didn't think it was possible to be that frightened."

"I don't think they were shooting at you," I said.

"I wasn't frightened for myself," she said, then lifted her face toward the ceiling, gently shaking her head, sighing deeply. I recognized the sigh from past encounters. It said, "What a jerk."

"Did you see anything?" I asked.

"Saw nothing, heard nothing. You started to fall, and I didn't know why, and then I saw the blood."

"It looked worse than it was," I assured her.

"No, it didn't," she insisted. "I tried to stop the bleeding," she added. "I didn't do a very good job."

"You did fine."

"I thought you were going to die," she said. "I almost had a drink because I thought you were going to die and to hell with AA. Went to Gallivan's after the paramedics took you away and had them pour me a double. But I couldn't do it."

"Good."

"Want to hear why? Two reasons. First, I didn't want to be drunk when they told me you were dead."

"And the second?"

"I didn't want to die with you."

WHEN I WAS in high school, I broke my wrist playing basketball. Other than that, all my injuries have been job related. I've been knifed several times, shot in the back, had my head cracked open twice, lost three teeth when a perp hit me in the mouth with a hammer, and have been beaten up more times than I will ever admit. Now I've taken a round in my leg. Yet there I was, more or less in one piece. If I didn't hate disco so much, I would have broken into the old Gloria Gaynor song, "I Will Survive." I was actually pleased with myself. "Yep, survival of the fittest," I heard myself proclaim aloud. And then I went searching through the magazines Cynthia had supplied, looking for something, anything, to occupy my mind so I would not linger on the cold hard truth: I was a lucky sonuvabitch, and one of these days my luck was going to run out.

STEPHANIE WAS CLEARLY still angry. But she knocked on the door and asked permission to enter as I had requested. She examined my leg without comment, then told the nurse, "Get him up slowly. And get him a walker. I want him to keep moving, but I don't want any weight on his leg. I'll send Tommy down tomorrow."

"Who's Tommy?" I asked.

"Physical therapist."

I nodded in agreement. It was time I was up and about.

"No restrictions on food," she told the nurse and headed for the door.

"Hey," I called, stopping her. "Thanks for knocking."

She didn't reply.

"Mr. Taylor," the nurse said before exiting herself, "Dr. Sampsell is probably the kindest, friendliest, most generous doctor in this hospital. And you, sir, are a jerk." And then she was gone, too, leaving me alone to ponder my prejudices.

ANNE SCALASI STOOD at the foot of my bed. "I was going to make you squirm for a while, but I think I'll just come out and tell you," she said.

"Tell me what?"

Anne made a production out of looking at her watch, then announced, "The bullet they took out of your leg was a thirty-two caliber. It was fired from the same gun that killed Levering Field."

She smiled, watching me watch her. Finally, I said, "That doesn't make sense."

"Something else," she added. "The Chicago cops got a line on Storey's friend, Mike," Anne added. "His full name is Michael Zilar. His sheet reads like the table of contents to a volume on criminal statutes: arson, assault, bookmaking, theft by credit card, drug trafficking . . ."

"Murder?"

"Questioned twice, released twice."

"Mob?"

"Chicago doesn't think he's connected, but you never know."

"Where is he?"

"Witnesses told Chicago PD that he left town, that he left immediately after he learned what happened to his friend."

"He's here," I said.

Anne supported my supposition when she told me, "We did a search of the downtown loop after you were shot; we found a plastic two-liter pop bottle stuffed with rags, a hole in the base."

"A bullet hole?"

"Jam a barrel of a gun into the neck, you have a home-made suppressor, good for two, maybe three shots with a small caliber. Chicago found the same kind of homemade suppressor at the scene of both murders Zilar was questioned about. That's awfully thin, I know. You can learn how to make a suppressor watching *NYPD Blue* on TV but—"

"I don't believe in coincidences," I told her.

"Neither do I."

Anne glanced at her watch again.

"Are you in a hurry?" I asked.

She smiled in reply, folded her arms, leaned against the wall, and waited. She was waiting for me.

"You never found the money?" I asked.

"You mean the two hundred and eighty-seven thousand dollars he withdrew from his bank earlier that morning to pay you off?" Anne shook her head. I wasn't surprised by how well informed she was. Anne Scalasi was, after all, a trained investigator. But I wondered who had told her.

"Cynthia?" I asked.

"Monica Adler," Anne answered. "She's scared silly. She claims she and Levering didn't set you up at Rice Park. She claims she was there to offer you half the money Field allegedly stole—an honest offer, she said. After the assassination attempt, she said Field decided to pay it all because he thought that you thought that he tried to have you killed—which he didn't, or so she claims."

"Wait, wait, wait," I protested. The facts were coming a little too fast for me. I paused to catch up. Anne looked at her watch.

"If Zilar came here to shoot me, to pick up the contract where Storey left off, he'd have no reason to shoot Levering," I said, thinking out loud.

Anne shrugged.

"If he killed Levering for the money, he'd have no reason to shoot me."

Anne still refused to speak.

"If he came here for revenge because of what happened to his buddy Storey, he would have shot Freddie."

Anne glanced at her watch again.

"Which means he came here for the both of us, Levering and me. The money was just a bonus Zilar lucked into."

"If it was Zilar," Anne cautioned.

"Yeah."

Anne looked at her watch, said, "And it only took you four minutes and forty-one seconds to figure it out." She smiled.

"How long did it take you?"

She smiled and held up three fingers.

"But who would have motive to kill us both?" I asked. "Who is your primary suspect?"

"Who is always our primary suspect?"

"The spouse. Amanda Field."

Anne grinned. "We always kill the ones we love."

"She had motive to kill Levering. He was cheating on her. But why hire someone to kill me? What did I do?"

"Gee, Taylor, I don't know. Think maybe you might have done something to piss her off?"

I closed my eyes, rubbed my face, refused to answer.

"'O what a tangled web we weave when first we practice to deceive!'"

I tried to ignore the remark and changed the subject. "When he killed Field, Zilar picked up two hundred and eighty-seven thousand untraceable dollars. You have that kind of money, would you hang around for a couple of days to shoot someone else for ten thousand more?"

"No," Anne admitted.

"He did."

"Yikes."

"Don't you just hate conscientious hitmen?"

TOMMY SANDS, NO relation to the singer, was tall. He had to lower his head when he walked into my hospital room to avoid bumping the top of the doorframe. And he was wide. You could play handball against him. Yet he had the softest hands I've ever felt. He wrapped one around each ankle, pulling my legs gently apart and pushing them in again.

The way Tommy explained it, the bullet caused only minor damage to my quadricep muscles, the muscles that lift the leg. Most of the damage was done to my adductors, the muscles that bring the legs together—but not so much that reconstruction was necessary. After scar tissue formed on the muscle where the bullet went through, it should heal up and be as good as new. But it was going to take a while.

"The body heals in its own time, and if the mind wants to argue, it'll act like a pissed off auto mechanic," Tommy said. "The body will find a few extra problems. Understand? It'll take every day of six weeks. If you push it, it'll take longer."

I didn't want to hear that, but I took his word for it.

We started with range-of-motion exercises. First Tommy put me in the correct anatomical position—flat on my back, arms straight out, palms up; legs straight, toes pointed—just the way da Vinci drew it. Then he slipped a folded towel under my knee and told me to bring the knee gently to my chest.

"Not all the way," he cautioned. "We'll start with about seventy-five degrees. If it's too painful, stop."

Next, he helped me bring my leg out to the side, about twenty degrees. He slipped a bread board underneath it to lessen resistance, but he claimed a large garbage bag would do as well. I winced at the movement.

"Where does it hurt?" he asked.

"Where I was shot, where do you think?" I answered.

We worked like that for an hour.

The next day, too.

I wondered when he thought I would be ready for out-patient therapy.

"Funny you should ask," he said, taking a typed sheet from his clipboard. "I've prepared a schedule—the exercises you should do, when you should do them."

I read the list carefully. It began with straight leg raises and terminal knee extensions the first week, then graduated to adductor exercises against resistance in weeks two and three.

"You should be walking without crutches by week four," Tommy told me. "Maybe sooner."

"AM I RESPONSIBLE for this?" my father asked me.

"What do you want me to tell you, Dad?" I replied.

"Tell me the truth."

"Yeah, you're responsible. Indirectly, anyway. But no more so than any client who's ever put me in harm's way. I take the money, I take the risks. I'm not bitter if that's what you're asking."

"But I'm not paying you," he reminded me.

"Let me rephrase what I said about being bitter."

"I still feel responsible," Dad confessed. "Your mom sure as hell blames me for getting her little boy shot."

"As well she should," I said and smiled. It was nice of him to take the trouble to fly up and visit me. My brother and sister-in-law had neglected to make an appearance, and they lived only across town.

"Well, at least it's over."

"Not exactly," I told him, then explained about Michael Zilar and the fact that he was probably still out there. And then there was whoever had hired ol' Mike in the first place. You couldn't let people get away with such things, I told him. It was bad for business.

"What have I started?" Dad asked, sorrow in his voice. I admit I liked seeing him that way. For too long I've thought of him standing on a pedestal, carved from marble.

"Don't worry about it."

"At least come home with me."

"I am home."

"I mean to Florida, to Fort Myers."

"No, this is my ground. I'll have a better chance here. I won't see him coming in Florida."

"You think he'd follow you to Florida?"

"I know nothing about the man except that he likes to finish what he starts."

Dad began to pace, his hands clasped behind his back, his head down.

"Besides," I told him as he walked back and forth at the foot of my bed, "I haven't gotten Mrs. Gustafson's money back yet."

Dad stopped at the window and looked through the blinds. "I haven't told her about any of this," he said.

"No reason why you should."

He was silent for a few moments, then told me, "Your brother said he was sorry he couldn't come. He was busy."

"Screw him," I announced. He didn't visit the last time I was in the hospital, either.

Dad continued to stare out the window. After a few moments he said softly, "My sons, so different," like he was speaking to himself. "Your brother was the best student, the best athlete—never in trouble. But he was always so needy. Always needed help and advice, always needed someone to tell him what to do. I worried about him all the time.

"You, on the other hand, you were always in trouble for

one prank or another, like putting the assistant principal's Volkswagen on the school roof; I still don't know how you managed that. And your grades—A's if you cared, C's if you didn't, and mostly you didn't. But you never asked for help. Not even for a ride to hockey practice or to your job at the car wash. You always took care of yourself. And that's why I never worried about you. That's why I never had long talks with you like I did with your brother. Why I didn't say anything when you quit college to become a cop and your mom went bananas. I figured you would be all right.

"Even now," he added, "your brother is safe in his big, beautiful house, with a nice job and a thick bank account and a caring wife while you're in a hospital with a bullet hole in your leg, telling me that a paid assassin is hunting you. Yet I'm more worried about him than I am for you. Why is that?"

"I don't know," I told him, without adding that I'd always been jealous of the attention he showered on my brother.

He didn't say anything for a while, just continued to stare out my window. Finally he said, "I don't think I ever told you how much I love you."

"Sure you have," I said, although if pressed for times and dates I doubt I could supply them.

"I do, you know," he added, still looking out the window, a catch in his voice.

"Let it go, Dad," I said, interrupting him. I decided I liked him up on that pedestal after all.

He took a deep breath and moved away from the window. "I met your girl," he said. "Spent time with her in the cafeteria while you were getting your therapy."

"Cynthia? What do you think."

"Beautiful."

"She is that."

"Smart, tough. Very confident."

"That, too."

"She's the kind of woman I would have been involved with—except they didn't make them like that when I was young. At least not many."

"Do me a favor. Tell Mom that."

He looked shocked. "Are you crazy?" he asked.

Looking at Freddie's large, bulky winter coat I observed that it must be pretty cold outside.

"Nah," he said. "It's more like lukewarm."

Then he handed me a Summit Pale Ale, easily hidden in the right pocket of the coat. He took another from the left pocket.

"This is strictly forbidden," I reminded him, twisting the top off the bottle.

"Yeah, I know," Freddie said. "The nurses find out, they might throw me out of here—and you know how much I like visiting folks in hospitals."

Actually, I didn't know. The only conversation of any length we ever had took place the day before he saved my life. "Considerate of you to come," I said.

"I was in the neighborhood," he told me, taking a swig of the golden liquid.

"Damn considerate, anyway," I said, and he shrugged.

I was amazed to see him, couldn't figure why he was there until he announced, "I hear the cops are lookin' for a guy named Zilar, Michael Zilar."

"I hope they're looking for him," I agreed.

"I hear he's some kinda buddy of this Storey guy I popped in Rice Park."

"You have good sources," I told him.

"So, you think he'll come after me next, lookin' for pay-back?"

I was disappointed that Freddie had only come to the hospital seeking information, that he was only looking out for himself. Although I couldn't tell you why. All things considered, his behavior seemed entirely reasonable.

"I honest-to-God don't know, Freddie," I answered him. "All I know is, the bullet that clipped me came from the same gun that killed Levering Field."

"Yeah, that's what I heard, too" he said and drained his ale. "Sounds like a real mystery," he added, setting the bottle on the table next to my bed. "Let me know how it turns out."

He then pulled a third bottle of Summit from his pocket, handed it to me, and left the room without a backward glance.

"I WANT OUT."

"What's the matter?" Stephanie Sampsell asked. "Don't you like the beer we serve here?"

"I want out," I repeated, not even pretending that I hadn't violated hospital regulations.

"I want you to stay another day."

"I want to thank you for your kindness and concern."

She sighed and started scribbling on my chart. "Taylor, you're an arrogant sonuvabitch, and I hope not to see you again."

"Is that what you're writing?"

"Take this to the nursing station, and they'll complete your discharge."

I took the paper from her hand. She moved toward the door.

"Hey," I said, swinging my legs over the side of the bed, rising to the occasion. She turned back, and I offered my hand.

"Thank you, Doctor," I said.

"Do you realize that this is the first time you've called me 'doctor'?"

"Yes," I admitted.

She smiled, took my hand. "Take care of yourself, cowboy."

"You too . . . Sam."

She was chuckling when she left the room.

I TOOK A good look at the wound while the nurse changed the bandage for the last time. Then I looked away.

"Not too bad," she said.

"No, not bad at all," I agreed, still looking away.

Cynthia and Anne watched the process with intense curiosity. When the nurse left, Anne gave me a sheaf of papers. "Sign these," she said.

"What am I signing?" I asked as I wrote my name on the forms.

"A confession."

"I didn't think I'd get away with the Lindbergh thing forever." I handed her the papers. Anne dug into the huge bag she called a purse and withdrew my Beretta 9mm parabellum, the official sidearm of the United States armed forces and law enforcement agencies throughout the country. She handed it to me.

"Careful, it's loaded," she warned me.

I choked a round into the chamber. Cynthia withdrew to the window and looked out.

"The assistant county attorney still wants to speak with you," Anne told me. "He's subpoenaed your bank records, phone records. . . ."

"He tried for a search warrant for both your office and home," Cynthia added. "Judge turned him down. The ACA couldn't adequately explain what he was looking for, and the judge wouldn't approve a fishing expedition. But he'll probably try again."

"Why?"

"He still considers you a suspect," Anne said.

"For shooting myself?"

"Stranger things have happened."

"I know, but still . . ."

"He ordered me not to cooperate with you in any way," Anne said. "He told me that considering our past relationship, it would be a felicitous if I withdrew from the investigation and let McGaney and Casper work it."

"'Felicitous'?" Cynthia asked from the window. A moment later she was writing down the word on the back of an envelope.

"He ordered you?" I asked, not believing it.

"Let's just say he strongly suggested it," Anne said. "And he was right to do so."

"So what are you telling me?"

"Good luck," Anne said.

TWELVE

CYNTHIA HELD THE front door open for me as I slowly climbed the outside steps of my house, using the crutches to swing my right leg up, my left leg hanging limp. I hobbled through the doorway and saw the debris. I dropped my right crutch and pushed Cynthia back toward the open door, hissing, "Stay out."

With my right hand, I pulled the Beretta from its holster, activating it. I headed into the living room, moving slowly, leaning on the left crutch. The contents of the house were torn and smashed: paintings and photographs ripped from the walls; lamps, tables, and chairs tipped over and smashed; cushions slashed, their contents dumped on the floor. Even my aquarium had been overturned, twenty-nine gallons of water warping my hardwood floor, the dried, discolored bodies of golden barbs, black mollies, pearl gourmis, red swordtails, and silver angelfish littered among shards of broken glass and gravel. The sight left me nauseous with rage, anger, and sorrow churning my stomach. The only thing that could've made it worse would have been fire. But it wasn't just willful destruction. My house had been searched.

I heard Cynthia call my name. I told her to come in. She looked at me and then the living room. "Wow!" she said. It got worse as we went from room to room.

SERGEANT JOHN HAWKS was a New Mexico range cop come to Minnesota; a man who fit all of Hollywood's criteria of what an ideal law enforcement officer should look like: tall, tanned, wearing a perpetual squint. He did not like Roseville, he did not like Minnesota, he did not like the entire Midwest for that matter. However, he did like his wife, a Roseville native who was once homecoming queen at Alexander Ramsey High School, and that's why he had moved here.

"Anything missing?" he asked.

"Not that I can see," I told him. I flashed on my guns, left undisturbed in the drawer of the pedestal of my waterbed, the drawer hidden by the sheets, blankets and pillows ripped from my bed and piled in front of it. "I'll know better after I clean up the place."

"We're not going to catch who did this," Hawks told me.

"I know."

Hawks tapped my left foot. I was sitting on a rocking chair, my foot resting on a hassock. "You're sure having your problems," he said.

"So it would seem."

"I'll send you a copy of the report for your insurance company."

I nodded.

"I'll also have my patrols keep a close eye on your place for a while."

"I appreciate it."

Hawks did a quick three-sixty, pausing briefly on Cynthia who was stacking my CDs on the dining room table. "See you around," he said.

"Take care," I told him. And then he was gone.

Cynthia left the table and moved to the rocking chair, kneeling next to it, her hands resting on the arm. I didn't mind that she saw the tears in my eyes.

"The bastards wrecked my wife's house," I told her.

I SENT CYNTHIA home. She wasn't happy about leaving. She wanted me to go with her, spend the night at her place. I declined the invitation, telling her I wanted to be alone for a while, telling her I would be fine. She kissed me before she left and said she was sorry about everything.

After Cynthia had gone, I started sweeping the glass off my dining room floor into a dustpan—not an easy thing to do on crutches. That's where they got in, the dining room, through a window they'd smashed. Amateurs. A professional doesn't smash anything. A professional goes through the door.

I sat on my good leg and pushed myself across the hardwood floors, dragging a kitchen garbage pail behind me, tossing what was irreparably broken, returning to the shelves and tables what was not. It was painful work, and not just because of the throbbing in my leg. It occurred to me as I went that none of the photographs of friends and family, the vases, ancient tea pots, candleholders, antiques, and collectibles were mine. They had all belonged to Laura. I had displayed nothing of my own. Four years after her death, the house still belonged to her. It still bore her personality, her taste. The sofa and chairs, drapes and rugs, tables and lamps: She had chosen them all. My contribution was merely a nod, a shrug, a curt "Whatever."

Suddenly, I felt like a stranger in my own home, like I needed to introduce myself to the rooms and closets and furniture—like I needed to somehow make them my own. And I wasn't sure I wanted to. They had belonged to Laura, not to me. Laura and my daughter were the only things in the house that I had truly considered my own.

With them gone . . . What was I going to do? Gut the house and buy new stuff? Carve my initials in the door-frame? For the thousandth time since my wife and child were killed, I seriously considered moving.

IT WAS PUSHING eight P.M., and I was still working on the ground floor. When my stomach started making gurgling sounds, I thought about stopping and fixing something to eat—the kitchen was largely undamaged; shattered plates and glasses, my silverware dumped on the floor, that was about it. That's when I heard the loud knock on my front door. The Beretta was in my hand before its echo died. Using one crutch, I hobbled to the door, turned on the outside light, and peeked through the spy hole. It was a pizza delivery man, dressed in the red, white, and blue colors of a national franchise.

I opened the door tentatively, hiding the Beretta behind the frame.

"Yes?"

"Mr. Taylor?" he asked. "I have your sausage, Canadian bacon, and pineapple. Thirteen-fifty."

"I didn't order a pizza."

A pained expression crossed the youngster's face—this sort of thing must've happened to him all the time.

"Are you sure?" he asked.

"Course I'm sure," I replied.

"Holland Taylor?" he said and recited my address.

"That's the place, but I didn't order a pizza."

"Sorry to bother you," he said and started down the steps.

"Wait!" I called, the aroma from the box causing my stomach to scream louder. "What kind of pizza is it again?"

THIRTEEN

I SAVORED THE pain as I shuffled to my Chevy Monza. A little pain was good. It was God's way of reminding me that I came *this close* to meeting Him face to face, and wouldn't I have to pay hell then.

Nick walked with me through the Park Service lot, slowing his gait so that I could keep up. Nick was not a happy man. I had kept his loaner for nine days without a word to him. He would have called the cops if he hadn't read that I had already been arrested. As it was, his loaner had been held for ransom in the St. Paul Police Department's favorite impound lot. It took me four hundred and twelve bucks to set it free, including towing charges.

He led me to the Monza. "Get 'hold of yourself," he said, then popped the hood and unscrewed the radiator cap. "Look," he said.

I did. Instead of rich green coolant, I found greasy black oil. "What are you trying to tell me?"

"I'm sorry, Taylor. She's gone."

"No way!" I cried.

He put his hand on my shoulder. "There's nothing I can do," he told me.

For a moment I was seized with panic, would not believe him, vowed to get a second opinion. He nodded. He understood. He went into detail, listing damaged car parts and prices, but I only heard his voice, not his words. *She's gone, she's gone*, my mind repeated as I stared at the Monza. Tears welled up in my eyes. She was gone.

"Hey, Taylor. Taylor!" Nick shouted at me. "You're not going to go postal on me are you, whip out an Uzi and start spraying the joint?"

I shook my head.

"Need a ride home?"

I nodded.

"Come on," he said and led the way back to the shop, moving quickly. I followed on the crutches. I heard him muttering several steps in front of me, "Man, get a grip. It's only a car."

I FOUND A young man and his fiancée circling my house when Nick dropped me at my front door. The man smiled and approached with his hand extended, the woman following behind. I took his hand and then hers.

"Can I help you?" I asked. If they were clients, why had they come to my home instead of my office?

"It's a beautiful house!" the woman exclaimed.

"Thank you."

"We'd like to see the inside," the man told me. "Your ad said you have hardwood floors?"

"Ad?"

A SECOND SET of house hunters was leaving just as Cynthia pulled into my driveway.

"Who were they?" she asked. Instead of explaining, I gave her a wet, sloppy kiss. "So, what's the word on your car?" she asked.

After I explained about the Monza's demise, Cynthia smiled.

"What?" I asked her.

"Do you realize that tomorrow is our twenty-third anniversary?"

"Excuse me?"

"Twenty-three weeks to the day since we started seeing each other."

"How do women remember that stuff? Men never remember that stuff."

"It's genetic," she answered. "Speaking of anniversaries, I think a gift is in order."

"What do you give on twenty-three-week anniversaries? Paper? Cotton?"

"Cars."

That stopped me.

"Cars?"

Cynthia smiled. "Let me buy you a car."

"Are you serious?"

"I'm rich, sort of," she reminded me. "Let me buy you a car. C'mon. You need a car, and my buying it will cheer up both of us."

Now, some men might have been offended by such a suggestion. And others might have been hurt. Me? I looked deep into Cynthia's eyes. They were the color of Hershey's Kisses, and sometimes I could see everything I ever wanted in them. Like now.

"Sure," I said.

"Really?"

"Why not?"

"No macho nonsense?"

"None."

"Honestly?"

"It's a small sacrifice to make for the good of our relationship."

"Thank you," she said.

"You're welcome."

WE WENT CAR shopping. Cynthia drove, sitting erect, her hands in the ten and two positions, her gaze shifting regularly from the street ahead to the rearview mirror to the side mirror to the street. She was twenty-four when she had learned to drive. I was sixteen, riding with my dad. When Cynthia was sixteen, she was riding the pole in a Minneapolis strip joint.

We cruised the lots on Highway 61. The dealer at the first lot spoke with the voice of an overtrained radio announcer. He could have been from anywhere or nowhere. And he all but ignored Cynthia, which must have taken a great deal of concentration considering how attractive she is. The only time he spoke to her directly was when he pointed out the vanity mirror under the passenger-side visor.

"What do you think, dear?" I asked.

"I wouldn't buy a car from this primping peacock of a sexist pig if he threw in the Hope diamond."

As we drove away, I asked her, "'Primping peacock of a sexist pig'?"

"I'll do better next time."

I didn't give her much of a chance. I hustled Cynthia back to her vehicle after only a brief tour of the next dealership on the highway.

"Didn't you see anything you liked?" she asked.

It wasn't the cars, I told her. It was the salesman. "I wouldn't buy crap from a man wearing a toupee," I announced. "A man who wears a toupee, you've got to question his judgment."

"I take it you don't approve of hair replacement systems."

"System my ass. It's a toup. If I lose my hair—and I

probably will—I intend to take it like a man. You don't see Sean Connery wearing a toupee."

"Except in movies."

"That's different."

"If you say so."

The third dealership was the charm. Cynthia got it into her head that she had to buy me a Saturn. She liked Saturns. But we had never actually sat in one. As we crossed the lot, I spotted a vehicle in the used car section.

"What is that?" I asked.

The dealer steered me right to it, bypassing the shiny new Saturns all in a row without comment. The car was a 1991 four-door Dodge Colt, ninety-four thousand miles, terrific condition. It was a light tan and if you squinted, you could see a Honda or a Toyota or a couple of the Ford series. It was an automatic, but with my leg I wasn't going to be using a clutch for a while, anyway. I took it for a test drive. I liked it. I said, "I'll take it."

"You're kidding," Cynthia said.

"It's perfect."

Cynthia stretched out her arms as if taking in the dealer's entire inventory of new Saturns. "You can have any one of these," she announced. "I'm buying."

"I'll take this one," I said, tapping the hood of the Colt.

"But why?"

"Neutral color, small, unobtrusive . . ."

"Exactly."

"Cynthia, you've forgotten what I do for a living."

"What, you can't follow people in a Saturn?" she wanted to know.

THE DEALER WAS very efficient; he wrote us up in a hurry. No lowballing, no double dipping, no grounding or flipping—none of the tricks that make customers mistrust car dealers with such a passion. I told him, the next time my girl wants to buy me a car, he's going to get my business. He liked that.

Cynthia walked me to my new Colt, kissed me good-bye, and said she'd call later that evening. I opened the car door, and the interior light flashed on. I took a moment to disconnect it. I sat behind the wheel, rolled down the window, took a deep breath of early spring. That's when I heard Cynthia scream my name. I was out of the car and hobbling toward her as quickly as I could, cursing my slowness, putting more weight on my left leg than I was supposed to, ignoring the pain. She was standing several yards back from her car, her hand over her mouth like she was silencing herself.

"What?" I asked breathlessly, the Beretta in my hand. She just pointed. All four tires were flat, an ice pick still imbedded in one of them.

I BOUGHT FOUR steel-belted radials from the Goodyear shop down the highway. Saturn put Cynthia's car on a hoist, mounting and balancing the tires. The dealer was very apologetic, claimed that nothing like that had ever happened on his lot before. He didn't charge me for the work.

Cynthia waited in a small room with a television and about ten thousand magazines, none of them current. She was surprisingly calm. At least that's the way she played it. She said only one word.

"Why?"

I replied in three words.

"I don't know."

I PUT CYNTHIA in her car and sent her to her office. I watched her leave the lot, catch Highway 61, and drive south toward downtown St. Paul. No one followed. Then I left, also heading south, driving to St. Paul Ramsey Medical Center for some work on the CIBEX machine to strengthen my quads. It hurt like hell—I refused to take pain pills since the mysterious visit from the pizza man. I figured it would be healthier to keep my head clear. After I finished, I drove to the newspaper and had them pull the ad offering my house for sale. The woman behind the counter apologized profusely. She claimed such a thing had happened only once before. Seems a couple of weeks ago someone had run a bogus ad selling a house near Mississippi Boulevard. She hoped it wasn't the beginning of a trend. And no, she couldn't identify the person who had placed either of the ads.

I went home. I had planned to go to my office, go back to work. But my leg was throbbing, and quite honestly I was exhausted; I felt like a wet rag. I went to bed early.

IT WAS TWO-FORTY A.M. when the phone rang.

"Yes?"

"You're not getting away with it," someone told me. The voice sounded like it was coming from the other end of a long sewer pipe.

"Excuse me?"

"This is just the beginning."

"Whom are you calling?"

"I'm calling you, asshole. And I'll be calling again."

With that the caller hung up, leaving a buzzing sound in my ear. I fumbled around in the dark for a few moments, trying to return the receiver to the cradle, then heaved myself out of bed and hobbled downstairs. My caller ID unit was attached to my kitchen telephone. The display read: PAY PHONE, only this time it listed a number, one with a 644 prefix.

I jotted down the number and returned to bed.

FOURTEEN

I WAS AWAKENED at 6:20 by the sound of sirens. I recognized them immediately. Fire trucks. I listened as they tore along Cleveland Avenue, expecting to hear the sirens fade as they passed my house. But they did not pass. I rolled out of bed and hopped on my good leg to the window. The Roseville Fire Department was parked in my front yard, looking for smoke. When they didn't find any, they charged me two hundred and fifty dollars for a false alarm.

THE BUILDING MANAGEMENT had piled all my mail into a brown box and set it inside my office door. Attached to the box was a note telling me to inform them the next time I went on vacation. I set the box in the middle of my desk, next to Sara's cell phone. I took it up, punched out her number. Steve answered.

"I'm glad you're all right," he told me. "Did you get my card and flowers?"

I told him that I did, thank you. He wanted to know who shot me, asked if it had had anything to do with Field, and wondered what happens next. My answers weren't particularly illuminating.

"Can you do me another favor?" I asked him. "I'll pay for this one."

"What?"

"I want you to work your magic with the telephone company; get me the exact location of a pay phone." I gave him the number.

He told me he'd call me back. And he did, about ten minutes later.

"It's on the corner of Marshall and Cretin in St. Paul," he said. The address placed the phone in the Midway district about a half mile from the Fields' residence.

"What's going on?" Steve wanted to know.

"Payback is what's going on," I told him.

THE PRESIDENT OF the Dakota County First National Bank was astonishingly cooperative. He could have told me to go to hell, probably should have. Instead he told me everything I wanted to know. I guessed he wanted to make sure that no one blamed him or his bank for Field's death.

"I handled the transaction myself," the president told me.

"You knew Field was coming?"

"No. I was here because I like to work Saturday mornings; fewer distractions, I can get a lot done. He walked in a little after nine A.M.—we're open from nine till one Saturdays—and told the cashier what he wanted. The cashier came to me."

"A man can just withdraw two hundred eighty-seven thousand dollars in cash?"

"Why not?" the president asked. "It's his money."

"Did you ask him why he wanted it?"

"Yes, I did. I told him no legal business transaction required cash."

"What did he say?"

"He said it was personal."

"Didn't you try to talk him out of withdrawing the money?"

"Of course we did. We tried to get him to take a cashier's check. He wanted cash."

"Do you usually have that much on hand?"

He shrugged. "It's a bank."

"And you gave it to him?"

"He was an important client; this isn't the biggest bank in the world, you know. If he says he wants cash, we try to talk him out of it. If he insists, we ask him how he wants it. He wanted twenties."

"That's what? Ten thousand . . ."

"Fourteen thousand three hundred and fifty twenty-dollar bills," the banker rattled off the top of his head."

"You have that many on hand?"

"No. He had to take sixty-three thousand in fifties."

"How many packets?"

"Fifty-seven of five-thousand dollars each and one more worth two thousand."

"Where did he put it?"

"In a black briefcase."

"Just like the movies," I suggested.

"If he didn't have his own briefcase, I would have given him mine. That kind of money, what? You expect him to carry it in a grocery bag?"

"After you gave him the money, what then?"

"Then I made him sign a Currency Transaction Form for the IRS, Form 4789. That's mandatory anytime you're dealing in amounts over ten thousand."

"OK."

"Afterward, a guard and I escorted him to his car."

"Was he alone?"

"Yes."

"Did he call anyone?"

"Not while he was here."

"After he got to his car, did he lock the briefcase in his trunk?"

"No. He set it on the seat next to him."

"Then what happened?"

"I waved good-bye."

"When was that?"

"At exactly ten-oh-five A.M."

"You're sure?"

"I insisted that the guard note Field's departure in his book."

"Why?" I asked.

"I just had a bad feeling about the whole deal."

THE BANK PRESIDENT did not wave to me when I left. Just as well. I activated my stopwatch and maneuvered the Colt out of the bank's parking lot and into traffic. I caught Highway 110, followed it to 35E, went south to Shepard Road, and followed that to Mississippi Boulevard and the street where Field lived. Twenty-two minutes.

I drove back to the bank, this time taking Cretin Avenue to Randolph, then east to 35E. Eighteen minutes. And the lights were against me.

Finally, I went the long way, taking 35E to I-94, 1-94 west to the Cretin-Vandalia exit, Cretin south about a mile, two rights and a left to Field's driveway. Twenty-six minutes.

I made a few notations in my notebook: Field leaves bank at 10:05. Arrives home at 10:50 (according to police). Trip takes maximum twenty-six minutes, minimum eighteen. Nineteen to twenty-seven minutes unaccounted for.

"YES? CAN I help you?"

"My name is Holland Taylor," I told the man through

the screen on his front door, flashing my ID. "I'm investigating the Levering Field murder."

"Yes," the man said. "I was told that an officer might come by to ask follow-up questions."

He opened the screen door, and I went inside the house. It was one of three where a man working in his front yard could wave at Field as he moved from his driveway to his door. I had guessed right the first time.

"May I offer you a cup of coffee, Officer?"

"No, thank you, sir," I answered. Obviously, he was under the impression that I was a cop, and I thought it would be bad manners to correct him.

"Well, then, how can I help?"

I consulted my notebook. "You indicated that you saw Mr. Field arrive in his car—"

"Yes."

"And walk into his house—"

"Yes."

"At approximately—"

"At exactly ten-fifty A.M.," he said confidently. "Like I said, there was a program I wanted to see at eleven, and I was keeping track of the time."

"The program was . . . ?"

"*The X-Men*. Yes, I know it's a cartoon. But I've been a fan since I was a kid reading Marvel comics. I still read them. Course, they're more expensive now, but I can afford it," he added, waving a hand at his opulent home. "My wife thinks I'm nuts."

"I was into *Spiderman* myself," I confessed.

"Yeah?"

"And *The Avengers*."

He nodded his appreciation.

"One more question, sir," I said.

"Hmm?"

"When you saw Mr. Field move from his car to the house . . ."

"Yes?"

"Was he carrying a briefcase?"

"No," he said without hesitation. "He was empty hand-ed."

UNDER ORDERS FROM the assistant county attorney, Anne Scalasi wasn't supposed to speak with me, and I didn't want to push her luck. So I contacted Martin McGaney. McGaney had been promoted to the Homicide unit from Narcotics, as I had. It was about the only thing we had in common, but it was enough.

"Taylor, what are you doing?" he wanted to know.

"Levering Field put the money in a briefcase and put the briefcase on the passenger seat in his car when he left the bank," I reminded him over the telephone. "You did talk to the banker, right?"

"Are you looking for an obstruction charge, 'cuz the ACA—"

"Field did not have the briefcase when he entered his house."

"Who says?"

"The neighbor who saw him. The question is—"

"Are you sure?" McGaney asked.

"The neighbor's sure," I answered. "The question is, did he leave the briefcase in his car?"

McGaney didn't answer.

"Martin?"

"Why would he leave two hundred and eighty-seven thousand dollars in his car?" he asked tentatively.

"Jesus Christ, didn't anyone bother to look?"

"We never checked his car," McGaney admitted.

"Where is it now?"

"His wife must have it."

"I see," I said trying hard to make the words sound like, "Sloppy!"

After a moment I added, "Tell me. While I was in jail expanding my circle of friends, did anyone bother to ask Mrs. Field where she was Saturday morning, say around eleven o'clock?"

"She claims she was shopping with her daughter."

TOMMY SANDS WAS a big believer in the maxim "No pain, no gain." And since I wasn't grinding my teeth in agony as I worked out on the CIBEX machine, he decided to increase the resistance. I ended up breaking my promise and downed a couple of pain killers. They didn't seem to help much. Yet, although I felt like something the dog dragged in and the cat dragged out, Tommy was pleased. I was making greater progress in my therapy than he had hoped.

"Tomorrow we'll move on to the adductors," he said, smiling like it was the most fun we could have.

I USED TO believe only wimps drive an automatic clutch. After I pulled into my garage and shut down the Dodge, I wondered how I'd managed so long without one.

I was hurting. My leg was throbbing, and so was my head. Not to mention my confidence. Zilar was out there. Somewhere. Waiting. Watching. Looking for an opportunity to strike. He wouldn't get one while I was driving. I was careful about that—driving defensively, guarding against tails. My house was a different matter. It was a static target. Vulnerable. And so was I when I was in it.

I dragged myself out of my car, shifting my weight from my right leg to my crutches. I stood at the gaping door, hiding in the shadow, looking out. I didn't see any plastic pop bottles anywhere. I hit the automatic garage door button, then ducked down and moved forward quickly before the door could shut on my head.

The back door to my house was inside a three-season porch made mostly of glass; three concrete steps lead to a metal and glass door. I hobbled to it slowly, putting some weight on my left leg but not much. I climbed the steps and opened the door. Inside, on a rubber mat embossed with the word WELCOME, I found a cat. It was dead, its white fur stained with blood, its body torn and ripped, its eyes open.

"Oh, God," I whispered, stooping, holding the doorframe to keep from falling, and stroked the dead animal behind the ears. Its body was still warm.

I backed away, lost my balance, and fell off the steps, landing on my right knee and tearing a hole in my jeans.

"Shit, shit, motherfuck, shit . . . !" The obscenities flowed loud and fast as I fought to keep down the contents of my stomach. After a few minutes, I pulled myself to my feet, leaning heavily on the crutches. I looked back at the porch but did not go inside, wondering who the cat had belonged to. "Bastards!" I spat at whoever had mutilated it.

The huge lilac bushes that separate my neighbor's property from mine rustled noisily. I turned toward the sound and saw a body trying to push through. I dropped my crutches—both of them—putting weight on my right leg, reaching for the Beretta on my hip. My leg couldn't support the weight, and I went to my knee again as I brought the Beretta up, pointing it at a young girl carrying a basketball.

Tammy looked at the gun, frowning like this sort of thing happened to her frequently. Tammy Mandt, the daughter of my neighbor, the girl who had given me Ogilvy. "What's the matter?" she wanted to know.

"Dammit!" I yelled too loud. The sound of my voice startled the eleven-year-old. "Sorry," I added quickly. I returned the Beretta to its holster, then used the crutches to get to my feet.

"You OK?" Tammy asked.

I nodded. "Listen. I want you to do me a favor. Keep Ogilvy for a while longer." As I spoke I slipped my money clip out of my pocket and peeled off two twenties.

"Sure," she said, then added, "What's this?" when I handed her the bills. "You don't have to pay me to take care of Ogilvy."

"That's for food and litter," I told her. "Keep the change."

"OK."

"Something else. I want you to keep away from my house. Don't go near here until I tell you. No shooting hoops in my driveway. All right?"

Tammy stared at me for a few beats, a concerned expression on her face. Then she asked again, "Are you OK?"

I flashed on the dead cat in my porch, but did not mention it. "Just stay away for a while," I said. "Oh, and watch out for strangers. Tell your mom if you see anyone suspicious hovering about."

Tammy promised that she would, then added, "You're in trouble again, aren't you?"

FIFTEEN

It wasn't the explosion that woke me at three-thirty in the morning. Or even the flames. It was the squealing tires of a car as it accelerated out of my driveway. I bumped my sore leg as I went to the window, but I did not have much time to contemplate the pain. The front of my house was on fire!

The fire never actually reached the structure; it stopped about a half-yard short of my stucco walls, consuming instead the hedge of shrubs and low-growing trees that Laura had planted and a fifteen-foot wide oval of grass. The Roseville fire crew doused the front of my house just the same—better safe than sorry. A deputy chief sidled up to me while I watched. He was holding the neck of a broken beer bottle in his gloved hand. It reeked of kerosene.

"This landed about six feet short of your house and blew backward," he told me. "Whoever threw it had no arm whatsoever. You were lucky."

Funny, I didn't feel lucky. Especially after the Roseville cops arrived, followed by the media.

The cops wanted to know if the attack had anything to do with Levering Field's murder and my subsequent arrest. "Probably," I told them, but not much else. They weren't pleased by my reticence and did not go away happy.

The media was not happy, either, but for an entirely different reason—the fire had been extinguished before their trucks arrived; there were no action shots of the Roseville firefighters to be had. One cameraman asked the firemen to start the blaze again. He was genuinely upset when the firemen told him to go to hell. But not as upset as me. I had to stand there, leaning on my crutches, shivering in the thirty-two degree morning temperature, answering questions, trying to explain that it wasn't a hate crime, suggesting that it was probably just a kid's prank, that April Fool's Day was—what? Tomorrow?

The only way to make the news media go away is to give them a story. If you try to stonewall them, try to argue your rights to privacy, they'll stay camped on your doorstep until hell freezes over. That's just the way they are. So I stood outside, answering their questions until dawn. To my general astonishment, no one asked about my leg, no one said, "Hey, aren't you the guy who was arrested for murder a couple weeks back?" And I certainly wasn't about to volunteer the information. Still, I felt a little like day-old bread.

After they had been satisfied, I took the telephone off the hook and went back to bed, saying a little prayer before dropping off: "Dear God. Bring me the head of Michael Zilar."

I slept until noon.

I RETURNED THE receiver to its cradle and went about fixing lunch. Well, breakfast actually. The telephone rang thirty seconds later. It was Cynthia.

"You're in the news again," she told me.

"I'm like Princess Di. The media can't get enough of me."

"A Molotov cocktail?" Cynthia asked.

"Can you imagine?"

"Why is this happening?"

"Payback for what I did to Levering Field. And I figure Michael Zilar is trying to soften me up before the kill."

Then I told Cynthia what I told Tammy the day before. "Stay away from my house for a while. Stay away from me."

"How long is a while?"

Good question.

IT WAS MUCH too early for gardening. The ground wasn't ready and the nighttime temperatures were still dropping below freezing. But Amanda Field was out there just the same, digging in the three-foot-deep strip of dirt that ran from the front door to the corner of her house. She did not see me approach and jumped when I said, "Excuse me, Mrs. Field."

"Who are you?" she demanded to know, still on her knees, holding a trowel like it was a weapon.

"Excuse me for intruding," I repeated. "I'm hoping you will answer a few questions for me concerning your husband's murder." I was uncomfortable as hell speaking with her, but what could I do?

"I have spent days answering your questions. Haven't you had enough?" By then she noticed the crutches. "You're not with the police, are you?"

I shook my head.

"Who are you?" Amanda repeated. "Are you with the media?"

"I'm Holland Taylor," I admitted.

"Holland Taylor," she said slowly, like a curse, then lunged at me with the trowel, the business end pointed at my groin. I pivoted on my left leg—probably causing me greater pain than getting stabbed in the nuts—and parried her thrust with my right crutch. The blow drove the trowel from her hand. I dropped both crutches, fell to my right knee, and grabbed her hands, trying to keep my bad leg straight. Her face, her eyes . . . You've heard the expression "She looked like an animal"? Well, she looked like an animal. A big one. A predator. But she did not make a sound except for the hissing of her breath. That painful grunting you heard? That was me.

"I didn't kill your husband, Mrs. Field. I swear to God I didn't."

She turned her wrists this way and that, trying to break my grip. "Then who did?" she wanted to know.

"Michael Zilar," I answered looking directly into her eyes.

"Who's he?" she asked without beating so much as an eyelash.

"A contract killer from Chicago." As if she didn't know, I was thinking.

Her pupils narrowed, and she stopped struggling. A calmness settled around her like a comforter on a cold night. She smiled. "I think the neighbors have seen enough," she told me quietly.

I released her hands.

She rose to her feet, picking up my crutches and handing them to me. Grateful, I pulled myself upright.

"Let's go inside," she said, wiping her hands on her jeans and moving toward the door. I almost didn't follow her. The look in her eye frightened me. Not the one I saw when we were struggling. The one that replaced it.

I made sure she was well inside, made sure I could see her empty hands, before I entered her home. The house looked exactly the same as when Levering had invited me over, except for the carpet. The carpet was new.

"I will not offer you anything," Amanda said.

Fair enough.

"Who would hire someone to kill my husband? The only enemy he had was you."

"Levering was having an affair," I told her.

"So I discovered. It was you who sent the flowers, wasn't it?"

I refused to admit it, to apologize, for fear there was a tape machine nearby. Instead, I said, "You didn't know until then?"

Amanda shook her head slowly.

"Swell," I said.

"Indeed."

I pushed on. "Where were you Saturday morning?"

"Shopping with my daughter."

"No, you weren't," I said.

"Yes, I was. Look, I went over all of this with the police. They seem satisfied."

"Why did your daughter come into the house alone?" I pressed on. "You didn't arrive until an hour later."

"I dropped her off, then went to visit my friend."

"What's your friend's name?"

"The police have the name of my friend."

"Is this the same friend you met at a hotel in Bloomington just a couple of days before your husband was killed?"

"I met my friend at his office, and we went to the hotel for a drink. The hotel has a bar—or didn't you know that?"

I refused to let it go.

"Did Levering know you were having an affair?" I asked.

Amanda was standing next to a telephone table with a drawer large enough for a telephone directory. She had moved there slowly while we were talking and I hadn't noticed—not until she flung open the drawer and pulled out a .38 Smith & Wesson. I instinctively went for my Beretta and managed to get my hand around the butt before I heard the *click* of the S & W's hammer being thumbed back. I froze.

"Go ahead. Take out your gun," Amanda told me calmly, the .38 looking as big as a grenade launcher in her small hands. "After everything that's happened, no one will call it murder."

I straightened up, leaving the Beretta in its holster. No sense making it easy for her. "You might get away with having your husband killed, but not this," I warned her.

Amanda was six feet away, her feet spread, weight evenly distributed, a two-handed grip holding the gun steady, pointing it at my heart. I got the impression she knew what she was doing. I hoped to keep her talking, hoped the weight of the gun would bring her hands down. Then I would make my move. I didn't like my chances.

"I've never killed anyone, Mr. Taylor," she told me calmly. "Certainly not my husband, though I admit I thought about it. I've never been angry enough to kill anyone. Except now. Except you. You threatened my family. You killed my husband. You ruined my life. . . ."

"I didn't—"

"Now you dare come to my home, accusing me, looking to save yourself."

I heard the key in the lock behind me. So did Amanda. I turned my head just so, hoping to draw her gaze to the door as it opened. She didn't move, didn't take her eyes off mine. She was good. And she was going to kill me unless whoever came through the door stopped her.

There was a gasp behind me, then silence. Then the rustle of a jacket. I saw the girl first out of the corner of my eye. It was Emily Field. She moved next to her mother, the jacket draped over her arm. "This is Holland Taylor, isn't it?" she asked Amanda.

"Yes," her mother said.

"I can go back outside," the sixteen-year-old volunteered. "Later, I can tell the police I didn't see anything."

"No," Amanda said. "That's not necessary. Mr. Taylor was just leaving."

"Are you sure?" the girl asked, just as cool as can be.

"I'm sure."

I left the house as quickly as I could without running. No pronouncements, no wisecracks, no bray of last words. I got out of the house and beat as fast a pace to my car as my crutches would allow, cursing myself with every step. Letting a woman get the drop on me like that, an amateur to boot . . . I had no business working as a detective. I should become a baker. Get a job with McGlynn's. Beat up on some bread dough. That was about my speed.

I started up the Colt and drove away without looking at the house, my hands trembling on the steering wheel.

CRYSTALIN WOLTERS WAS not in school. Somehow I didn't expect that she would be. I went to her apartment. The door was open to the hallway, so I knocked loudly on it and walked in, leaning on a single crutch, calling her name, my right hand in my jacket pocket—the pocket containing a 9mm Beretta. I had no intention of making the same mistake twice.

I found her in the center of her living-room floor, kneeling before a large carton, wrapping the base of an expensive-looking lamp in newspaper. She looked up from the task when I entered the room but did not speak.

"The door was open," I told her, excusing myself.

"You're Holland Taylor," she told me. "You killed Ring."

"No, actually, I didn't. That's why the cops let me go. That's probably why I was shot."

She looked at my crutch like she was seeing it for the first time.

"You expect me to believe that?"

I didn't say if I did or didn't. Instead, I said, "Moving?"

"I am unless you want to pick up the lease."

I shook my head.

"I didn't think so," she said, placing the lamp inside the carton. Next, she picked up a crystal ashtray and started wrapping that. I took my hand out of my pocket.

"I take it Field didn't leave you anything."

Crystalin looked at me like I was the dumbest human being alive. Then she started to laugh. "No, he didn't leave me anything."

"Not much job security, being a mistress," I said.

"Not much," she admitted. "But it was fun while it lasted. I drove a nice car, lived in a nice apartment, wore nice clothes, even got a year of college out of it. I can't complain."

"Still, it would have been nice if he remembered you," I suggested.

"I suppose."

"How much was Field worth?"

"I have no idea."

"None?"

"He paid the rent, he made the payments on the Porsche, he covered my tuition and the credit card expenditures. That was all I cared about."

"Tell me," I said, "was Field here Saturday morning, around ten, ten-thirty?"

She didn't answer, still kneeling at the carton, wrapping.

"It's easy enough to check," I suggested. "This apartment building uses video cameras for security. We'll just call the office and ask to see the tape."

"Yeah, all right, he was here," Crystalin admitted, rising to her feet. "And you're a dick."

I've been called worse, I told myself, watching her move, making sure her hands stayed empty. "How long?"

"He stayed just long enough to tell me we were through, OK?" Crystalin said. "Ten minutes, tops. Long enough to tell me the apartment and Porsche were paid up only to the end of the month, that the credit card was canceled. Course, the card was canceled a few days before. He said you did that somehow. Did you?"

I ignored the question. "He broke up with you?" I asked.

"Yeah. Waltzed in without knocking, like usual. Told me he loved his wife. Told me he loved his daughter. Told me we were through. Bullshit like that."

"Maybe it wasn't bullshit," I suggested, not knowing why I was defending the man.

"Levering Field didn't love anything but money. I asked him once if his wife knew about us and he said she didn't. So I asked him what he would do if she found out. He told me that since she was having an affair, too, he didn't think it would be a problem. . . ."

Amanda had lied to me. Good.

"Do you know who Amanda was sleeping with?" I asked.

"No," Crystalin answered. "I didn't ask. It didn't interest me."

"No reason why it should."

"I've known a lot of men—trust me on this, OK?—I've known a lot of men who wouldn't think twice about cheating on their wives but who would have coronaries if their wives cheated on them. And I told Levering that. I told him most men would go nuts. Know what he said? He said, 'It's all right with me. It's good for business'."

"What did he mean by that?" I asked.

"I don't know," Crystalin replied. "I'm only saying, the man didn't give a shit about his wife or family, OK?"

"Then why did he leave you?"

"For another woman."

"You're kidding!" I said.

She smiled at me and said, "Thank you," like I was paying her a compliment.

"Are you sure?"

Crystalin nodded. "After he left, I went out on the balcony. It overlooks the parking lot. I'm going to watch him drive away, OK? A woman was leaning on his car, waiting for him."

"Ever see her before?"

"Can't say. She was wearing a hooded scarf—red, with matching gloves. Very stylish. The slut."

"His secretary?"

"I don't know his secretary."

"His secretary is blond."

"I don't know."

"His wife?" I was grasping.

She shook her head.

"What happened next?"

"They chatted, they got into the car, they drove off."

I nodded for no particular reason, then asked, "Was he carrying a briefcase?"

"A briefcase? Yeah, Ring had one. Black, I think. He had it when he walked in, never set it down. Why? What was in it?"

"Did he have it when he left?"

"Sure. He handed it to the woman before they got into the car."

"And you have no idea who the woman was?"

"Hey, if the wife is the last to know, where do you think that leaves the mistress? Next to last, that's where it leaves her."

I HAD PARKED in the second row of the lot outside Crystalin's building. In the front row, three stalls to the left, was a '91 Honda Accord nearly the same color as the Colt. In fact, if you were in a hurry, you might mistake it for my car. I did. Until I noticed that all the windows had been smashed, fragments of safety glass scattered everywhere.

I looked around the lot but saw nobody. Then I looked up at the building. Cyrstalin was on her balcony, looking down.

I PARKED IN the lot across the street from the Butler Square Building, but I did not go to my office. Instead, I hobbled over to Levering Field's building and took the elevator up. The doors to his office suite were locked, and a sign indicated that the previous occupant was no longer at that address.

"Nobody's home," a voice informed me as I stood outside the door. I turned toward it. It belonged to a woman, no longer young, who was carrying two white bags emblazoned with the name of a bakery down on Sixth Street.

"A young woman used to work here," I announced. "Miss Portia?"

"Penny? Sure, I knew her," the woman informed me as I walked with her to another suite of offices, this one occupied by architects.

"How well?"

"Well enough. We had lunch together a few times. Why?"

"I'm trying to find her."

The woman shrugged as I opened a glass door for her. "Try her at home."

"Where's home?"

"Ann Arbor, Michigan."

McGANEY AND CASPER were waiting in my driveway when I arrived home following my therapy.

"Let's go," Casper said.

"Go where?"

"ACA wants to talk with you," McGaney answered.

"Tell him to call my lawyer."

I went to walk past him. McGaney blocked me.

"We can do this easy, or we can do it hard," Casper said. "You won't like hard."

"You guys watch too much television," I told them.

They didn't so much as smile.

I went.

THE ACA DID not rise when I was ushered into his office. He did not extend his hand, did not say, "Hey, Taylor, how's it going?" Instead he left me and my police escort standing there while he scribbled in a file on his desk. It wasn't that he was ignoring us. We were simply beneath his notice.

After a few moments he said, "Do you know why you're not in jail?"

"You talking to me?" I asked.

The ACA shut the file, rolled his chair away from his desk, and shouted, "Lisa!"

Lisa scurried into the office, all blue eyes, short blond hair and skin like milk in a pitcher. An out-state girl from good Scandinavian stock. She reached around me and took the file from the ACA's hands. My eyes followed her out the door.

"I received a telephone call from Mrs. Field this afternoon. And another from her attorney," the ACA said. "Are you listening?"

"Hmm? Sorry, I was thinking about something else," I answered as Lisa closed the office door behind her.

"You don't want to mess with me, Taylor," the ACA warned, his face close to mine. "Because nothing will give me greater pleasure than to prove to you just how tough I am."

He stepped back, looking at me with a patient expression like he knew he was smarter than I was and was just waiting for the opportunity to demonstrate it. I didn't care for the expression.

"Yeah, yeah, yeah," I said. "You're tough as nails. So, tell me about the phone calls that got your Jockey's in a knot."

Ooooh, he didn't like that at all, and for a moment, I thought he really would throw me in jail. Instead, he returned to the chair behind his desk, tried hard to keep his voice calm, and nearly succeeded. "Mrs. Field claims you broke into her home and assaulted her."

"I was invited into her house, and *she* assaulted *me*; she pointed a Smith & Wesson thirty-eight at my heart."

"What heart?" Casper snorted.

The ACA chose to ignore us both. Instead, he reminded me, "The Ramsey County court issued a restraining order forbidding you to contact the Fields or go near them or their home. . . ."

Jesus, I'd forgotten about that.

"You violated that order. That's a misdemeanor in this county."

Oh, man.

"Ninety days, pal. Ninety days minimum," the ACA said, holding up nine fingers in case I was confused.

"I was acting within the scope of my employment as a private investigator," I claimed quickly.

"That's your defense?"

"It's the best I can do right now. Give me a few minutes."

The ACA surprised me by smiling. "Are you always such a smartass?" he asked.

"Only when I'm frightened," I admitted freely.

The ACA regarded me for a moment. Then he smiled some more. Then he shook his head. Then he said, "You're not in jail because I already thought out your position in this, and it just might have some merit. And because you did us a favor with your information about the briefcase. It was something we had not considered," he said, glancing at McGaney and Casper.

"That's what you get when you take a veteran investigator off the job and replace her with a couple of trainees," I told him. "These guys, they couldn't find Canada on a map of North America if you spotted them Mexico."

I did not look at McGaney and Casper, but I could feel their eyes burning holes in my back.

"There are approximately twenty minutes unaccounted for after Field left his bank," the ACA said. "We're trying to determine where he went. Do you know?"

"Levering had a mistress," I volunteered.

"Crystalin Wolters, age twenty-two, Cathedral Hill Apartments," McGaney recited behind me. I wasn't surprised. I was joking when I said they couldn't find Canada. Sort of.

"My money's on Amanda," I announced.

"How much?" McGaney asked, like he was looking to cover my bet.

"Mrs. Field was shopping with her daughter when Field was killed," Casper said.

"Who says?" I asked.

"Her daughter," said McGaney.

"And two video cameras at the Rosedale Shopping Mall," Casper added.

That stopped me for about three seconds. "Doesn't matter," I said. "I figured she paid to have it done, anyway. Michael Zilar."

"Whom nobody has seen or heard from," McGaney said.

"That doesn't mean he's not out there," I reminded him.

The ACA was smiling again. "An upper-middle-class woman from St. Paul, outraged that her husband is having an affair, hires a professional killer from Chicago, brings him to the Twin Cities, and has him shoot her husband in her own living room. Is that your theory?"

"It's done all the time," I replied.

"Uh-huh. And exactly why did she also have you shot? I forget."

"I indirectly told her about the affair."

He continued smiling, adding a head shake.

"Kill the messenger," I added. "Haven't you ever heard that phrase before?"

The way he and the detectives looked at me, I had a feeling they weren't impressed by my deductive reasoning. Truth be told, neither was I. Amanda could have killed me and probably would have gotten away with it, but she didn't. That had to count for something. I decided to try a new theory.

"Has anyone interviewed Field's secretary?"

"Penny Portia?" McGaney asked. "She's clean."

"Sure of that are you?"

He didn't say if he was or wasn't.

"She might have the money," I volunteered.

McGaney yawned.

"How did you get so smart?" the ACA asked me.

"It's amazing what you learn just by paying attention," I answered, trying to bluff my way through.

"Well, pay attention to this. You are not to go near Mrs. Field again. Or her daughter. You are not to contact them in any way. Understand?"

"I understand."

"You violate the restraining order again and it's no longer a misdemeanor. Uh-uh. It becomes a gross misdemeanor. I'll put you away for a year and make you serve every blessed day."

"I understand."

"You had better because honest to God, I get another phone call, you are his-tor-y."

THERE WERE SEVENTEEN messages on my answering machine. A few callers wanted to buy my house or my car or my baseball cards featuring the 1927 Yankees. One was confirming a dental appointment I hadn't made. Another wanted to thank me for volunteering to go door-to-door to collect money for the Clean Water Act and asked when they could get their materials to me. Five callers had read my file at the dating service and wanted to arrange dinner—all of them were men. A plumber, cable TV technician, and an interior decorator complained that no one had been home to receive them as promised. And a member of a storefront church said he could feel my pain and wondered when he could come over and comfort me.

The tape was rewinding when the telephone rang again. I answered it.

"This is Finnegan Siding. You called about an estimate for your house."

"No, I didn't."

"Sir, we have your name and—"

"Listen. I have stucco walls. Why would I want fucking aluminum siding?" I was shouting now.

"Sir, there is no reason to be abusive."

I hung up the phone. The doorbell rang. I opened the door. A delivery man from a home shopping service stood on the other side, holding a box of groceries.

"Your order, sir."

"I didn't order anything! Get away from me! Goddammit!"

I slammed the door. My breath was coming fast. I pressed my head against the wall. "Relax," I told myself. I've always found it easier to control my emotions in a crowd than when I was alone. When alone, it required more effort, somehow. Often, I answered my anger or frustration by shooting hoops in my driveway. Only my wounds wouldn't permit it. So instead, I stood there, reciting the roster of the 1987 Twins by position: "Bert Blyleven, Tim Laudner, Kent Hrbek, Steve Lombardozzi, Greg Gagne, Gary Gaetti . . ."

The phone rang again. I let the machine answer it: "Mr. Taylor? This is Hakala Painting and Supplies. You told one of my salespeople that you wanted to paint your house purple? Really? Purple?"

"You sonuvabitch!" I screamed at the machine. "You goddamn, mother-fucking sonuvabitch!"

"I'm going to hold this job order until you call me," the voice on the machine continued.

IT TOOK ME three trips to deposit my recyclables on the curb. Usually it took only one, but the damn crutches . . . I wasn't a happy man, and hobbling back to the house after the third trip, I couldn't help wondering what mischief my assailants had scheduled for that night. I was shivering when I mounted my front steps. The temperature was dropping along with the sun. That's when I had an idea.

THE MOON WAS bright. You could read your watch by it and I did. Two-thirty A.M. I stretched and felt the pain of inactivity; it was a pleasure I did not expect. But I enjoyed it only for a moment, and then hunkered down among the lilac bushes that I had allowed to grow fifteen feet tall along my driveway. The air was crisp and cold; my fingers were numb, even in my pockets. I wasn't wearing gloves so that I could work my gun. But the rest of me was toasty warm in a black-and-gray snowmobile suit and Sorel boots. It felt like old times, running all-night stake outs on various miscreants. Boring and exciting at the same time.

Ten years a police officer, four in Homicide. How many stake outs? Who knows. The memories came back as I sat quietly, watching the few cars that traveled the street where I lived. I remembered my first homicide case. It was the case that turned me into a true investigator. A five-year-old child had been stuffed inside an old refrigerator in the garage by his mother who claimed the child had been abducted from a local playground; who cried herself into a hospital room for fear of his safety while literally hundreds of her neighbors searched the area. That was when I truly became aware of the magnitude of human corruption—of what, as individuals, we are capable of doing. And from that day until this, I've accepted nothing at face value. I never assume someone is incapable of anything.

AT TWO-FORTY, a Ford pickup running on parking lights stopped at the curb in front of my house. The driver got out, leaving the engine running, and quietly, nervously, looked all about before moving toward my recyclables. He trained a small flashlight on the recyclables, checking them over. He turned off the light, slipped it into his pocket, and picked up a grocery bag. That's when I pushed through the bushes, a crutch under my left arm, the Beretta in my right hand.

"Freeze!" I yelled just like in the movies, holding the gun unsteadily, my weight leaning on the crutch.

"Don't shoot!" a voice squealed. The driver was a woman. "For God's sake don't shoot."

"Turn on your flashlight," I commanded. She did, pointing it at my face. "Get it out of my eyes," I ordered. "Point it at the ground." She did.

"You can't shoot me for this! You can't shoot me for this!" she repeated.

"What do you want here?" I demanded.

"Your cans. Just your cans."

"My what?"

"Your cans. Your aluminum cans."

"Are you serious?"

"Of course I'm serious."

I started waving the gun around like it was a wand. "Why?"

"For the money. Why d'you think?"

"Shine the flashlight at your face," I told her. She did. She looked about sixty. Someone's grandmother.

"For the money?" I asked.

"You know how much aluminum cans sell for in the Twin Cities these days? Eleven hundred bucks a ton."

"So you go around stealing people's cans?"

"Well, it's not exactly stealing. After all, you are throwing them away."

"I'm putting them out to be recycled."

"That's what I'm doing with them."

"You're stealing my cans!" I insisted loudly.

"And you're pointing a gun at me. Which is worse?"

She had me there. I deactivated the Beretta and returned it to the pocket of my snowmobile suit.

"Go away," I told the woman.

"Sure," she said, then reached for the grocery bag filled with empty pop cans.

"Leave my cans alone!" I shouted at her. "I catch you around here again, I'll have you arrested."

"You know, you have a real attitude problem."

"Just go away," I told her.

She moved to the open door of her pickup. "Some people's children," she muttered.

"Hey!" I called.

"What?"

"How much do you make doing this?"

"About twelve hundred bucks a week."

If you live long enough, you'll see everything. I waved her on, watching her red taillights disappear as she turned a corner, her headlights off. Probably looking to loot someone else's recycling bins, I decided.

"Twelve hundred a week," I repeated to myself. "Man, am I in the wrong business."

I CALLED IT a night and went to bed. When I woke the next morning, my aluminum cans were gone. And a huge white swastika was spray painted across my front door.

SIXTEEN

I HAD TO wait until noon, until the temperature reached about sixty degrees, before I could paint over the swastika. There was a can of brown exterior paint in my basement left over from the last time I painted the doors and trim, but not enough. I had to buy another quart, and even then I ran out—the damn swastika required three coats. I was just finishing when Cynthia arrived. The way she drove into my driveway—fast—and the way she stopped at the top of the horseshoe in front of my door—really fast—startled me, and I instinctively reached for the Beretta. When I recognized my visitor, I hid the gun beneath a rag next to the paint can.

"I've been worried about you," Cynthia informed me even before saying hello. "I've been trying to reach you all day."

"I took my phone off the hook."

"Why?"

"Because I didn't want to take any calls."

"Why didn't you let your machine pick up?"

"Because I didn't want to. Is that OK with you, Counselor?" I was angry now. Angry at her. Angry at everyone. But mostly I was angry at the stalker. Why didn't he show himself?

Cynthia studied me for a moment, gauging my mood. I don't think she liked what she saw. She took a step backward and folded her arms across her chest, a defensive posture.

"You're painting your door," she informed me, just in case I hadn't noticed.

"It needed it," I replied, finishing the job with a couple of short strokes.

"You can still see the swastika," she said.

"No way. Really?"

I backed away from the door and gave it a hard look. She was right. *"Sonuvabitch!"* I yelled, throwing the brush at the steps, splattering the top step with paint.

"Oh, that was good, that was smart," Cynthia told me.

"What do you want?" I asked, surprised at how the words spilled out with a snarl. "I told you to stay away."

"I thought you might need help," she replied calmly.

"Help doing what? Messing up my life? I can manage that all by myself."

"I'll say."

"I'm not in the mood for visitors, all right?" I said as I bent to the paint stain, trying to wipe it up with the rag, leaning on my left hand, the rest of my weight on my right leg and my left leg straight out.

Cynthia noticed the awkward position and asked how my leg was. She didn't mention the gun, left uncovered when I grabbed the rag.

"The leg is fine," I told her sharply.

"How about the rest of you?"

I tossed the rag down, straightened up, and turned toward her. "I've been better," I admitted.

"This guy, this, this—"

"Stalker," I said.

"He's giving you a hard time," Cynthia said.

"Very hard," I agreed.

"Why? Revenge because of Levering, do you think?"

"I don't know anymore. I thought I did, but now I'm not sure."

Cynthia unfolded her arms and moved to the base of the steps. "I'm sorry," she said.

"Yeah, thanks," I said as I put the cover back on the paint can, rapping it home with the butt of the Beretta. Cynthia said nothing, and her silence caused me to look back at her.

"It gets worse," she said.

"What?"

"I received a call from Monica Adler this morning," she said. "Monica told me that the Field family is filing suit against you for intentional infliction of emotional distress. Jesus, Taylor, you violated a restraining order. What were you thinking?"

"Truth is, I forgot all about the damn thing."

Cynthia sighed and turned her head away, like a woman who had just discovered that her daughter was dating an idiot.

I sat down. "How much are they asking?" I wanted to know.

"What difference does it make? Whatever it is, you can't afford it." Cynthia sat on the step next to me. I scooted over to give her room. "Besides," she added, "even if it's only a nickel, Monica said she's going to make sure that the Department of Public Safety is informed of the verdict. You could lose your license."

"If they win," I reminded her.

"They're going to put a shattered, weeping widow on the witness stand and have her recite all the terrible things you did to her and her family in front of six middle-class jurors who would rather be somewhere else. What do you think is going to happen?"

"Shit."

"Exactly."

"What can I do?"

"You can prove Levering Field was a thief; you can prove that you had just cause for what you did."

"Then they'll drop the case?"

"No. Then we'll have a shot at convincing at least one juror that you're not a sadistic maniac."

"No problem," I told myself, not really believing it. I closed my eyes and rubbed my temples with paint-stained fingers. What a headache. "It all seemed like such a good idea at the time," I said.

"It was never a good idea," Cynthia countered.

"I was wondering how long it would take you to say it."

"Say what?"

"I told you so."

Cynthia didn't reply.

"I did what I had to do," I insisted.

"Baloney," Cynthia told me, making the word sound like one of the more vulgar obscenities. "There were other things we could have done to collect Mrs. Gustafson's money. Only you had to be clever and cute. You decided that since Levering Field was abusing the system, you would go 'head and ignore it altogether. To hell with the law, to hell with common decency."

"I don't need you to tell me I made a mistake."

"You didn't make a mistake," Cynthia reminded me. "Two plus two equals five, that's a mistake. You made a considered decision. You were going to get the job done; get the job done and not worry how, just like Daddy wanted. Well, you got the job done. And now someone's doing a job on you. How does it feel?"

I didn't need this, I really didn't, Cynthia coming over and telling me what a jerk I've been. Hey, I know what kind of jerk I've been. And I sure as hell didn't need her to blame my father for my actions. I'm responsible for my actions. Me and no one else. Yeah, I know all about childhood. Your childhood makes you; the things you learn as a child stay with you always. I understand that. But the things my father taught me, they were all good things, positive things. Honor. Loyalty. Pride. He taught me that a man's word is his bond. He taught me that winners never quit, and quitters never win. He taught me you do what you have to do. . . . Ahh, dammit to hell!

"You're one to talk!" I lashed out. "You've lived such a perfect, pristine life, right, Counselor? You've never done anything to be ashamed of."

"What I did, I did to myself!" she yelled back at me. "What you did, you did to someone else."

"Now I know why you always dress in black and white," I told her.

"Fuck you!"

"Levering Field was dirty," I insisted. "He deserved everything that happened to him."

"Sure he did." Now it was Cynthia's turn to mock me. "In the world according to Holland Taylor, eventually we all get what we deserve. Isn't that your favorite saying?"

"It's true."

"Yeah," Cynthia agreed. "It is."

I had nothing to say to that. And Cynthia wasn't waiting for a reply. She was off the steps, rounding her car, going away mad. Ahh, man. I was making another mistake, lashing out at her to cover my own guilt; pretending I'm right and she's wrong when I knew damn well it was the other way around. Besides, who would I have on my side if I didn't have her?

"Wait!" I shouted.

She stopped and looked over the roof of her car, the door open. I left the crutch on the steps and hopped across the grass to the car, resting against the hood.

"You're right, I'm a jerk," I admitted.

"Is that an apology?"

"I'm sorry I'm a jerk."

"So am I."

"Please, Cynthia," I pleaded. "Don't be angry with me. Without you, I'd be outnumbered."

Cynthia sighed heavily.

"I'm sorry," I told her. "You're right. I have no one to blame for my problems but myself. I should have listened to you in the first place. I should have. . . . Cynthia, I'm sorry."

"I'll see you later," she promised. And then she was in the car, her door shut.

THE MINNESOTA SECRETARY of state's office was located on the ground floor of the Minnesota State Office Building, a few hundred yards from the state capitol. The woman behind the counter was very helpful. I gave her twenty-five dollars, and she gave me a copy of the Certificate of Partnership for Willow Tree, LP.

Prove Levering Field was dirty, Cynthia had said. Prove he was a thief and had stolen Mrs. Gustafson's retirement fund. To do that I had to follow the money. And the money led to Willow Tree.

IT WAS A long walk across the capitol mall to where I had parked my car at a meter. At least it seemed that way, hobbling along on my crutches, fighting pain with each step. That's when I saw the man approach—small, thin, dressed in a black suit, black tie, and white shirt. He was carrying a Bible in his hand, a red ribbon marking his place. I stopped, my hand moving to the Beretta on my hip.

"Have you been saved?" he asked matter-of-factly.

"Many times," I answered, my eyes locked on the Good Book. It made me more nervous than a .44.

He stuck a red sticker to my lapel without asking, white letters popping out of the red, proclaiming JESUS SAVES.

"The Lord be with you," he said.

"And with you," I replied.

He continued toward the capitol; I went to my car. On the way I found myself admitting that Michael Zilar could have killed me a dozen times by now. Then asking, *Where is he? Why hasn't he made a move? Is he really out there?*

"Maybe the Lord *is* with me," I said aloud as I unlocked my car door.

When I was secure in my new Colt, I studied the Certificate of Partnership. It listed as "agent of service and process," Peter Dully, President, JPD, Inc., a general partner for Willow Tree, Limited Partnership. It also listed JPD's address: a Wayzata office building. I called 411 for a phone number, using the cell phone Sara had lent me. But directory assistance did not have a listing for JPD. So I called the building's management office. A pleasant woman with a high-pitched voice informed me that JPD had closed its doors several months earlier; there was a waiting list of businesses that wanted their space, so the building management hadn't held JPD to its lease. I asked her what JPD did, but she didn't know.

"Damn," I said aloud after deactivating the phone. I glared at the State Office Building. "Damn, damn, damn," I repeated.

I lumbered back to the secretary of state's office at a much slower pace than before. For some reason I carried this image of one-legged Long John Silver trudging across Treasure Island. I can't tell you why. Long John was a nimble fellow whereas I was about as agile as a hippo on skates. Probably looked it, too, considering how much exercise I'd been getting lately.

Another twenty-five dollars later—I paid by check this time—I had the Articles of Incorporation for JPD. It listed two officers: Peter Dully, president, and Joan Dully, vice president/treasurer. They lived at the same address in Golden Valley.

AFTER COMPLETING MY therapy I drove out to Golden Valley. The house was strictly nouveau riche—a two-story brick job with a distinctive roof that rose from gently sloping sides to a spectacular peak. What wasn't brick was glass—you live in this house, you don't throw stones.

I parked, slid out of the car, and looked around as the dusk turned to night. My car was the only one I could see. The street and driveways were empty. Nor was there any sight or sound of children or pets or electric motors. No one was walking. No one was working in their garage with the door up, their radio on. The only sign of life came from the light that streamed from nearly every window of every house. These people conserved energy the way Don King conserved hair spray. And the houses, while they were all of different designs, seemed strangely similar. It was as if they were all constructed of the same materials by the same builder at the same time. You could bet that come summer, the height of each lawn wouldn't vary so much as a quarter inch from yard to yard.

I used both crutches to negotiate the cobblestone sidewalk and the three steps that led to the Dullys's front door. The doorbell was lit. I pressed it twice. A few moments later the porch light flicked on. "Who is it?" a man's voice inquired from beyond the closed door. I identified myself, and the door opened. Peter Dully surprised me by inviting me inside without first asking why I was there. Either he already knew, or he was anxious to get me off the street before his neighbors noticed.

"What happened to your leg?" he asked as though we'd been buddies since the third grade.

"I was shot," I answered.

"Dangerous job, your profession," he declared.

"Not usually," I told him.

He said, "I guess it's true what the life insurance sales-man says: 'We're all going to die, we're all going to die'." And then he started laughing.

The inside of the house was very sleek, very sophisti-cated, with cedar floors, posts, and beams. A large fire-place stood in the center of the living room, triangular in shape with glass doors on each side. White sofas and chairs and glass-topped tables were arranged in front of two sides of the fireplace. The third side faced five cedar steps that led to an elevated dining area featuring what looked like a black marble table.

"Let's go in here," Dully said, leading me through slid-ing cedar doors into a large den. The den also had a fire-place—this one was working—with a sofa facing it. Off to the side was a mahogany desk, papers of various sizes and colors piled on top. A PC, set on an ergonomically correct work station, and a fax machine, set on a small table, were positioned where Dully could reach them both by swiveling his desk chair around.

As we walked in, Dully began noting the heads of the dead animals he had mounted on his walls. "Got this ram in Wyoming, got this moose in Canada, got this elk in Montana." Above the fireplace was the head of a large buck with a magnificent ten-point rack. "Ever see antlers like these?" Dully wanted to know. "I got 'im in Wisconsin. One hundred yards with the three-oh-eight."

"Impressive," I admitted. But, not to be out-done, I added, "I once took a twelve-point buck in northern Minnesota, up near McGregor."

A pained expression crossed Dully's face. "The hell you say! What'd you use?"

"'79 Chevy Monza."

"What?"

"I hit him with my car."

"The hell you say!" Dully was laughing again. His was a rough, deprecating laugh that knew neither courtesy nor tenderness. "How'd it happen?"

"It was dusk," I told him. "I was driving Highway 65, about ten miles over the limit. He jumped out of the ditch, I hit him. . . ."

"That's funny," Dully said, laughing some more.

"Smashed up my car; damn near killed me."

"Funny story. A '79 Chevy. I gotta remember it."

Dully was still chuckling when he sat on the sofa in front of the fireplace, motioning me to the chair beside it. There was just too much of him. Too much voice, too much size, too much money spent on clothes—too much effort to impress someone he'd never seen before and probably would never see again.

"Private investigator," he said, looking straight at me. "PI, gumshoe, shamus, rubber heel, dick." He gave the last word too much emphasis for my taste, but I tried not to show it. "You're here because of Willow Tree. Tell me if I'm wrong."

"You sound like you've been expecting me."

"Hell, yes. Well, not you specifically. But someone like you. Joannie and me—Joannie, that's my wife and partner—Joannie and me figured someone would be along. Someone representing a disgruntled investor who doesn't like the way things went. Hell, we don't like how it went, either. But what are you going to do? It's business."

"How *did* it go?" I asked.

He answered, again without taking his eyes off me. "The politicians, the social workers, everybody talks about the need for low-income housing. Low-income housing for the elderly. Low-income housing in the 'burbs so we can get the minorities out of the inner city. But when it comes to putting up or shutting up, suddenly everyone's a mute. We were working with six separate counties, putting up the money for environmental impact studies and community presentations and God knows what else. But when we were ready to go, the counties weren't. They stalled us. Let's wait until the spring. Let's wait until after the elections. We couldn't get the zoning, the proper building permits. And while we were waiting, construction materials and labor costs skyrocketed." Dully shrugged. "We ran out of money, couldn't find additional investors. . . . Say, you want a beer or something?"

Dully was being surprisingly candid, and I suspect most people would have found his straightforwardness disarming. Not me. As my dear old dad used to say, never shoot pool with a man named after a state, and never trust anyone who looks you straight in the eye and never looks away.

"No, thank you," I said to his offer. "What I would like is to see your business records."

"What for?"

"Oh, Peter," a woman's voice called. "I think the answer to that is quite obvious."

We both turned.

Joan Dully had the look of a woman well-acquainted with the pleasures that money could buy. She stood just inside the doorway, removing a deep-brown beret, careful not to muss her hair. The beret matched her pencil-slim skirt and contrasted well with her two sweaters, a blush pink job with jeweled neck under a fitted long-sleeve cardigan. She might have been returning from an evening swapping tales with Hemingway and the gang at some Parisian café. The clothes were tight on her; she was a few pounds overweight. But she had dark, handsome eyes and legs that reached well into your imagination.

Dully and I were both on our feet. He skipped around

the sofa as she moved deeper into the den, taking her hand like he was going to shake it.

"This is Holland Taylor," he introduced me. "He's a private investigator."

She extended her hand after freeing it from Dully's grasp. It was soft to the touch. "A pleasure, Mr. Taylor," she said as if she actually meant it. "Excuse me just a moment," she added and stepped outside the study. I watched her as she opened the closet nearest the front door and hung her hat on a wooden peg. Hanging on the peg next to it was a red hooded scarf.

Joan Dully returned to the study and sat in the spot formerly occupied by her husband, crossing her arms and her legs. "If I may impose on you, sir, could you tell us which of our many long-suffering limited partners has solicited your services?"

I nearly missed the question, distracted by her magnificent legs. "Mrs. Irene Gustafson," I replied, then hesitated. Had I meant to say that? Didn't matter, I decided, adding, "She was a client of Levering Field."

Joan turned to Peter, who was hovering above her, just behind the sofa. Peter shook his head slightly, and Joan returned her attention to me.

"Mr. Taylor, does this have anything to do with Ring's murder?" she asked.

"Mrs. Gustafson is an eighty-five-year-old widow living in Fort Myers, Florida," I said in reply, careful now, not wanting to give anything away. "Mrs. Gustafson lost everything when Willow Tree went bust," I added.

Joan closed her eyes and rubbed her temples. "I'm sorry," she said. "Truly, I am." Then she opened her eyes again. "She shouldn't have put everything into the business. Was that Levering's idea?"

"You tell me."

"I have no idea," Joan said. "We solicited limited partners to sell them on Willow Tree, on what we were trying to accomplish. We spoke with Levering Field for some time. He seemed enthusiastic, said he had a few clients who might be interested in Willow Tree. But that's as far as it went. He didn't name names until he bought the LPs."

"Did you know Levering well?" I asked.

"Not well."

"How did you meet?"

Joan turned to her husband. "How did we meet?"

He shrugged. "Someone must have given him our name. I don't remember who."

"A guy knows a guy who knows a guy. . . ." Joan told me.

"You didn't know him before you started Willow Tree?"

"No," Joan said. She then added, "This does have something to do with his murder, doesn't it?"

"This has to do with Mrs. Gustafson," I replied. "Field can't answer my questions, so I need to get information where I can."

Joan and Peter nodded simultaneously. But that didn't mean they believed me.

"How did Levering react when Willow Tree went bust?"

"He was angry like everybody else," Peter claimed. "Well, maybe not quite as angry. After all, it wasn't his money."

"I see."

"No, Mr. Taylor, I don't think you do," Joan told me. "Willow Tree was a good idea, a smart investment. It should have worked. It would have worked if it had not become embroiled in Roosevelt County's financial affairs."

"Roosevelt County?"

"Roosevelt County Housing and Redevelopment Authority was in deep trouble," Peter volunteered, still hovering above his wife. "It was facing a large balloon payment on a debt for a housing project similar to the one we were proposing. We lent them the money to cover it."

"If you read the newspapers back then, you know what happened," Joan added.

"The authority went bankrupt," Peter said.

"And so did we," Joan said.

"I would still like to see your business records," I told her.

Joan smiled, uncrossed her legs. "Mr. Taylor," she said, "Peter and I fully appreciate that some of our disgruntled investors are going to sue us. We've been expecting it. But if you think we are going to help them, you're crazy."

"I'll settle for a list of your limited partners," I said.

"Not a chance, Mr. Taylor," Joan told me. "We will, of course, respond to the demands of a court order. But unless you have one, you're wasting your time. We have no intention of voluntarily turning over our records to someone who is merely seeking grounds to sue us. Would you?" Then she shook her head. "No one wants to take responsibility for their actions anymore. Everyone dreams of being rich, but few truly appreciate what the dream can cost. And fewer still are willing to pay it."

"Mrs. Gustafson paid it," I reminded her. "She lost everything."

"We, too," Peter said.

I glanced around the room. "If you don't mind my saying so, you wouldn't know it to look at you."

"Mr. Taylor, we can barely make the minimum payments on our credit cards," Joan claimed. "We are literally one paycheck away from financial disaster."

"You got jobs after Willow Tree crashed?"

"It seemed like the prudent thing to do at the time."

"Whom do you work for?"

"Mr. Taylor, our employer is not responsible for us," Joan replied.

I admit Joan Dully sure seemed like the real thing. Every word she spoke sounded honest enough. But remember what I said about not trusting someone who looks you in the eye and never turns away? The same holds true about people who insist on using your name in every sentence.

I thanked them for their time. Joan walked me to the front door, her arm linked through mine like we had been high school sweethearts in a previous life. Peter following behind. As we walked, I told Joan how much I admired her home. She shrugged the compliment away. "Ten percent down can buy anything these days," she said.

Then, at the door, I turned slowly, going into my Peter Falk impersonation: "There is one more thing. It's silly, really; don't know why I'm asking. But Saturday morning? The Saturday morning when Levering Field was killed? Where were you?"

"I was here," Joan said. "Making love with my husband."

Peter didn't miss a beat. "We like it in the morning," he said.

"I'm a night person myself," I admitted.

IT WAS PAST nine when I reached Cynthia Grey's home. I would have been there sooner, but I had to make a few stops first. She answered the doorbell after the third ring.

"Hi," I said.

"Hi."

I nearly gasped when I saw her. She was wearing colors: a red cotton tunic over faded blue jeans.

"I like your outfit," I told her.

She frowned and shifted her weight. "Red is the color of luck," she told me.

She carried a law book in her hand—*Minnesota Statutes Annotated, Volume Seven, Sections 62C to 69*—her finger holding her place.

"May I come in?"

"What's in the box?" she asked, motioning toward the small black case I held in my hand.

"Do you know what day it is? It's our twenty-fourth anniversary. Twenty-four weeks exactly since we started seeing each other."

"Is it?" she asked.

I opened the box. It contained a string of pearls. Cynthia looked but made no move to take them. Then she sighed, a sigh of resignation. She removed her finger from the book and said, "Yes, you may come in."

SEVENTEEN

When I arrived home the next morning, I found my house, my lilac bushes, and my willow tree smothered under roll upon roll of white toilet paper. It looked like the place had been hit by a blizzard. And the sight pushed me beyond reason. Mutilated cats on my doorstep, my house ransacked, Molotov cocktails, swastikas, punctured automobile tires, harassing phone calls, even getting shot . . . yet somehow this childish prank angered me more than all those other violations combined. I was out of control, looking for something to hurt, to destroy.

Tammy Mandt, in front of her house waiting for the school bus, said, "Don't use a hose. My friend Shelia, someone TPed her house, and they used a hose to knock it down, but the paper got all soggy and stuck to the branches and stuff. You should take it down with a rake or something."

And for that friendly advice I would have screamed at her, would have gladly wrung her neck, especially after she added, "Shelia's dad acted the same way as you."

While she spoke, a car stopped in front of my house. A woman got out, took a photograph, then drove away.

"Ssshhhhhhh . . ." I was so angry I couldn't even get the obscenity out of my mouth.

I PARKED AT the corner where I could watch the Dully residence through my rearview mirror and waited. What I was waiting for I couldn't tell you. Courage, perhaps. Or maybe I was just trying to relax. It had been an emotional morning. I had changed clothes and left my home without even considering the toilet paper—I just didn't want to deal with it.

It was half past ten. I had called the Dully's several times on the cellular and always reached their answering machine. I decided to give them a few more minutes.

While I waited, I fiddled with my car radio, setting the AM buttons. It wasn't hard to pick five stations: WCCO broadcasts the Twins and the Minnesota Gopher basketball and football games, KFAN has the Vikings and Timberwolves, KKMS has the St. Paul Saints games, KSTP broadcasts the Gopher hockey games, and WMNN is all news all the time. Finally, I turned the radio off, removed my key from the ignition, and slid out of the car.

Burglars don't wear black leather jackets. They don't carry prybars in their back pockets. They don't wander the neighborhood with ski masks covering their faces, stopping periodically to peek through a window. Instead, they wear khakis and topsiders and carry grocery bags. They try real hard to be nondescript. But how nondescript can you be on crutches? I knew I was taking an awful chance, but I needed to learn more about Willow Tree's financial dealings and Levering's relationship with the Dully's, and I figured I was on to something—especially after I saw the red-hooded scarf hanging in Joan Dully's closet.

I was pleased with the neighborhood's layout. The houses were all staggered so that the house across the street wasn't looking directly at the Dullys' front door.

When I reached the cobblestone walk I turned right in, went to the front door, and knocked. I backed away, looked at the house. I went to a window, peered inside, then back to the door, and knocked some more—classic "Hey, where is everybody? I'm expected" behavior. I made my way around the house to the back door. Not once did I turn around to look up and down the street. When I reached the backyard, I slipped a pair of latex surgical gloves from my pocket and put them on. Then I took out my tools—my pick and wire—and attacked the back door. A real burglar would have hit it with a crowbar and bolt cutter. But I didn't want the Dullys to know anyone had been there.

Once inside I waited. Ten minutes. No sirens, no police dogs. If the neighbors had seen me, the cops would have been there by now, guns drawn.

I went directly to the den. The computer was a standard IBM with a 20-megabyte hard drive and a printer. A simple setup, already old, used mostly for word processing I guessed. I booted up the computer and started racing through the icons. There was nothing in the memory relating to Willow Tree. You'd have thought there would be, wouldn't you?

For a moment I felt totally defeated. I started going through the desk drawers. In one I found a plastic box filled with 3.5-inch disks. There were a dozen, all neatly labeled—four of them carrying the title WILLOW TREE. I loaded them one at a time. They were empty. It was apparent that the Dullys had erased their records. Maybe they thought they were getting away with something. If they did, they don't know the law like I do. While a potential litigant is under no obligation to keep every document in his possession, the very act of failing to preserve evidence that is reasonably likely to be requested during discovery is seriously prejudicial to the litigant. It's like refusing to take an intoxalyzer test when you're stopped for drunk driving. As far as the court is concerned, it's the same as pleading guilty.

I went through all the other disks. Most contained games. One, labeled ACCOUNTING, detailed the Dullys' personal finances. I perused it carefully. Looked to me like they were doing pretty well, what with at least eight hundred thousand dollars scattered over a wide range of investments.

"Liar, liar, pants on fire," I muttered, remembering Joan Dully's insistence that they were on the cusp of financial ruin.

There was nothing else of interest in the disks, at least not to me. The defeated feeling was back with a fury. I started searching the desk. Like the disks, the vertical files in the bottom left drawer of the desk were neatly labeled. I thumbed through them quickly. My breath was coming hard and fast now. I didn't even want to guess at my heart rate—I had been in the house much too long.

The files didn't reveal much. But I noticed a short stack of papers at the bottom of the drawer. They looked like they had slipped down there by accident. I pulled half of the vertical files to get at the papers, which seemed to be mostly scrap. *Wait, what's this?* A crumpled white sheet, like someone had scrunched it into a ball to toss but then thought better of it, contained a long list of names. After each name was the notation: $250,000. One of the names belonged to Mrs. Irene Gustafson.

I took the sheet to the fax machine. It had a copy function. I used it, then returned the crumpled sheet to the bottom of the desk drawer and replaced the files. I deactivated the IBM, grabbed my crutches, and went out the back door, locking it behind me.

The walk back to my car seemed to take twice as long as the walk to the house. I kept telling myself to slow down. You run, people might ask why. And Lord knows, I didn't do anything wrong.

IT TOOK A long time for my stomach to uncoil—the half-hour drive to my office and another hour after that. I tried to eat but couldn't manage it. Drinking wasn't a problem, though. I slammed back three Summit Ales in about six minutes. After that I switched to Dr Pepper.

Man, how do burglars do it?

I was still buzzing when I turned to the list. I copied it off the fax paper on to regular paper, using my small Canon. Then I burned the fax copy—don't ask me why. Nerves, I guess.

There were thirty-five names on the list, all of them followed by addresses, telephone numbers, and the amount $250,000. And you didn't need a pocket calculator to figure out the total since that was also notated: $8,750,000.

The first letter of both the first and last names of thirty-two of the entries was printed in boldface. Three names—Irene Gustafson, Sam Boyd and Michael Landreth—were printed in regular type. However, each of those names was followed by the boldface initials **LF**.

I called Boyd first. He lived in St. Paul. Or at least he used to. He had died of cancer four months earlier—alone, according to the caretaker of the nursing home where he'd spent his remaining four years. No family, few friends. His bills had been paid by Field Consulting, Inc.

Landreth was living in Minneapolis, if you could call it living. He was suffering from acute Alzheimer's and hadn't spoken a coherent sentence in about six months. He, too, was in a private nursing home, although that was about to change. The director told me that Landreth's invoices had been marked INSUFFICIENT FUNDS and returned to the facility by Landreth's conservator: Field Consulting.

The other thirty-two names were fictitious: A Woodbury address had a North Minneapolis zip code; a Coon Rapids address had a Highland Park telephone prefix. I tried each number just to make sure, dialing them in turn, then used the telephone directories to assure myself that the names did not match actual addresses.

Three real names surrounded by thirty-two fakes. What sense did that make?

"Must be some kind of code," I decided. I played with the names, the phone numbers, the addresses, but my efforts revealed nothing. Then I noticed the initials. There were only ten sets: two LMs, two SDs, two DGs, two KDs, three LFs, four CSs, four CDs, four TLs, four KSs, and eight BBs. I wrote amounts next to each set:

LM=\$500,000;   SD=\$500,000;   DG=\$500,000;
KD=\$500,000;   LF=\$750,000;   CS=\$1,000,000;
CD=\$1,000,000; TL=\$1,000,000; KS=\$1,000,000;
BB=\$2,000,000.

Staring at my notes, I figured I had found part of the answer. Unfortunately, I didn't know which part.

I decided to shift gears. The Dullys had claimed that much of Willow Tree's money had been siphoned off by a bad loan to Roosevelt County. That was easy enough to check. I reached for the telephone. But it startled me by ringing before I could pick up the receiver.

It was Anne Scalasi.

"I want you to come over right now and answer a few questions," she said.

"Why?"

"So I don't have to send a team of detectives to pick you up."

"Annie?"

"Bring your lawyer," she told me.

CYNTHIA GREY WAS sitting at my side when Anne Scalasi asked, "Can you account for your whereabouts at ten-thirty this morning?"

"Don't answer that," Cynthia commanded.

It seemed like good advice to me. Especially since I'd been breaking and entering the Dully residence at ten-thirty. My left foot started to beat a nervous rhythm against the leg of the interrogation room's wooden table. I originally had been happy to see that Annie had been returned to the case. Now I wasn't so sure. What did she know?

"I decline to answer on advice of counsel," I said, trying to keep my voice down.

Anne slumped in her chair. "This isn't fun anymore," she told me.

"It stopped being fun a long time ago," I agreed. "What happened at ten-thirty?"

"Someone shot at Amanda Field."

Without thinking about it I rose from my chair, putting all my weight on my wounded legs. I didn't feel a thing.

"Is she . . . ?"

"No," Anne said. "Just a scratch."

"My God!" I muttered.

"From what we can determine, it was a drive-by. Mrs. Field was working in her garden, her back to the street. She didn't hear the first two shots. They pancaked against the house just above her head and tossed out a few splinters; one caught her cheek. She heard the third shot, though. She said it sounded like a low pop."

"A suppressor," I volunteered, retaking my seat.

"Yeah. Homemade. The same as when you were hit. A plastic two-liter pop bottle stuffed with rags, the bottom shot out. We found it two blocks away. No prints."

"The third shot?"

"In the dirt," Anne said.

"Ballistics?"

"Thirty-two."

"Does it match?"

"Oh, yeah."

"Oh, God." I was up again, my hands on my hips, staring at the empty tabletop. But there were no answers there.

"Taylor, I have to ask—"

"I didn't do it, Annie, and I wish to God I had an alibi to give you."

"So do I."

"Did Mrs. Field see the car?" I asked.

"No."

"Neighbors?"

"Uh-uh."

"Dammit."

Anne paused, decided there was something I should know. "Mrs. Field received a telephone call a half hour before the shooting. A man threatened her. She said the man sounded like you."

I shook my head.

"She said the man said he was going to get her for stealing his money."

"What money?"

Anne didn't answer.

"The two hundred and eighty-seven thousand?"

"The caller didn't say." Anne looked me up and down, pursing her lips.

"What?" I asked.

"We put a trap on her phone after she reported that you violated the restraining order. The ACA insisted. The call originated at a pay phone on Edgerton Street near the Merrick Community Center."

"Railroad Island," I said, invoking the nickname for that depressed neighborhood.

"Mean anything to you?"

A spark of recognition flickered in the back of my head, then went out. "I don't think so," I answered.

"Do you intend to hold my client?" Cynthia asked.

Anne shook her head.

"Then we're leaving."

Anne spread her hands wide, like she didn't give a damn what we did. So we left. During the elevator ride down, Cynthia whispered, "So, Taylor, tell me. Where exactly were you at ten-thirty this morning?"

"Searching for evidence to prove that Levering Field was dirty."

"And was he?"

"He and a lot of other people it seems."

"You know what the good thing is about being a private investigator?" Cynthia asked.

"No, what?" I answered, anxious to hear her opinion.

"A private investigator doesn't have to discover who's guilty, only prove that his client isn't."

"Ahh."

"In this case the client is you, right?"

"Is that a hint?"

"The point is to get out of trouble, not cause more."

"I'll take that as a yes."

THE EXECUTIVE DIRECTOR of what was left of the Roosevelt County Housing and Redevelopment Authority did not want to speak with me, but it wasn't personal. It had been painful for him when the agency was forced into bankruptcy, and he would have rather discussed a more pleasant topic. But I insisted, and after a few minutes he gave me the short version of the story.

"We couldn't pay our debts," he said with a kind of grimace. "The HRA built several low-income housing projects. Lincoln Park. Crystal Pond. We built Lincoln Park six years ago for seven and a half million. One hundred units. But by the time the doors opened, the debt on the project was fourteen million dollars."

"How did that happen?" I asked.

"The debt was financed at nine-point-seven-eight percent. When the market dropped, it became impossible for the HRA to meet interest payments, let alone pay off the principal. We tried to refinance the debt, tried to convince the bond holders to devalue the property, but we couldn't get anyone to go along. Finally, we were faced with a six hundred and sixty thousand dollar balloon payment that we couldn't meet, and it was over. Sad thing is, all the units at Lincoln and the Pond were occupied and renting at the market rate."

"What about the money Willow Tree loaned you?" I asked.

"I don't follow you."

"I was told that Willow Tree agreed to loan the Roosevelt HRA a considerable sum of money to help you meet your obligations."

"No, that's not true. We spoke with Willow Tree about some additional low-income projects. But that was before our financial problems became acute. We had no discussions with them following that. Certainly we did not discuss a loan. I'm not sure that would have been appropriate in any case."

"Are you sure?"

"Of course I'm sure. Why do you ask?"

I didn't tell him that I was merely surprised that Joan Dully would tell me a lie so easily uncovered.

IF YOU'VE EVER borrowed money from a bank, a mortgage company, a credit union or a credit card company, you will be listed with at least one and more likely all of the nation's major credit bureaus—whether you like it or not. Most of the information the bureaus compile, especially your credit history, is restricted by the Fair Credit Reporting Act, and, at least in theory, guys like me can't get at it. However, for a price we can gain access to your "header" information, your noncredit data such as name, address updates, DOB, social security number, employment history, et cetera.

I was back in the office now, researching Dully, Joan, and Dully, Peter. It took about five minutes to discover that up until they formed JPD, Inc.; both had been employed by Saterbak Incorporated, he as CFO and she as VP-sales manager. A few months ago they returned, getting their old jobs back. But that wasn't what interested me most. What interested me most was the location: Saterbak was headquartered in the Adolph Point Office Complex. That's where Amanda Field had gone after I sent her flowers addressed to Crystalin Wolters. That's where she had met her friend.

I punched up *Dunn's Direct Access* and dragged its bank of Twin Cities businesses. It told me that Saterbak, Incorporated, was an investment firm specializing in start-ups. It had been founded and wholly owned by Carson Saterbak of Minnetonka, Minnesota.

CS. I wrote the initials on a yellow legal pad and circled them several times. Then I referred to the list I had stolen from the Dullys. Yep. CS. $1,000,000.

Carson Saterbak was easy to access. He must have been listed in a dozen data bases: the *Dialog & Knowledge Index*, *BRS Information*, *Newssearch*. I printed out twenty-three pages on him, although I probably would have been satisfied with just one—the page that told me Carson Saterbak had been cocaptain of the football team at Irondale High School his senior year—the same year Amanda and Levering Field had graduated.

I NEEDED MORE information, and I knew just where to look. But I couldn't go after it until the following day at the earliest, so I pushed the thought out of my mind as best I could, concentrating instead on the adductor exercises Tommy Sands was so gleefully subjecting me to.

"Let me see some sweat," he demanded, and I showed him plenty. My T-shirt clung to my body like the skin of a banana. Apparently Tommy approved of the effort because following the exercises, he announced that I could start walking without crutches if I took it easy. But not too easy.

"You want to avoid a limp," he told me. "You want to walk through the pain. The tendency is to take short steps with your strong leg and long steps with your weak leg. The tendency is to take the weight off your weak leg as soon as possible. Don't do it. Don't shift your shoulders and pelvis to one side as you walk. Maintain an honest step. If the pain is too much, then get back on your crutches."

I told him I would.

"You won't have speed or power, so don't look for any," Tommy warned. "Walk normally. Concentrate on using your hurt leg. Don't be afraid of it."

I told him I wouldn't.

I walked out of the St. Paul Ramsey Medical Center into bright sunlight, carrying my crutches. The snow had long since melted, gone from even the shadowed areas, gone for at least seven months, knock on wood. And baseball season had begun. The Minnesota Twins were playing their home opener that evening against the White Sox, although not as many fans seemed to care as did before the strike—including me. Lately I've been thinking of baseball season as the weeks between Memorial Day and Labor Day, when the St. Paul Saints play minor league ball at Midway Stadium. Still, there was something about opening day that filled me with optimism.

I took a deep breath and exhaled slowly. Life was good.

Putting the crutches in my back seat, I slid behind the wheel of my Dodge Colt and for a moment regretted buying an automatic. I felt like "peeling out," as we used to say when I was a kid: popping the clutch and leaving about a ten-foot strip of rubber behind me. Only you just can't do that with an automatic. Pity.

TO MY GREAT disappointment, the toilet paper draped over the branches of my willow tree and lilac bushes had not disappeared. So, bad leg and all, I was out in the yard trying to clean it up. I first used a lawn rake to pull down from the tree and bushes what I could reach, then a snow rake for what I couldn't. But the snow rake, designed to remove heavy snow from roofs, was much too long and top heavy; it was difficult to maneuver. I ended up pulling down more tree branches than Charmin, which caused me to curse the contraption. Yeah, I know—it's a poor workman who blames his tools.

In the ninety minutes I was out there, my mood had shifted from supreme optimism to outrage. With every stroke of the rake on my tree, I found a new target for my wrath, shifting from the sonuvabitch who had vandalized my home to the house itself to Irene Gustafson to my parents and eventually to the president of the United States for not being tougher on crime. Even my fourth grade teacher took a few of licks. And my mood wasn't helped much by the fact that, after all my hard work, the willow tree still looked like it had been topped with whipped cream. There was nothing I could do about it except wait until the toilet paper degraded.

While I was raking, a car carrying a young couple pulled into my driveway. The man got out and the woman stayed inside. The man said, "I read the ad in the *Pioneer Press*, but I don't see any signs. Is this house for sale?"

Well, was it or wasn't it? I had been thinking about sell-

ing since the day I arrived home from the hospital. I had
been thinking about the property taxes and the mainte-
nance and the size. It was so much larger than I needed;
there were rooms I hadn't stepped into in weeks. And I'd
been thinking about my vulnerability. So was it for sale?

Standing there, a rake in my hands, a throbbing pain in
my leg, I surprised myself by telling the young man, "No,
it's not."

The answer actually made me feel better.

I WENT TO bed early. But the facts I had gathered that
day were making a helluva racket in my head; I couldn't
sleep. I ended up in my kitchen at two A.M. drinking milk
and munching Old Dutch potato chips. The telephone
rang. It didn't startle me at all. I knew who it was before
I picked up the receiver.

"Had enough?" a muffled voice asked.

"More than enough," I told it. "Exactly what do you
want?"

"You know what we want."

I jumped on the "we" like a fumble on the goal line.

"No, I don't know," I answered truthfully.

The voice chuckled. "All right," it said. "Have it your
own way."

"No, wait!" I yelled, but it hung up.

I checked the caller ID: PAY PHONE. The number was
UNAVAILABLE.

EIGHTEEN

"Sure about the time?" Steve asked while he stared at his screen, his long, elegant fingers working the keyboard.

"Yes."

"Here you go," he announced triumphantly. "The call originated at two-oh-two A.M. from a pay phone on East Lake Street and Forty-eighth in Minneapolis."

"Hmmm."

"What?"

"That's just across the Lake Street Bridge, on the Minneapolis side of the river."

"Yeah?"

"Less than a half mile from Levering Field's house."

"I don't get it," Steve admitted.

"I think Amanda's playing games," I told him, before adding, "I need a favor."

"What do you want me to do?"

"Actually, it's Sara's help I need."

WE WALKED ARM in arm down the street, a pleasant-looking couple taking a stroll through the neighborhood. I told Sara to talk, to switch her smile on and off, to pretend we were husband and wife enjoying a pleasant conversation. And she did a good job of it. But I ignored my own advice. I was too wired to do anything but watch the street, my head perfectly still, my eyes darting quickly from one side to the other. When we reached the Dullys' cobblestones we turned in. This time I did not bother with the front door, instead maneuvering Sara quickly around the house to the back. When we reached the back door, I pulled a police scanner from the tennis bag I carried, switched it on, and handed it to Sara.

"What's this?" she asked.

"Listen carefully to the calls," I told her in way of explanation. "If you hear the name of this street, you tell me."

I took two pair of surgical gloves from the bag and gave Sara one pair, telling her to put them on while I pulled on the other. Then I bent to my task, slipping the pick into the keyhole of the door lock, the tension wire directly beneath it.

"What are you doing?" Sara asked, rather stupidly I thought.

"*Ssshhhhh!*" I hushed her, trying to feel the vibration of the pins in my fingers, listening for a distinctive click. It was a long time in coming. I know burglars who can pick a lock in seven seconds. Even locks with high-security pin tumblers. It took me about two minutes. But I got it done.

I opened the door and pushed Sara inside, closing the door behind us.

"Now what?" she asked.

"*Ssshhhhh!*" I told her again, standing just inside the door, waiting, listening. Maybe I expected the air to be filled with sirens, to hear a dozen K-9 units surrounding the house, the German shepherds straining against their leashes, barking their heads off. But I heard nothing. I wiped the sweat from my brow with the sleeve of my sports jacket. I must have been out of my mind returning to that house.

"How did you learn to pick a lock?" Sara asked me.

"Practice," I told her. "I bought about fifty locks and kept working on them until I got it right."

I led her to the den and the Dullys' personal computer, gesturing at it with a flourish. "Your turn," I told her.

Sara smiled and went to the machine, sitting in Peter Dully's chair.

"How long?" I asked.

"Ssshhhhh!" she told me.

The Dullys had attempted to wipe the Willow Tree files from their system. But employing the delete function on a computer does not actually eliminate the files from the computer's memory. All it does is delete the names of the documents from the index of files. As any hacker will tell you, the files remain in the hard drive—or on floppies, hard disks, optical disks, and magnetic tape—unless they are written over by new data. Until then, the documents can be easily retrieved by anyone with the proper expertise and software programs. Like Sara, say.

I watched as she set to work, humming to herself. The only words she spoke were these: "DOS is pretty lazy when it comes to erasing a file."

I left the room.

I paced, staying far back from the Dullys' massive windows, my Nikes squeaking on the polished cedar floors. My leg throbbed with pain. But I remembered Tommy Sands's advice and walked it off. The various coaches I'd had over the years would have been proud of me.

The only sound in the house came from the police scanner I carried, and it was mostly silent. You don't get many calls that time of the morning. I regarded the Dullys' furnishings, but touched nothing. I considered going upstairs but couldn't think of a reason why I should beyond a prurient curiosity and vetoed the idea. I continued pacing, glancing at my watch every thirty seconds or so. We had been in the house far too long.

"Hurry up, Sara!" I called.

"Do I tell you how to pick locks?" she replied.

I discovered I was thirsty. It probably had something to do with the sweat that poured down my back and drenched my shirt under my arms. I found myself looking in the Dullys' refrigerator. Milk, OJ, and Diet 7Up. I almost took a can of pop, caught myself, and shut the refrigerator door.

"What are you doing?" I asked myself loudly. "Are you nuts?"

Almost in reply, I heard Sara shout, "Taylor, Taylor! Look at this!"

Tommy hadn't said anything about running, so I did, surprised that I could. I circled the Dullys' desk, looking at their computer screen over Sara's shoulder. She had called up a list of ten names and corresponding dollar amounts:

Brian Burke	$2,000,000
Carl Defiebre	$1,000,000
David Doll	$ 500,000
Levering Field	$ 750,000
Peter Grotting	$ 500,000
Phillip Jaeger	$ 500,000
Tim Lemke	$1,000,000
Katherine Moralas	$ 500,000
Carson Saterbak	$1,000,000
Kennedy Slavik	$1,000,000
	$8,750,000

"My God!" I said, reading the names.

"Some of the richest people in the Cities," Sara said softly.

"Brian Burke . . ."

"Owns about eight banks," Sara noted.

"Katherine Moralas . . ."

"Operates all those fast-food Mexican joints."

"Dave Doll . . ."

"Former United States senator and ambassador to Germany." Sara added, "This Slavik guy? He's a friend of my dad's. He owns a company that manufactures medical devices."

"I once did a consulting job for Phillip Jaeger," I volunteered. "He wanted to test a security system set up to protect his computer software company."

And then there was Carson Saterbak's name. And Levering Field's.

I pulled from my pocket the copy of the list of names I had stolen from the Dullys' earlier. The initials matched. So did the dollar amounts.

"Print this out," I told Sara, indicating the list on the screen. "Then bury it."

She did as I asked.

"Why?" she wondered. "Why would people like this get involved in something like Willow Tree?"

"I'm surprised to hear you ask a question like that. You of all people."

"Huh?"

"They did it for the money, Sara. They did it for the dough."

I DROPPED SARA at her loft, then drove to Monica Adler's law offices. She wasn't happy to see me and at first refused to speak with me alone. She was rooted in the center of her reception area, looking down at where I was sitting. A second lawyer and a legal secretary stood passively next to the receptionist's desk.

"What is it you want here?" she demanded to know.

"Are you afraid of me?" I asked calmly.

"Yes," she replied.

"Why?" I asked. "Is it because you tried to have me killed and think I've come looking for revenge?"

I caught the expressions on the faces of the lawyer, legal secretary, and receptionist over Monica's shoulder. They exchanged glances, looking at each other like they had just walked in on the middle of a movie.

"I told the police—" Monica started.

"Yes," I interrupted her. "I know what you told the police. They believe you, and who am I to argue? Don't worry, I'm not bitter. I've come here for an entirely different reason."

Monica took great comfort in my remarks. She even invited me into her office, closing the door behind us. But that didn't mean we were friends.

"It is inappropriate for us to speak while litigation is pending unless you are being advised by an attorney," she told me, then waited for my reply.

"Sound advice," I agreed. "But that's not why I'm here, either."

"Well, then . . ."

"I would like to speak with Amanda Field. I was hoping you could arrange it."

"You must be joking. After everything you've done?"

"I've done nothing to her," I protested.

"Oh, really?"

"I don't expect either of you to believe me," I admitted. "But I think I'm close to learning who killed her husband and who shot me and who tried to shoot her yesterday. I'm asking for just a few minutes of her time. That's all."

"Not alone," Monica insisted.

"She can have the Mormon Tabernacle Choir with her for all I care."

Monica studied me for a moment, chewing on a thumbnail. I offered an additional incentive.

"If I'm right, it'll help prove you had nothing to do with what happened at Rice Park."

"Give me a moment," she said.

I waited in the reception area while Monica placed a telephone call. Minutes passed. Monica emerged from her office, a spring coat draped over her arm, a purse in her hand.

"Amanda will give you ten minutes, and I'm going, too."

"Agreed," I said, and we headed for the door.

"Don't push her, Taylor," Monica warned. "She's very close to the edge. You can't imagine, what with her husband being murdered and someone shooting at her."

"Yes, I can."

"And now trouble with her daughter."

I flashed on Emily's boyfriend, the kid with the ancient Cadillac. Was he the source of the trouble? I asked.

Monica shook her head. "He's only part of it," she said. "To protect himself financially, Levering put all his assets in Emily Elizabeth's name. Now that he's dead, Amanda is being forced to sue her own daughter for half of his estate."

"What was it Tolstoy wrote in *Anna Karenina*, about unhappy families being unhappy each in its own way?"

"You read all those damn Russians, don't you?"

AMANDA FIELD SAT me in a chair near the entrance to her home. She stood next to the telephone table, the one with the .38 Smith & Wesson in the drawer. Monica Adler was leaning against the wall between us. We did not waste time on pleasantries.

"Tell me about your relationship with Carson Saterbak," I told Amanda.

She glanced at Monica, then back at me. "What is this?"

"You went to the same high school at the same time,

Irondale in New Brighton. Carson and Levering were cocaptains of the football team."

"That's right," Amanda admitted. "Years ago."

"You were good friends?"

"Very."

"How long did the friendship last?"

"It's never ended," Amanda told me, then added, "Congratulations, Taylor. You discovered the name of the man I had drinks with in the hotel in Bloomington. I knew you could do it."

"Mrs. Field, I'm not accusing—"

"The hell you're not."

I gave it a few beats before starting again. "Were Levering and Carson good friends?"

The question seemed to catch Amanda off guard. She stumbled over her answer. "They–they were . . . but that changed."

"When did it change?"

"When Levering and I were married."

"Why?" I asked. "Was Carson jealous?"

"No, it was the other way around. Levering was jealous. Carson and I remained good friends. We had lunch together, spoke on the phone. I confided in Carson. Told him things I never told Levering."

"That upset Levering?"

"Yes, it did."

"Why didn't you give up your friendship?" I asked.

She shook her head like she wasn't sure herself.

"Were you and Carson having an affair?"

"Absolutely not!" Amanda shouted. "We were friends. That's all."

"Is that what you told Levering?"

"Many times."

"Did he believe you?"

Amanda didn't answer.

A few moments of dead air passed before I asked, "How long were Levering and Carson business partners?"

"Business partners?" Amanda repeated, genuinely surprised by the suggestion. "Never."

"Are you sure?"

"Not a chance." She was adamant now. "Carson might have been willing to work with Levering. But Levering work with Carson? No way."

"Are you sure?" I repeated.

"Yes. Why?"

"I was under the impression that Levering was steering investors to one of Carson's start-ups."

Amanda shook her head. "He would have starved first," she insisted.

I THANKED AMANDA for her time and told her I was truly sorry for her troubles. I don't think she believed me. Monica Adler escorted me out the door and walked me to my car. Something was on her mind. When we reached the Dodge Colt, she told me what it was.

"Are you involved with Cynthia Grey?"

"I am," I answered, not caring that it was none of her business.

"What do you see in her?"

"I'd tell you, Monica, but it would take me several hours to list her virtues, and I simply don't have the time."

"Virtues? Did you know she was a stripper?" Monica asked, a little girl telling tales.

"A very good one, too, I'm told."

"By whom? The Minneapolis Police Vice Squad?"

She was annoying me now, dissing my main squeeze, as the kids would say. I tried to keep my growing anger to myself. "You're a little old for this kind of schoolgirl nonsense, aren't you?" I said.

Monica came back hard. "She's a fake, a fraud, a phony," she vehemently insisted. "There's not one thing about her that's real, that's honest."

"On the contrary," I replied. "She's easily the most honest person I've ever known."

"She's a stripper! Probably a hooker, too!"

"Maybe, in her youth," I agreed. "Today she's someone entirely different. Someone to be admired."

"Why? Because she dresses better than she did? Because she speaks better?"

"Because she's exactly the person she wants to be. How many of us can make that claim?"

I unlocked my car door and slid inside, rolling down the window so I could hear Monica say, "She'll never be as good a lawyer as I am."

"I wouldn't know about that," I said out the window as I started the car, putting it in gear. "But there's something that she is that you'll never be."

"Oh, really? And what's that?"

"Tenth in her class."

THE RINGING TELEPHONE greeted me as I unlocked my office door. I rushed to it, not bothering to remove my jacket.

"Taylor Investigations," I spoke into the receiver.

"Mr. Taylor?" a woman asked curtly.

"Yes."

"I am calling for Mr. Carson Saterbak." The name shook me; I was glad the caller couldn't see my face. "Mr. Saterbak would like to meet you at his office at one-thirty P.M. Please, do not be late."

"Why does he want to meet?"

She hung up, a loud *click* ending the conversation.

"Sounds like a good reason to me," I said to nobody.

I glanced at my watch. If I kicked it, I could be there with ten minutes to spare.

IT WAS HIM, all right. Amanda's friend. I identified him from the portrait that hung above the sofa in his ostentatious lobby. It was a nice enough painting, I suppose: head and shoulders against a neutral background. But somewhat self-aggrandizing for my taste. I don't think you should display a portrait of a company's founder unless he's retired or dead. At least that's what I told the receptionist when I identified myself. She didn't say whether she agreed or not. Instead, she told me to take a seat, that Mr. Saterbak would be with me in a moment. That was at 1:25. At 1:40 I was still sitting. I reminded the receptionist that I had an appointment. She told me she knew. I waited some more.

I've met guys like Saterbak before. Some make you wait because it makes them feel important: "See, I can make you waste thirty minutes of your precious time." Others make you wait to wear you down, believing it gives them an advantage in negotiations. Maybe it does. Only I had grown tired of the waiting game and decided to make a move of my own. At exactly 1:50 by my watch, I tossed my business card on the receptionist's desk. She looked up.

"Man calls me," I said, "and tells me he wants to meet, tells me not to be late, then stands me up for twenty minutes? I don't think so."

"I'm sure Mr. Saterbak . . ." the receptionist began, but I wasn't listening. I turned my back on her and went through the door into the long corridor beyond, stopping at the elevators and hitting the down button. The receptionist rushed into the corridor just as the doors opened.

"Mr. Saterbak will see you now," she told me.

I waved good-bye and stepped onto the elevator.

THE PHONE WAS ringing when I returned to my office. I let it, pulling a Summit Pale Ale from the fridge. My answering machine picked up. It was Saterbak's secretary, beseeching me to return the call. I sat behind my desk, reviewing the latest edition of *The Sporting News*, a special issue on the opening of baseball season. I ran down the list of teams, starting with the American League. Baltimore looked good in the East, the Angels should run away with the West, and the Central was up for grabs. At least that's what the pundits claimed. We'd have to wait one hundred sixty-two games to learn if they were right.

The telephone rang again. This time I answered. "Holland Taylor Private Investigations. Holland Taylor speaking."

"This is Carson Saterbak," a voice replied. The voice was angry. I said nothing and waited. Finally the voice said, "Well?"

"Well, what?"

"We had an appointment."

"I know," I said. "How come you didn't keep it?"

Saterbak was almost sputtering with rage as he yelled, "I'm a busy man!"

"Not me," I said. "I have all the time in the world to waste."

Saterbak hesitated, then said, "I don't like your attitude."

"I don't care." I told him. "You want to see me? I suggest you keep your appointments."

"Is that what all this is about? You want to teach me a lesson in punctuality?"

"Something like that."

"Fine," Saterbak said. "I've learned my lesson. Now, if you please, I will see you at *exactly* three-thirty. How's that?"

"I'll be here," I told him.

"No, I meant at—"

I hung up before he could tell me I was expected at his office. Then I took the phone off the hook.

I went back to *The Sporting News* and managed to get through the National League East. But my concentration wasn't there. My stomach was softly churning, and my head ached. It was as if my body wanted to tell me something. I tried to ignore it, but when a light sweat broke across my forehead I decided it would be a good time to start listening. I returned to the telephone and called Freddie.

"AP Criminal and Civil Investigations. May I help you?"

"How come you don't use your name?" I asked him.

"Huh?"

"Sidney Poitier Fredricks Investigations, something like that?"

"I used to be an AP, remember? At Clark Air Force Base in the Philippines."

"So?"

"So I'm sentimental. Besides, it puts me first in the telephone book."

"Now I hear you."

"So what do you want, Taylor?"

"There's an old Chinese proverb. I don't remember the exact words, but what it says is, if you save someone's life . . ."

"Yeah?"

"You're responsible for it."

After a few moments of silence Freddie said, "I ain't Chinese."

CARSON SATERBAK POUNDED on my door like he was trying to knock it down. I made him do it twice, made him wait while I slid open my top right-hand drawer—the one with the 9mm Beretta in it.

I bade him enter and in he walked. He was wearing a black lambskin jacket over a mohair sweater, black jeans, and black loafers with tassels. Yet he had the bearing of a man who wore a tie.

"I'm Carson Saterbak," he announced.

I'd guessed as much but did not say so. Instead, I gestured at a chair in front of my desk, not rising myself, not offering my hand, not speaking.

After a few moments of silence, Saterbak said, "I am by nature a patient man."

I did not reply, waiting to see if that were true, sipping coffee from my mug without offering him some. It was. He knew exactly what I was doing—trying to anger him into making mistakes—and the strategy didn't bother him a bit. He smiled at me, then asked if he could have coffee. I nodded, and he went to the machine and poured himself a mug. His manner was smooth now, and indifferent, like a shopper with plenty of cash browsing the merchandise, not caring if he made a purchase or not.

He returned to the chair and smiled some more. "You have been disturbing several of my friends these past few days," he said at last. "I wish for you to stop."

Saterbak seemed intent on a reply, the way he stared at me after speaking, so I gave him one. "You want to hear my personal definition of success? Success is making a comfortable living, doing what gives you pleasure, and not taking shit from anybody."

He smiled, almost laughed. "We all take shit from somebody," Saterbak insisted.

"Yeah? Who gives it to you?"

"Right now, you are," he replied. Then he did laugh. When he was finished, he said, "It shouldn't be this difficult."

"What?"

"I want you to leave Amanda Field alone. I want you to stay away from Joan and Peter Dully."

"If I don't, what are you going to do? Give me shit?"

Saterbak set the coffee mug on top of my desk, went into his inside pocket. I flinched at the gesture, shooting my hand into the drawer. When his hand came out holding a sheet of paper, mine came up empty. Saterbak unfolded the sheet and began to read from it. The paper contained the facts and figures of my life right down to the limit of my credit cards. He told me what schools I'd gone to and what grade point average I'd acquired, when I married Laura and when she died, how much we paid for our home, my employment record, health record. . . . I let him read without interruption. If he was trying to impress me or frighten me, he was failing. I compile dossiers like this on people all the time; I wasn't surprised that someone could do it to me. But I was angry. Not at the information. At the fact that I was now convinced Saterbak was responsible for stalking me, for trashing my house. Which meant he was also responsible for the telephone call to Amanda Field just thirty minutes before someone took a shot at her.

I let that slide for now, waiting for Saterbak to finish his recitation. When he did I asked, "What about the guns?"

That caught him off guard. "Guns?"

"I own eight," I said, then listed them by caliber. "Your report missed several names, too," I added, reciting four.

"Who are they?"

"The men I've killed," I replied. "I thought you should know. Keep your files up to date."

He stared at me and I stared at him. As conversations went, this one was going nowhere fast. And that did not fit my plans. I drank some more coffee, then asked, "Are we done playing now?"

Saterbak smiled like a man who understood perfectly the grand scheme of things and liked his place in it. "Done," he said.

I studied him for a moment, then played my ace. "Brian Burke, two million dollars."

Saterbak did not reply.

"Carl Defiebre, one million."

"Excuse me?"

"Tim Lemke and Kennedy Slavik, one million dollars each."

"What are you saying?"

"Senator Doll, Peter Grotting, Phillip Jaeger, Katherine Moralas—half a million each."

"My God."

"And then there's you and Levering Field."

Saterbak shook his head like he had a pain he hoped would fall out of his ears.

"Aspirin?" I asked.

"No, thank you."

"Would you like some more coffee?"

"No, thank you," Saterbak replied, again.

I didn't get any, either. I didn't want to leave my opened drawer.

"So you have a list of names," Saterbak pointed out. "Means nothing."

"C'mon Saterbak. You think you're bulletproof? I could take you out with a spitball. A scam like yours works only if no one looks real close. A phone call is all it would take to convince the IRS to put Willow Tree under a microscope."

"Are you going to turn us in?"

"I don't work for the IRS," I assured him.

"Who do you work for?"

"A little old lady in Fort Myers, Florida."

"One of Levering's investors?" Saterbak guessed.

"What were you thinking?" I wanted to know. "You and

your rich friends hire Joan and Peter Dully to set up a dummy corporation in which to make dummy investments. I figure you paid them ten percent. That's about their net worth."

Saterbak nodded.

"You buy up all thirty-five limited partnerships at quarter of a million bucks a pop. Then you pretend the company goes bust and you've lost your investment, when in fact, you're just putting the money back in your pocket. You report the paper loss to the IRS. Now you and your friends have a capital loss for the full amount of your investment plus a deduction that you can use to offset the gains from all of your other investments. The entire scheme was devised so you and your rich friends wouldn't have to pay taxes on your sizeable investment incomes."

"Tax avoidance," Saterbak said.

"Tax fraud," I said. "And it should have worked."

"It still can," Saterbak insisted softly, looking me straight in the eye.

"Maybe," I answered encouraging him.

Saterbak smiled. He was in control again. "How much do you make?" he asked.

"Four hundred a day plus expenses."

"How does forty thousand dollars sound?"

"It sounds like a number that came off the top of your head."

Saterbak smiled some more. "I'm open to negotiation," he said.

"Tell me something," I asked, returning to the subject. "Levering Field didn't invest his own money in Willow Tree. He invested other people's money, people who might want to know what happened to it. Why did you let him?"

"We were using Willow Tree to avoid paying taxes, as

you said," Saterbak confessed. "Levering was using it to fleece his clients."

"Why did you let him?" I repeated.

When Saterbak didn't answer, I asked, "Was it because of Amanda?"

He sighed.

"Levering thought you two were having an affair, but Amanda denies it."

Saterbak inhaled deeply, then spoke quickly, like it was his last breath and he wanted to get the words out while he could: "I've loved Amanda since we were sixteen years old. And I think she loves me. But she was married to that jerk and wouldn't even consider having an affair. Never."

"If she loved you, why did she stay married to him?"

The smile on Saterbak's face was one of admiration. "Amanda is an old-fashioned girl," he said. "Not long ago, people used to stay in bad marriages for the kids. Amanda is one of those people."

"So you remained friends."

"Sometimes you have to settle for what you can get," Saterbak said.

"But you and Levering weren't friends."

"No."

"Then why did you let him in on Willow Tree?"

Saterbak was on his feet now, pacing my office, his hands behind his back. I watched his hands while making sure mine never strayed far from the desk drawer.

"He came to me with an offer. What's the saying, an offer you can't refuse? He told me that since I loved Amanda, I could have her. He said he was tired of being married to her, anyway; said she was boring. He said he would divorce her—clear the decks for me, he said—for one million dollars."

"He offered to sell you his wife?"

"Nice guy, wasn't he?"

"Helluva human being," I agreed.

Saterbak kept pacing, but now his arms were folded across his chest. "I didn't have a million dollars lying around," he continued, "so I told him about Willow Tree."

"He was in to it for only seven hundred-fifty thousand," I reminded Saterbak.

"That was his choice," he told me. "Apparently those were the only investors he was sure of."

"The only ones he thought would soon die intestate."

Saterbak shrugged.

"You people—"

"Us?!" Saterbak shouted. "Your hands aren't so lily-white. You tried to blackmail Levering."

"I tried to force him to give back the money he stole from my client!" I shouted back. "And that's not the same thing."

"You threatened his life."

"I did not."

"That's what Amanda said."

"I admit to making his life miserable, but I did not threaten him with violence," I announced as if that absolved me of all sins.

"He thought you were going to kill him. That's why he asked me . . ." Saterbak stopped walking and talking simultaneously. I filled in the blank.

"That's why he asked you to supply him with the name of a killer, preferably an inexpensive one."

Saterbak looked at me like he was going to deny it. I didn't let him.

"I've been to the pony rides before, pal," I insisted, tapping my chest.

Saterbak defended himself: "He said you were trying to kill him, and I couldn't very well tell him to go to the police."

"Course not," I agreed.

"I knew some people in Chicago."

"Don't we all?"

Saterbak sat down again. He looked defeated. I found his expression encouraging. But then he perked up, announcing, "You can't prove any of this."

He was right, of course. "But I can prove what I need to prove," I told him. "And the Dullys will probably prove the rest when the IRS leans on them. Joan is a woman who likes company. Do you think she'd be willing to go to jail alone?"

"What do you want?"

"Let's start with some honest answers. Why did you have Levering killed?"

"I had nothing to do with that."

"And when I was shot afterward . . . ?"

"I wasn't involved that time, I tell you."

"Why did you try to have Amanda killed?"

"Now, wait a minute!" Saterbak said.

"The cops matched the bullets," I told him. "Whoever shot Levering and me used the same gun on Amanda."

Saterbak was on his feet now, his hands resting on my desk top.

"Sit down!" I shouted at him.

He did.

I waited a few moments then asked, "Why?"

"I had nothing to do with any of that," Saterbak claimed.

"Have it your own way." I didn't believe him, but that was OK. I had worked out my plan before Saterbak arrived, and whether or not he confessed to murder was immaterial at this point. I just needed to ratchet one more bolt into place before I turned on the machinery.

"Two hundred and eighty-seven thousand dollars," I said.

"What?"

"That's how much Levering stole from my client to invest in your Willow Tree. That's how much I wanted from him. That's how much I want from you." Saterbak did not so much as blink, so I added, "You have until noon tomorrow."

And then he blinked plenty.

"Are you insane? You think I can get that kind of cash overnight?"

"Yeah, I do." I shrugged. "And if you can't, ask Joan Dully. I bet she has the exact total all packed up in a brief-case and ready to go."

Saterbak studied me hard, like I knew he would, his lips drawn into an angry line. "I'll be in touch," he said, then turned and left my office, leaving the door open behind him. I was up quickly, the nine in my hand, went to the door, closed it, and locked it.

NINETEEN

I WAS WEARING a gray sweatsuit with the emblem of the University of St. Thomas emblazoned on the shirt and pants. Over the sweatsuit I wore a green-and-blue down vest. Hidden in the vest was my four-and-a-half-inch long .25 Beretta. I would have preferred something with a little more range, accuracy, and stopping power, but it was the only weapon I had that didn't make the vest look like I had a gun in the pocket.

I had chosen my ground carefully. I wanted a location that was secluded, where civilians were unlikely to be hurt—where a shooter would be encouraged to take his chances. Yet, I also needed a natural setting; a place where my presence would not cause suspicion. I did not want the shooter to know that I knew he was coming. And he was coming—between now and noon tomorrow. Carson Saterbak wasn't going to pay me two hundred eighty-seven thousand dollars. No way. Not at this late date. Not after all the trouble he'd gone to to protect himself and the other Willow Tree investors. I knew that before he came to my office, before he even *called* my office.

I had picked the time, and now I chose the place—the asphalt jogging path that hugged the modest lake in Central Park in Roseville—and waited.

The lake was in the center of the park; the jogging path followed its shoreline. The east and west sides were open to playground equipment, tennis courts, softball diamonds, volleyball pits, a pavilion, and a band shell. They were usually populated, even late on a cold April afternoon with the sun about to set. But the north side of the path that ran between the lake and the railroad tracks and the south side that cut through a thick grove of trees were not. I dismissed the tracks. Michael Zilar could shoot me from the tall grass between the tracks and park, but then he'd have a lot of open space to negotiate before he could get to a car—all of it in the shadow of several apartment buildings. The grove was more secluded and was bordered by residential streets. It was not uncommon for joggers to park their cars along them.

Yeah, he would try to hit me in the grove. I'd bet my life on it.

I LEFT MY car in the lot off Victoria Avenue. Experience told me that that was the most populated area of the park and therefore the safest. I walked slowly down to the shore, stopping at the wooden pier that reached one hundred feet into the lake. A couple of white kids dressed like gang bangers, who knew only what they saw on MTV, were leaning against the railing, playing the part, talking loud, not caring who heard them.

"You smokin' too much grain, man!" the first shouted unnecessarily. "Your head is juiced."

"Don't wanna hass, man," answered the second. "Whaddya say we nee-go-she-ate? Maybe throat some beverage, do some sub if 'n you a mind. Talk it over."

I was stretching, my left leg propped on the top rung of

the railing, my body leaning into it. I was trying hard not to be obvious as I scanned the area around me, my eyes everywhere at once, seeing everything, watching nothing. I must not have done a very good job of it because the first kid waved his companion quiet and moved down the railing to where I was standing. He didn't say a word. Just locked onto my eyes with his, mad-dogging me, not moving, not even blinking, like a prize-fighter trying to put the fear of God into an opponent.

There was a time you caught a kid goofing, you'd straightened him out, maybe cuff him upside the head. (It takes a village to raise a child, isn't that what Hillary Clinton says?) Now when a kid gives you the business, you turn away, say nothing, for fear the kid will put a bullet in your heart. But this guy and his buddy? They knew the jargon, knew the look, but they weren't bangers. There was too much life in their eyes. They were wannabes; kids who might actually be impressed—and fearful—at the sight of a gun.

I did not speak to the kid. Instead, I showed him the inside of my vest, showed him the butt of the .25 sticking out of the pocket. When he saw it, he glanced back at his companion and said real low: "He's packed."

The second kid asked me, "You iron?"

I nodded my head. Public or private, a cop is a cop is a cop to them.

The first kid asked, "You ever trace anyone?" There was a hopeful expression on his face. The idea that I might have actually killed someone excited the bejesus out of him. Man, just like TV! And it was that hopefulness that made me think he had a chance, that Mom or Dad or a teacher or coach could save him. Some kids you meet, they can be just twelve years old and you already know they're history; no way to turn them around, no way to save them. It's only a matter of how much pain they inflict, how much suffering they cause before we put them into a cage; out of sight, out of mind. But to these kids it was still cops and robbers; life was still a game with rules.

I gestured with my head for the kids to vacate the pier. To my surprise, they did.

I WAS RUNNING now, actually running. Not fast, not without pain, but I was picking them up and laying them down nonetheless. It would have given me great pleasure had I not been so totally scared to death.

I was rounding the northwest corner, moving at a slow pace past the volleyball pit, heading east, nearly parallel with the tracks. I put my hand inside my vest, gripped the .25, then took my hand out again. Nobody runs with their hands in their pockets. I relaxed just a tad as I approached the area where the path and the track came closest. The grass was still lying flat, beaten down by the winter. I was right, it wasn't a good place. Just the same, I picked up the pace as I passed it, which was hard to do, holding my breath as I was.

The park opened up on my left as I moved around the northeast corner. It offered iron barbecue grills unused since last fall, another volleyball court, a few tennis courts, a pavilion and a maze of playground equipment. In the distance a pond, its water level low, sparkled in the setting sun. I continued on for another hundred yards, slowing my pace as I made the turn, my feet thudding against the wooden bridge that spanned the creek connecting the pond to the lake. It was not my intention to slow down, but it had been weeks since I last ran, and while the spirit was willing, the flesh was weak. Besides, my leg had set to throbbing, and I was fearful of blowing it out.

Three full strides past the bridge, and I was in the grove. The leaves were just buds on the trees, and the undergrowth was dormant, yet it was still thick enough to obscure the streets and houses that line the park and, in some areas, block out the lake. I went deeper. My breath was coming hard now, and not just from exertion. The pain in my leg had increased, and I found myself wanting to stop and rub it away. I didn't. I stayed close to the right edge of the jogging path, the edge nearest the lake. I expected Zilar to come at me from the left. If he attacked from the lake side of the path, he would have to cross over to make his escape, and for a few brief moments he would be visible to, say, another jogger. So I guessed he would stay on the left—"guess" being the operative word. I went deeper.

Up ahead was another jogger, a woman, moving toward me at an easy pace, her hands inside white athletic socks. I gave her plenty of room. She nodded as we passed.

The path climbed gradually up a hill, then just as gradually fell away into a small valley. *There*, I thought as I crested the hill. *That's where it'll happen.*

I began my descent, and with each step I lost confidence. *Are you out of your mind?* I asked myself. *Are you nuts? Do you have some kind of death wish?* I couldn't believe that I had actually thought this was a good idea, dangling myself as bait, daring a professional killer to shoot me. A professional! Man, I wasn't going to see him coming. I wasn't even going to hear him. He was going to pop me using his homemade suppressor, and I was going to fall, and some unfortunate jogger would find me laying facedown in a pool of my own blood, and Anne Scalasi would be called to investigate, and she would go, "Tsk, tsk, I wonder what he was thinking."

The pain in my leg grew worse, my steps shorter and slower.

I hit the valley and immediately started to climb out of it and nothing happened. I tensed, anticipating the hard punch of a bullet, but there wasn't one. No *pop*. No *zing* of a round buzzing past my ear. At first I felt relief. Then I was irritated. What the hell was he waiting for, an engraved invitation?

I followed the path out of the grove. Again the park loomed before me. More playground equipment, more barbecue grills. In the distance a lone batter took hits at a softball diamond, a half dozen guys in the outfield shagging his flies. The path curved with the lake, leading me past the band shell. I remembered the last time I had been in the park. It was the Fourth of July before my wife and daughter were killed. We had lolled on the hill surrounding the band shell with a couple of hundred other natives, listening to the local orchestra bang out march tunes while fireworks exploded above. But there were no fireworks today. Zero. Zip. Nada.

He's a professional, I reminded myself. Zilar isn't going to hit me on my terms; he's going to do it on his. He'll take me when I go back to my car. Or maybe he's waiting for me to pull into the driveway at home. How many other ways could he do it?

I was past the pier, taking the turn at the volleyball pits before I realized it. "Well," I decided, "one more time around. The exercise will be good for my leg."

Only my leg didn't agree, and it told me so with each step I took as I recircled the lake, again meeting the female jogger, this time along the tracks. She smiled and nodded, and I smiled and nodded back. She wasn't particularly attractive, but, man, was she in good shape. Better than me, anyway.

The sun was sinking fast when I hit the grove. Again I ran along the edge of the path closest to the lake. And again my stomach tightened when I crested the hill and began my descent into the valley. But I did not expect Zilar to make his move there. And of course that is exactly what he did.

WHOOM!

I heard the explosion and knew instantly what made it—you hear the sound once and you remember. I dived off the path into the trees, rolled, and turned toward the sound. The deep, piercing pain in my leg convinced me I had been shot again, but I wasn't. It was the old wound, protesting my shabby treatment of it.

WHOOM!

I rolled some more until my legs were in the lake, icy water soaking through my sweatpants. The 25-caliber Beretta was in my hand, for all the good it did me. I couldn't see a thing. I thought about crawling toward the path but resisted the idea. Let him come to me. And he did. I detected movement out of the corner of my eye, up the path toward my right. He was squatting behind a tree wearing a black jacket zipped to his throat, jeans, and boots.

How did he get over there? I wondered. I would have bet the ranch that the shots had come from my left side, from down the path.

I lay in the water. I didn't trust the .25 from that distance, but I didn't want to move, didn't want to reveal myself the way Zilar had. Besides, he was the one in a hurry. I waited. Finally, Zilar was on the move, dashing from tree to tree, keeping low, his eyes down the path. He stopped a few feet from the edge, leaning against a tree, giving me an opportunity. I lined him up, took a deep breath, let half out, held the rest, was about to squeeze the trigger. . . . But Zilar jumped. The woman jogger! She was closing in on his location, about to go past. Zilar turned toward her, the gun leveled.

"No!" I screamed.

Zilar saw me and double-clutched. I was on my knees now. He brought his gun up. I did the same.

WHOOM!

The tree Zilar was leaning against exploded just inches above his head, sending splintered wood flying everywhere.

He instinctively pulled his head in.

The woman screamed.

I fired one round. The bullet caught Zilar high in his left shoulder. The force of the blow, even from a .25, was enough to bounce him off the tree. He lost his gun, which clattered on the asphalt.

The woman screamed again.

I was on my feet now, limping fast toward Zilar. I kicked his gun off the path—it was a .38—then drew a bead on his head.

"Don't shoot me again!" he begged. "I'm hurt. I'm really hurt. Don't shoot me no more!"

The woman screamed yet again. For someone dressed for running, she sure wasn't going anywhere very fast. But I didn't hold it against her. Fear has a way of paralyzing you.

"Call the police," I told her. But she didn't move, so I shouted, "Get the cops!"

She nodded and started running through the grove toward the houses hidden beyond.

"Nice ass," Freddie said as he watched her scamper through the woods, fall, regain her feet, and hurry on. I didn't answer, my gun still trained on Zilar's head. "This the guy?" Freddie wanted to know.

"Yeah," I said.

"Gonna shoot him?" he asked as if he wanted to know whether I preferred butter with my popcorn.

"I'm thinking about it," I admitted.

"I'll do it," Freddie volunteered. "No problem."

"Don't shoot me! Don't shoot me!" Zilar pleaded. "You got me, man. You don't need to shoot me no more."

"Who hired you?" I asked.

"I'm hurt bad," Zilar replied, his right hand pressed against his shoulder, both the hand and the jacket red with blood.

"Who sent you?" I asked again.

"G'ahead, take 'im out," Freddie urged me. "We can tell the cops anything we want; who's gonna know?" When I didn't reply, Freddie added, "Man, what are you? A pussy?"

I took Zilar's left wrist, stretching his arm and causing great pain to his shoulder. I pressed the muzzle of the .25 to his elbow and said, "First this one and then the other. You don't tell me what I want to know, I make it so you'll have to ask strangers to unzip you whenever you need to take a whiz."

Zilar yanked his arm away. "Jesus, Mary, Joseph!" he said. "You don't need to do that. I'll tell you what you want to know."

"And then tell the cops something else?" Freddie volunteered. "Shit, Taylor. Kill the fucker."

"Jesus, Mary, Joseph!" Zilar hissed again, slumping against the tree. "Oh, Jesus!"

Freddie leveled his gun at Zilar's face. "Say, Taylor?" he asked me. "Did I show you my new gun, yet?" He was holding a 50-caliber Desert Eagle, just like the one Zilar's buddy had tried to use on me at Rice Park. Freddie—the man's a slave to fashion.

Zilar was shaking his head now with a calmness I found mystifying. "There isn't any need for this. I get it," he said. And apparently he did because he straighted up, his hand clutching his shoulder, and said, "I roll on Saterbak, turn—whaddaya call it—state's evidence, and maybe they let me plead down to simple assault with a sentencing recommendation. You've got some nice, cushy prisons in this state. Clean. Modern. No gang rapes. No sodomy unlessin' that's your pleasure. Yeah, I can do a year in Stillwater or

St. Cloud, no problem. So, tell me, what is it exactly you guys want to know?"

I looked at Freddie. He looked at me.

"I told you this was a good idea," I said.

SERGEANT JOHN HAWKS studied Freddie's Desert Eagle carefully after unloading it, shook his head in disgust, and said, "Compensating for a small penis, are we?" I don't know what he thought when he examined my tiny Beretta.

We gave him a statement at the scene, after which he was kind enough to remove the handcuffs his patrolmen had wound around our wrists. He then took me, Freddie, and the female jogger to the Roseville Police Department, where the three of us gave our statements again, first to the city attorney, and then to a stenographer. After we signed them, the woman was offered a ride home. Freddie and I were asked to wait. And so we did, while Michael Zilar was treated at the St. Paul–Ramsey Medical Center. His wound wasn't particularly grievous. My bullet had torn away part of his deltoid muscle just below the shoulder joint. It was what people who haven't been shot call a "flesh wound."

After a couple of hours, Hawks loaded Freddie and me into a patrol car and drove us down to the Ramsey County Annex in downtown St. Paul. We were installed in separate holding cells and waited some more. Eventually the assistant Ramsey County attorney arrived. He watched me through the round peephole in my door, gave me a hard look, then left.

When he came back—it was either early or late depending on your sleep habits—he informed me that Zilar had been true to his word. After negotiating a deal, Zilar spilled his guts about Carson Saterbak, starting with Saterbak's original call to Chicago on behalf of Levering

Field. He confessed that Saterbak brought him to town following Tom Storey's untimely death in Rice Park, putting him up in a hotel near the Mall of America. He confessed that Saterbak had contacted him on what was now yesterday afternoon and promised to pay him twenty thousand dollars if I was dead by noon the following day. (Later that evening, after learning the price tag, Freddie would nudge me with an elbow. "See, I told you you were worth twenty.")

Zilar even explained what little he knew about Willow Tree, which was little indeed. That's what the ACA wanted me to tell him now: more about Willow Tree.

"I can tell you that Willow Tree was founded by Joan and Peter Dully, who were Saterbak's employees," I said. "Beyond that, I can tell you nothing."

The ACA was furious until I explained.

"Most of the information I have on Willow Tree was obtained illegally," I confessed. "Anything I tell you now will probably be thrown out of court. A smart defense attorney will argue that I was acting as an agent of the police department and therefore am subject to the same rules of search and seizure, and the court of appeals will probably agree. You'll lose what evidence I give you and any evidence you develop because of it."

The ACA nodded. He knew I was right. He also knew he should have thought of it first.

"I promise you," I said, cheering him up, "everything you need will be right there in plain sight." Then, remembering the size of the names on the Willow Tree investment list, I added, "All you need is a little nerve, and this could become the biggest, most important case of your career."

He was smiling when he left the room, probably wishing cameras were allowed in Minnesota courtrooms.

After a while they let Freddie and me out of the holding cells and gave us some coffee and donuts. Meanwhile, the

ACA had set an all-time land-speed record in obtaining arrest warrants for Carson Saterbak and the Dullys. Freddie and I were still there when Ramsey County sheriff's deputies brought Saterbak in, his hands cuffed behind his back. He stared at me for a long time while he was being processed. I smiled back. Words didn't seem necessary.

A half hour later, another squad of deputies ushered the Dullys past us. I turned to Freddie. "Our work here is done," I announced.

"Our work?" he grunted, his lips encrusted with tiny red-and-white sprinkles from a cake donut. He glanced at his watch. "I've got fourteen, fourteen and a half, make it fifteen hours you owe me for. I'll send a bill," he promised and took another bite of donut.

Of course, Zilar did not admit to shooting Field. Or me. Or of taking several pot shots at Amanda, for that matter. And the gun we took off him at the park—a .38 wheel gun manufactured by Charter Arms—most certainly had not fired the 32-caliber slugs they dug out of Field, me, and Amanda's siding. But let's face it, that would be a lot to ask. There was no way he could have plea bargained those charges away. Besides, I was satisfied. I was particularly pleased when the ACA told Freddie and me that we were free to go, leaning in real close and saying, "You lucky sonuvabitch, get out of my sight."

TWENTY

I TOLD FREDDIE that I owed him big time. He told me where to send the check. I offered to buy him breakfast—the sun was up, the birds were singing. He stretched, yawned, and said, "It's past my bedtime. I'll see ya around."

"Yeah, around."

I watched him walk away. The man had saved my life. Twice. And I wasn't even sure I liked him.

CYNTHIA GREY HAD been worried about me. After I retrieved my car and drove home, I found several messages on my machine, all from her. Before I could return them, she called again.

"Where have you been?" she wanted to know.

"In jail."

"What, again?"

I chuckled and explained everything, then asked if she wanted to meet for lunch. She had a prior engagement. Dinner? Same thing. But, maybe she could swing by afterward. I thought that was a good idea.

"It's too bad about the money, though," she said before hanging up.

"Hmm?"

"The two hundred and eighty-seven thousand dollars."

"Yeah," I agreed. "I would liked to have gotten the money for the old lady."

And then it hit me, really hit me. Everything that had happened since my father called me down to Fort Myers had been for nothing.

"Nuts," I said. "What am I going to tell my mom?"

I PUT FIVE CD's on my machine—a little Miles, some Bird, some Diz, two Coltranes—hit the shuffle button, and cranked the volume. I made some scrambled eggs. Ate the eggs. Then I lay down on my sofa in the living room to rest my eyes. I opened them again to silence and a dark house. The sun had set, and the only light I could see was the green dot that informed me that the CD player was powered up. I had slept ten hours.

I stretched and thought about some more eggs, maybe a slab of ham to go with them. The telephone rang. I answered it, expecting to hear Cynthia's voice telling me her meeting had broken up early. Instead, a voice, deep and sour, informed me, "This is your last chance, asshole. Where's the money?"

You know how sometimes when you first wake you feel like a car that's been left on the street over a cold winter's night? You might be running, but until you're warmed up you just don't want to go anywhere? Well, that was how I felt. And without even thinking about it, I answered the voice: "Listen to me, you prick. I've already shot one guy today, and I'll be happy to make it two."

The voice laughed at me.

I had thought that this problem had been taken care of. Then again, maybe the voice was working for Saterbak and hadn't learned that his employer had been jailed and the gig was over.

"Fuck you," I said and slammed the receiver home. But I did not let it go. There was something the voice had said. Christ. It said, "Money."

I limped quickly to the kitchen, the muscles in my leg complaining with each step, and checked the caller ID under my kitchen phone. Along with a familiar telephone number, it flashed a name I knew well: LEVERING FIELD.

And suddenly, I knew everything.

I WAS HALFWAY down the driveway before I realized I didn't have a gun.

Careless.

I raced—that's the correct word—I raced back into my house, to my bedroom, pulled open the drawer, took out a Beretta 9mm, checked the load, and ran out of the house, back to the car. I was on 280 heading south when it occurred to me to call the police, call Anne Scalasi, and tell them to hustle over to Amanda's. Only I had left Sara's cell phone on my kitchen table.

Careless, careless.

I stopped in front of Amanda Field's house and limped quickly to the door. I pounded on it, leaned heavily on the bell with my thumb. No answer. With the Beretta in my right hand, I tried the knob with my left. It turned. I pushed through the door, yelling Amanda's name. Still no answer. The house was dark. I went from the living room to the kitchen, racing again. Something caught my ankle and I went down, face first, my chin bouncing off the tile floor, my gun clattering beneath the kitchen table. I tried to rise, but a knee planted against my spine pinned me down. I heard the distinctive *click* of a hammer being thumbed back, felt the cold steel of a gun barrel pressed against my ear.

Careless, careless, careless.

"THIS IS SO great!" she shouted as I was led down wooden steps into a finished basement. "This is just so unbelievably great! I can't believe how great this is!"

Emily Elizabeth Field stood next to her mother, her mother's Smith & Wesson .38 in her hand, pointed at the floor. She was smiling happily, like she just received her heart's desire wrapped as a birthday present. Her mother was tied to a wooden chair, the thick twine cutting into her wrists. Her cheeks were stained with mascara. But she was not crying now, not making any sound at all. She was alive, but her face had the same hopeless expression that you see in the old photographs of Jews being herded into Nazi concentration camps. She wasn't dead, but she wasn't far from it.

Emily's boyfriend, the one with the rusted-out Caddy and Oakland Raider's jacket, pushed me ahead of him with his free hand. His other hand held a .32 Taurus revolver pointed at my spine. My gun was in his pocket. He was several inches taller than me, and his head just brushed the false ceiling.

"What?" he asked Emily, as he roughly pushed me into a wooden chair opposite Amanda.

"Don't you see?" Emily asked.

"I wouldn't ask if I—"

"We can shoot Taylor with Momma's gun, and shoot Momma with Taylor's gun," Emily told him. "The police will think they shot each other. No wait! Better yet! We'll shoot Momma with your gun and then put it in Taylor's hand so the cops'll think he shot Daddy, too. God, this is so great!" And then, in the mocking accent of the English gentry, she said, "So nice of you to come, Mr. Taylor. To what do we owe the pleasure?"

"Your boyfriend called me," I told her. "I traced the

call." Then I told him, "You live on Railroad Island, don't you? On Collins Street? I ran your plates. I should have put it all together when you threatened Amanda, calling her from Railroad Island." I was angry with myself. Working at a bakery was looking better all the time.

Emily glanced at her boyfriend and then at me.

"The cops will figure it out. The woman in charge is smarter than I am," I told them.

Emily shrugged. Traps and traces and MURs meant nothing to her. Yeah, you could see she was brains of the outfit.

"You want to kill both of 'em?" the boy asked.

"Why not?"

"I don't know. . . ."

"C'mon, Jerry. It's not like you haven't shot anyone before."

"But, both of 'em?"

Amanda slumped in her chair. If she hadn't been tied to it, she probably would have fallen out. I was somewhat more alert. Blood was pulsing through me like the oil in a Formula One, some of it dripping from the wound on my chin. I took a chance. "Don't be stupid!" I exclaimed. The outburst cost me a lump on the side of my head above the ear, delivered by Jerry with the butt of his .32. I didn't let it deter me.

"Look at her wrists," I told them, and they did. "You think the marks where the twine's cut into her flesh will go away? You think the cops won't notice them?" Jerry made another move toward me. "You think the medical examiner won't notice bruises and swelling on my head?" I added.

He stopped and looked at Emily.

"So?" she asked.

"So they'll know it's murder. And the first person

they'll suspect is the one who benefits most from that murder."

"That's you," Jerry told Emily.

"I know it's me," Emily replied, exasperated.

"With your mother gone, there's no lawsuit," I told her just in case she didn't. "You'll get to keep your father's entire estate. That's what all this is about, isn't it?"

Emily lightly tapped the .38 against her cheek, thinking it over.

"Your father put all his assets in your name to avoid taxes, and with him dead, it all goes to you unless your mother convinces a court to give her half."

Now Emily was brushing her cheek with the barrel; I doubted she was even listening to me.

"That's why your boyfriend, here, killed your father, wasn't it? Because your father intended to give me two hundred and eighty-seven thousand dollars—"

"It was *my* money!" Emily shouted. I guess she had been listening. "I told him not to give in to you. But he said it wasn't worth it anymore. He said it was easier to just pay you off. Easy for him, maybe. It was *my* money!"

Amanda moaned incoherently.

"It was!" Emily yelled at her. "Daddy had no business giving it to him. And you had no business trying to take it away from me." To emphasize her point, Emily slashed her mother across the mouth with the barrel of the gun, tearing her lip at the corner. Amanda didn't even bother to lick the blood away.

"I warned her," Emily informed me, "but she wouldn't listen."

"So you had loverboy try to shoot her in the back."

Loverboy shrugged. "She was out of range," he said.

"But you're not," Emily said, pointing the Smith & Wesson at my head. *"Where the fuck is my money!"* she screamed.

"What money?" I asked as calmly as possible. Jerry hit me again. "What makes you think I have your money?"

"'Cuz the ol' man said he gave it to you," Jerry said softly.

"Huh?"

"Before I spiked 'im, I asked, 'Where's the money?' and he said he gave it to you."

"That's not true," I said.

"Then where is it?" Emily screamed again.

I looked up at Jerry and smiled. "Ask the boyfriend," I said.

"Hit him again," Emily told Jerry, and Jerry did. Then she told me, "That ain't gonna work, trying to play us against each other. We watch TV, too."

I tried to rub my head where Jerry kept hitting me, but he rapped my knuckles with the barrel of his gun, and I pulled my hand down.

"Where's my money?" Emily repeated.

"You searched my house," I reminded her. "I haven't got your money."

That sent Emily to rubbing her cheek with the barrel of her gun again. After a few minutes she said, "OK, this is what we're gonna do."

"What?" asked Jerry, her obedient servant.

"We'll shoot Momma with your gun," Emily told him. "Cops will figure whoever shot Daddy shot her, too. OK, then we'll take Taylor out to the woods somewhere—"

"Where?" Jerry asked.

"I don't know. The woods. Itasca State Park. I don't know."

"Why?"

"We'll take him out there and torture him."

"Torture him? How?"

"Gouge out his eyes or something. Do I have to think of everything?"

"I was just asking."

"We'll torture him until he tells us where the money is, and then we'll kill him and bury him in the woods. Nobody will ever know what happened to him."

I looked at Jerry and thought about the wannabes I'd met on the pier at Roseville Central Park. They could never do what Emily suggested. But could Jerry? He looked at me without expression, with the dull flat eyes of a shark. Yeah. He could.

Screw this, I thought. After everything I'd been through, I'd be damned if I would let a couple of psycho kids kill me without a fight.

"God, you're stupid," I said. Just as I expected, Jerry moved toward me, his gun directed at my head, ready to strike. I shifted my head away from the line of fire and with my left hand slapped the gun behind me, holding on to it. I slipped off the chair to my knees and with my right hand punched him hard in the groin, one, two, three times in quick succession. That brought him down to me, and I followed with an elbow to his jaw. He weakened. I pulled the gun from his grasp and smacked him upside the head with it. He was on his side now, groaning, holding his head with both hands. I spun on my knees, transferred the .32 to my right hand, brought it up, and pointed it at Emily's chest. Emily had the Smith & Wesson in both hands, aiming it at me with one eye closed. I thumbed the hammer back, my index finger squeezing the trigger, when Amanda screamed, *"No, no, no, no, no!"*

Emily hesitated, glanced at her mother, looked back at me, and slowly let the gun slip from her hands onto the floor.

And because Emily had listened to her mother, I didn't kill her. I didn't put a big, bloody hole through her tiny, cold heart.

DESPITE EVERYTHING, AMANDA tried to save her daughter, inventing a story as she went along in which I was the bad guy, in which I had threatened her, and Emily had merely come to her rescue. The cops who arrived first on the scene listened closely. From their expressions, I guessed they were just as confused as I was. By the time Anne Scalasi arrived, though, Emily was doing all the talking, explaining how her mother and father—and I— had cheated her out of money that was rightfully hers and got exactly what we deserved, except that Amanda and I weren't dead. Amanda started crying again. And the more she cried, the louder Emily wished she had killed her mother when she had had the chance. After about ten minutes of it, Anne finally told Emily to shut up, to stop talking until Emily had a lawyer, until someone from juvenile services could advise her.

Meanwhile, Jerry sat on the floor, his back against the wall, arms folded across his chest and his eyes closed. He seemed genuinely surprised when a uniform yanked him to his feet and led him outside. No doubt when he opened his eyes, he had expected all of us to be gone.

Amanda wanted to ride to the cop shop with Emily, but Emily didn't like the idea. "You ruined my life," she told her mother—told her several times. And Amanda kept saying, "I'm sorry! I'm sorry!" She repeated the words even after the patrol car had taken Emily away. And then she turned on me. *"This is all your fault!"* she screamed. She slapped my face and would have slapped it again except two uniforms restrained her. I suppose I could have just stood there and taken it. Hell, turn the other cheek, where was the harm? Except I had almost been killed—three times now—and I was tired of taking abuse because of Amanda's dysfunctional family.

So while the cops held her arms, I leaned in real close and told her: "I did not steal from the sick and elderly, your husband did. I did not try to defraud the government, your lover did. I did not murder your husband or try to kill you, your daughter did. Don't blame me. Blame them. Blame yourself."

Amanda screamed again, this time more in pain than anger. If the cops hadn't held her arms, she would have collapsed. As it was, they had to carry her to a squad car and tuck her into the back seat. I watched from the front lawn, Anne Scalasi now at my side.

"I'm not responsible for any of this," I told her.

"No, of course not," Anne agreed. "You're as pure as a Christmas snow."

I WAS INVITED to the St. Paul Police Department again, but at least this time they let me drive my own car. And I spent a second consecutive night in various holding cells and interrogation rooms, talking to a wide array of law enforcement officials. Only this time they didn't offer donuts. Bad coffee, but no donuts. I finally emerged after rush hour traffic the following morning. When Anne sent me home, she said I should shower and shave before I went to bed unless I intended to wash my sheets real soon. I thanked her for her advice and drove to Minneapolis.

STEVE DID NOT smile when I walked through the steel door into his loft. I think he knew why I was there. He managed an unenthusiastic "Good morning," then an "Are you OK?" when he noticed the cut on my chin and the swelling on my head where the kid had hit me. But I was just too damn tired to be polite. I went directly to Steve's clothing racks and started pushing garments around.

"What are you looking for?" he asked.

I didn't tell him until I found it: a red hooded scarf.

"Very stylish, you slut," I said, repeating Crystalin Wolters's words to me. Steve cringed at the insult, and I tossed the scarf on the floor.

"Where's the money?" I asked him.

"What's happened?" he asked me. I told him. He turned his head away. "I didn't think anyone would get hurt," he said.

"What did you think would happen?"

He didn't answer.

"You knew when Levering was going for his money, didn't you," I told him more than asked. "You told me you had a sniffer working in the bank's computer system. You knew when Levering's accounts were being accessed, didn't you?"

Steve didn't respond.

"Didn't you!" I yelled.

He nodded.

"How did you know he would go to Crystalin Wolters's apartment?"

"I didn't," he answered. "I went to the bank. He was just leaving when I arrived. I followed him."

"And waited at Crystalin's until he left."

Steve nodded. "I told him that I worked for you. I told him that you didn't trust him to deliver the money at his home, that you thought it could be a trap. I told him I would take the money."

"And he gave it to you? Just like that?"

Steve snickered. "First he tried to pick up Sara—put his hand on her thigh. He was a pig. He deserved what happened to him."

"No, he didn't," I said. I stared at him for a few moments. He avoided my gaze. Finally, I asked, "Why? Why did you do it?"

"I was afraid."

"Of what?"

"My parents. I can't keep Sara from them forever. Sooner or later they're going to find out about her and when they do . . ."

"They're going to cut you off," I guessed.

"I can't live without money."

"You have plenty of money," I told him. "Your business—"

"I mean real money!" Steve shouted, adding in a soft voice, "Sara has expensive tastes."

I could only shake my head at that. Real money, Christ. Real money is what Sid and Bob made climbing in the damn gondola every day, washing skyscrapers for thirteen bucks an hour.

"You didn't have to steal from me," I told Steve.

"I guess I didn't see it like that. Stealing from you, I mean. The way I figured it, I was stealing—"

"From Levering Field," I volunteered.

"Yeah," Steve said, still avoiding my gaze. "That's what you were doing, wasn't it?"

"I guess I didn't see it as stealing, either," I admitted.

"I took a lot of big risks for that money," he told me, finally looking me in the eye.

"Didn't we all," I answered. "Where is it?"

Steve walked slowly across the warped floor to his bed, dropped to his knees, and slid Levering's briefcase out from beneath it. He brought it to me, and I opened it on his desk.

"Is it all here?" I asked.

Steve nodded.

I counted out eight five-thousand-dollar packets and the two-thousand-dollar packet—forty-two grand—and dropped them on his desk.

"I usually tip fifteen percent," I announced, then slapped the briefcase shut. I was at the door in four strides, stopped, turned. "I'll return your cell phone by parcel post," I said.

"No hurry," Steve said, counting the money, a disappointed expression on his face. "You can drop it here anytime."

"No," I told him. "I don't want to see you or Sara for a while."

THE BRIEFCASE DID not fit into my office safe, so I took out the cash and stacked it neatly next to my passport. Then I called Fort Myers. Mom answered.

"Let me speak to Dad," I told her without much of a greeting.

"He's not home right now, Holly," Mom said. "He just left for the funeral parlor."

"Funeral parlor?"

"Something about a mistake on the invoice."

"Invoice?"

"Your dad thinks they charged him for the wrong casket."

"What are you talking about?"

"Your dad thinks the funeral parlor charged him for the wrong casket."

My mother has this annoying habit of relating only little bits and pieces of information even when she knows you want the whole story. I lost my patience with her.

"Holly, watch your language," she told me.

"Whose casket?" I demanded, adding, "And don't call me Holly."

"Mrs. Gustafson's."

"What?"

"Didn't your father tell you?"

"Tell me what?"

"He said he was going to call; I told him he should." I could actually hear her shake her head in exasperation.

"He's always doing that, forgetting things. I keep telling him, you have to write things down. But does he listen?"

"Call about what?"

"About Mrs. Gustafson."

Mom apparently thought the conversation was over after that, and I had to yell, "Mother!" to get her talking again.

"Mrs. Gustafson died five days ago. Heart attack. Went just like that. I was telling your father—"

"Five days ago?!"

"Your father didn't tell you? See what I mean about forgetting things?"

"Dammit, Mother! People up here have been getting shot over this. I was shot. Again."

"Well, you certainly can't blame me for that. I didn't shoot anybody. If you would get a real job that kind of thing wouldn't happen."

What can you do? She's your mother.

"Have Dad call me," I told her softly. She said she would, and then she started telling me about poor Mrs. Gustafson's funeral. While she was talking I did something I had never done before. I hung up on my mother.

I FOUND CYNTHIA dressed all in white and waiting for me beneath my willow tree. It was a nice place to see a beautiful woman. I went to her after parking the car and hugged her hard, hoping she would hug me back. She did. And then she said, "Want to tell me about it?"

I told her about Amanda and her daughter. Cynthia shook her head and said, "Good God." Then I told her about Mrs. Gustafson. She seemed truly saddened by the news; saddened over the death of an eighty-five-year-old woman she had never met or spoken to.

"I love you," I told her. And I meant it. I kissed her, but I wasn't looking for romance. I was seeking absolution. "I botched the whole deal," I confessed. "I should have listened to you. If I had listened to you, if I had let the courts do their job, none of this would have happened."

"You're right," she agreed. "If it weren't for you, Levering Field would have gotten away with stealing three-quarters of a million dollars from his clients. Carson Saterbak and his friends would have bilked the goverment out of over eight-point-seven million dollars. Two professional killers would still be on the streets. And Emily Field would have killed her mother as well as her father."

I wrapped my arms around Cynthia's shoulders like she was a life preserver and walked her to my house.

"Don't be sorry for them," she told me.

"And Amanda?"

"It's a dangerous world. Sometimes bad things happen to good people. There's nothing you can do about it." Cynthia said it, but I knew she didn't believe it. She merely wanted me to feel better about what I had done to Amanda, and I thanked her.

"What are you going to do about the money?" she asked me.

"You mean after expenses? I don't know. What are my legal obligations?" I asked her.

"Legally, the money belongs to the State of Florida," Cynthia advised me.

I shook my head with disgust. "I don't like that idea at all."

Cynthia shrugged. "You might consider donating it to a worthy cause. Anonymously, of course, since the IRS, among others, might be interested in where it came from."

"Cash can be easily laundered," I told her.

"I wouldn't know about such things."

"I do."

"I'm not surprised."

We were on the front steps now. You could still see the faint outline of the swastika on the door.

"I could keep it, I suppose," I suggested.

"I suppose," she replied in a way that made me think she didn't like the idea at all. And she had a point. Ill-gotten gain just doesn't spend as well as money that belongs to you. Still, it was a lot of dough. Stash it in an IRA, in a tax-deferred annuity, I'd be sitting pretty by the time I retired. Course, I didn't really need the money. And I did have a rich girlfriend. . . .

"Maybe I'll donate it to a charity that provides low-income housing for the poor," I said, savoring the irony—wondering if I meant it.